Praise for the
CHARLOTTE GRAHAM MYSTERIES
by National Bestselling Author
STEFANIE MATTESON

MURDER AT THE SPA

"Clever, original, suspenseful!"
—**David Stout, Edgar Award–winning author
of *Carolina Skeletons***

MURDER AT TEATIME

"A gripping mystery, with a splendidly authentic
background of the magical Maine coast."
—**Janwillem van de Wetering,
author of *Inspector Saito's Small Satori***

MURDER ON THE CLIFF

"Sly . . . an ironic background for murder!"
—**Margaret Maron, author of *Corpus Christmas***

MURDER ON THE SILK ROAD

"Matteson's adventure will charm readers."
—*Publishers Weekly*

MURDER AT THE FALLS

"An offbeat heroine who is . . . the sophisticated
American woman sleuth that the mystery world has
been lacking."
—*Murder ad lib*

"You'll get hooked on Charlotte Graham!"
—*Rave Reviews*

MURDER
ON
HIGH

STEFANIE MATTESON

BERKLEY PRIME CRIME, NEW YORK

MURDER ON HIGH

A Berkley Prime Crime Book / published by arrangement with the author

PRINTING HISTORY

Berkley Prime Crime hardcover edition / November 1994
Berkley Prime Crime mass-market edition / November 1995

ISBN: 0-425-15050-X

Berkley Prime Crime Books are published
by The Berkley Publishing Group,
200 Madison Avenue, New York, NY 10016.
The name BERKLEY PRIME CRIME and the BERKLEY PRIME CRIME
design are trademarks belonging to Berkley Publishing Corporation.

PRINTED IN THE UNITED STATES OF AMERICA

10 9 8 7 6 5 4 3 2 1

In memory of
ROGER P. BEIRNE
August 16, 1911 to November 25, 1993

The tops of mountains are among the unfinished parts of the globe, whither it is a slight insult to the gods to climb and pry into their secrets, and try their effect on our humanity. Only daring and insolent men, perchance, go there. Simple races, as savages, do not climb mountains,—their tops are sacred and mysterious tracts never visited by them. Pomola is always angry with those who climb to the summit of Ktaadn.

—HENRY DAVID THOREAU, *The Maine Woods*

· I ·

IT HAD TAKEN her five hours and twelve minutes this year to reach Baxter Peak, the highest peak of Mount Katahdin, Maine's highest mountain. It was fourteen minutes more than last year, but still good by anyone's measure, for a woman of seventy-two. She had climbed the mountain every year for the last fourteen years at this time: *Diapensia* time, the second week in June. Her routine was always the same: up the Saddle Trail and over the saddle to the Tableland, a broad, plateau-like expanse on the south side of the summit, suspended nearly a mile above the surrounding countryside, to see the *Diapensia*. The Tableland, which had been molded by the retreating glacier, was one of the few places in the East where the unusual alpine wildflower bloomed in such profusion. There was a small colony on the summit of Mount Washington in neighboring New Hampshire, but nothing like here, where clusters of the dainty white flowers dotted the barren, windswept tundra, each a testimony to the ability of nature to adapt to near-arctic conditions. It took a plant eight to ten years to develop a taproot in the poor, thin soil, to say nothing of the twenty years it took to form the small evergreen cushion of tiny, leathery leaves, as dense as a clump of brain coral, that allowed it to survive the constant exposure to wind and snow.

Iris Richards felt a special sympathy with this tiny alpine wildflower, on whose habitat she had become something of an authority. She sometimes thought of herself in terms of a colony of *Diapensia*, alone on the tundra, drawn into herself, protected from an inhospitable environment by her thick, leathery skin. She supposed that's why she felt so protective of the plants. Though signs warned hikers not to stray from the trail, few knew the reason was to protect the *Diapensia*. One footstep could cause what botanists called a blowout in the center of a cushion, opening a chink in the plant's armor to a lethal invasion of the brutal winter winds that robbed it of life-giving moisture and causing it to die from the center out, thereby destroying a plant that might have taken thirty-five years to establish itself.

And even those who knew about the *Diapensia* didn't care. Like that man she'd run into on the rim, the same one who'd kept dislodging rocks on the Saddle Slide. He'd said he was a member of the Highpointers Club. Their goal was to climb the highest peak in each of the fifty states. He'd climbed thirty, he said—all of the easiest ones. Some he'd simply driven up, like Mount Washington. And some, like the highest point in Delaware, were nothing more than a crossroad. It was a goal so typically American: a goal that satisfied the compulsion to quantify. He'd showed her his tally card. Up and down, probably not even stopping to look around. What was he going to do when he had to climb McKinley? she wondered. He certainly hadn't taken any time to look at the *Diapensia*, hadn't even noticed he was stepping on it. She'd carefully explained to him about the delicacy of its root system, to which he'd replied, "Well, if it's so rare, I'd better take a picture of it," proceeding as he did so to squash another clump with a foot shod in a fancy new hiking boot. A member of the Highpointers Club indeed! When she'd chastised him, he'd retorted with the outrageous statement that being stepped on by hikers was the price it had to pay for growing so near the trail. Awful man! She should have beaned him with her hiking stick when she'd run into him again on her way up. Good thing she hadn't seen him on the Knife Edge. She'd have been tempted to push him right off.

Having added her rock to the rock monument at the summit, she now sat in a nest of lichen-clad boulders near the sign proclaiming Baxter Peak as the northern terminus of the Appalachian Trail. As she ate her snack (a cold sweet potato; she didn't believe in eating meat, didn't even believe in cooking her food because it was a waste of precious energy), she pondered the second part of her annual pilgrimage: across the Knife Edge to Pamola Peak. The Knife Edge: in length, slightly more than a mile; in width, as narrow as nine inches in places; in height, one mile, with a vertical drop-off of two thousand feet on either side. Getting across it was the test she set for herself each year. The Knife Edge was the ground on which she came to terms with herself. Courage, resolve, patience, fortitude, perseverance—it was a measure of the old-fashioned virtues in which she put her stock. It was also her opportunity to make her annual offering to the Indian god, Pamola, a ritual that she had created in recognition of the virtue in which she put the highest stock of all: sobriety. Others collected anniversary pins from AA; she, being intolerant of the society of others in general and especially so of the society of alcoholics, whose self-indulgent outpourings of guilt revolted her, waved a fifth of rum to the winds on Pamola's summit in observance of another year without a relapse.

The Knife Edge stretched away from her now toward Pamola Peak: a dark, sharp, undulating spine of granite, banked on either side by a sea of gray-white fog, and wreathed in ghostly wisps of mist. It looked more eerie, more threatening than she had ever seen it, but oddly enough, less frightening. The fog that had moved in during the last hour camouflaged how high up she really was, thus eliminating *down* as a direction to consider (as if *across* wasn't bad enough). It was this fear of *down* that provided much of the motive for her annual trek across the Knife Edge. It was a fear so severe that it reduced all thought to the question of where to put your feet next, and even that became too much to consider at times. Next to the Knife Edge, all of her life's tribulations, foremost among them her daily battle with temptation, became mere minor annoyances. It was a terror that reduced life to its most basic element: survival.

Having finished her sweet potato, she slipped on her ash splint backpack, picked up her hiking stick, and stood up. There weren't many other hikers on the peak today: a tall, handsome man passing by, a group of three young men eating lunch. She supposed the weather report posted at the ranger station at Chimney Pond had kept the hikers down below. Because of the fog and the chance of precipitation, park authorities had ranked this a Class II Hiking Day, meaning that the trails above the tree line were open, but not recommended because of potential weather deterioration. So far, the weather hadn't deteriorated to the point that she would have to consider turning back, but it had turned cold and windy. Taking off her pack, she pulled out the foul-weather gear that Jeanne had given her: a windbreaker and matching rain pants in a synthetic fabric. Though she appreciated the practical advantage of a fabric that was both lightweight and waterproof—she had waited out too many rainstorms in the discomfort of a heavy rubber rain slicker—she wished the manufacturers had produced it in more discreet colors. This was a neon green, almost a chartreuse, trimmed with black. She might have questioned Jeanne's judgment had she not noticed that all of these foul-weather suits seemed to come in similarly vivid colors. After donning the jacket and pants, she put her backpack on again, picked up her hiking stick, and set out.

She was glad the summit wasn't crowded. There was nothing worse than traversing the Knife Edge with someone breathing down your neck. She especially didn't want to be hurried today, tired as she was. She hadn't been able to get back to sleep last night after being awakened by the creature that had appeared at the front of her lean-to at the Chimney Pond Campground. She'd thought at first that it was a moose. She'd seen a moose grazing near the lean-to just before she'd gone to bed that evening. But then she'd realized that it was a man wearing a headdress of moose antlers. He'd been an eerie sight in the moonlight, against the backdrop of twisted white birches, softly shaking the

rattle he held in one hand. For a second, she thought he
was a hallucination. Then she remembered that she wasn't
drinking anymore. He'd disappeared the moment she'd sat
up, evaporated into the woods without even a rustle of the
underbrush. The ranger had appeared a moment later, dispel-
ling any doubts she may have had about the figure's reality.
He'd heard the rattle, he said. The man was a prankster pretending to be Pamola haunting the campground. The ranger
himself had heard him several times, but on each occasion
the man had vanished before he could be apprehended.
Though the ranger assured her that he wouldn't appear
again that night, she hadn't been able to fall back asleep.
The incident had been deeply disturbing. She was reminded
of the demons in Tibetan Buddhist rituals, symbols of the
personal demons that needed to be overcome on the path to
enlightenment. She had chosen the fierce, avenging storm
spirit as the symbol of her personal demon, and here he
was, taunting her, as if he were an emissary from her own
subconscious. "You thought I was dead," he said. "But I'm
still very much alive." It gave her the shivers just to think
about him. So she decided she wouldn't. Just put him back
in his box, and close the lid. Bam! Take that, you little nasty.
The deed done, she checked her watch—it read 1:32 P.M.—
and headed out onto the trail that led across the clouds.

The first part of the Knife Edge wasn't so bad, and she
crossed it easily. It was the jagged up-and-down terrain of
the stretch between South Peak and Chimney Peak that
always gave her the most trouble. She had once heard this
section described as resembling the spine of a stegosaurus,
with its row of pointed, upright plates. Adding to the difficulty was the fact that this was the narrowest section of the
ridge, the result of glaciers on either side having honed it
to a slender blade. After pausing for a few minutes on South
Peak to gather her courage, she continued on. From South
Peak, the trail turned to the northeast, and then descended
steeply to a low point. She could never decide which was
worse, down or up. Usually she thought it was down, but

today down wasn't that bad because there was no down to see. She was breathing deeply when she reached the notch between the first and second of the plates, and paused to remove her canteen from her pack. The bank of fog that clung to the headwall stretched out below her like a great white plain studded with snowy hills and mountains. Ahead, the rounded summit of Chimney Peak loomed out of the fog, and beyond it, the peak of Pamola. If the Knife Edge was a dinosaur's spine, Chimney Peak would be its hunched-up shoulders, and Pamola Peak the back of its head. After taking a drink, she returned her canteen to her pack—she liked the open packs because you could just reach around to take something out, though they weren't as practical in bad weather—and began her ascent of the next of the steep, narrow plates on the dinosaur's back.

This trip, up was definitely worse than down. The trouble with up was that there wasn't anything in the distance to fix your gaze on, to orient you in space. Today, there wasn't even a distant cloud; only the cold, damp vapors of fog. The solution, of course, was not to look out. To look only at the dark rocks at your feet, with their green and gray patterns of ring and map lichens. To plot the placement of each hand and foot with the precision of a brain surgeon deciding where to make the next cut. Only a few more steps now. One last lift over an outcrop. There, she had made it! Standing precariously on the tip of the dinosaur plate, she savored the cold, damp sting of the fog against her cheek. She took out her pocket spyglass, and lifted it to her eye. In the distance, the conical summit of Russell Mountain peeked out of the fog like a volcanic island, perfectly centered in her field of view. She put the spyglass back. Now for the next descent.

She was just turning when she felt a rush of air, then a sharp pain on the side of her neck. What was this! Stung by the force of the impact, she rocked back and forth on the pinnacle like an amusement park Kewpie doll that's been hit with a softball.

Then she fell into the soft bed of fleecy white clouds.

• 2 •

THE ASSISTANT RANGER at the Chimney Pond Campground, whose name was Chris Sargent, awoke at 5 A.M. with a sense of disquietude. In the mental confusion of first awakening, he thought at first it was the bed. He wasn't used to sleeping in the double bed on the screened-in back porch of the ranger's cabin, but rather in a hard, narrow bunk in the crew cabin on the other side of the campground. He was only here because his boss, the campground ranger, was on vacation. But when he opened his eyes and caught his first glimpse of the fog-shrouded headwall on the other side of the screen, he remembered what had caused him such an uneasy night. It was the hiker, Iris Richards: a seventy-two-year-old woman from Old Town, a hundred miles to the south. She had signed in at the hiker's register yesterday at eight, as all hikers to the summit were asked to do. But she hadn't signed out. Nor had she returned to Chimney Pond to meet her companion, a woman in her fifties named Jeanne Ouellette, who, being the less experienced hiker of the two, had chosen an easier route to one of the mountain's other peaks. Though they had set out together, Mrs. Richards had gone on ahead once they reached the rim of the basin, leaving Miss Ouellette to go off in another direction.

After arriving back at the campground at six, Miss Ouellette had waited at the ranger's office for two hours. When Mrs. Richards hadn't returned by eight, Sargent had notified the South District supervisor, whose name was Haverty, that Mrs. Richards was missing. Haverty had asked the Old Town police to check Mrs. Richards' home on the off-chance that she had returned there by some other means. Miss Ouellette had reported that a friend of Mrs. Richards' from Old Town, a man named Mack Scott, had announced his intention of climbing the mountain that day from the opposite side, via the Abol Trail. Mrs. Richards had discussed meeting him in the vicinity of the summit, and Miss Ouellette had speculated that perhaps Mrs. Richards had done just that, and had descended the mountain and returned to Old Town with him. For Mrs. Richards to leave her hiking companion waiting at the Chimney Pond Campground was highly inconsiderate, but certainly not out of character for a woman who tended to put her own needs ahead of those of others, and in particular ahead of those of the woman who had been her devoted companion for more than thirty years. It was also possible, confessed Miss Ouellette, whose annoyance had transmuted itself into worry as the hour grew later, that she had misunderstood, and that Mrs. Richards had been planning to go home with Scott from the start. But why, then, would she have given her descent route in the hiker's register as the Dudley Trail, a trail whose terminus was the Chimney Pond Campground? In any case, Iris Richards had not arrived home by eight when the police checked her house, though it was possible that she and Scott had stopped for dinner on the way back. Miss Ouellette had finally decided to spend the night in Millinocket on the chance that Mrs. Richards would still turn up. Without her companion's car, Mrs. Richards would have no way of getting home. But when Sargent had checked in with Haverty at eleven, Mrs. Richards still wasn't back.

As Sargent rolled over, he felt the stiffness of his muscles. The day before had been exhausting. A full day of clearing a blow-down from a trail had been followed by the search for Mrs. Richards. When she hadn't returned by eight, he had been directed by Haverty to give her route a thorough going-over—quote, unquote. Usually he would have begun by scanning the headwall with binoculars, but the fog that had moved in earlier that day had ruled out that option. Instead, he had walked around the pond to the base of the headwall, and tried to make voice contact from there. Voices carried well in the Great Basin, and extended conversations had been carried on in the past with stranded hikers from the base of the headwall. But this time his efforts had been to no avail. Finally he had surveyed her route, taking the opposite direction on the theory that a hiker who got into trouble would most likely have done so on the way down. But he hadn't found anything. Wasn't likely to in that fog.

All the time, he had been considering what might have happened to her. Though he never would have admitted it, a part of him was hoping it was something serious. He wasn't wishing for a fatality, mind you; but a broken leg wouldn't be bad. An accident victim on the headwall would give him a chance to show off his training in mountain rescue techniques. As a member of the University of Maine's Dirigo Search and Rescue Team he had participated in several exciting rescues in New Hampshire's Presidential Range, and he was eager to do the same here. A chance to show off his rappelling skills might even result in a promotion. The campground ranger wasn't taking time off to visit relatives, as she had told Haverty, but was interviewing for a job at Denali National Park. If she got it, and she seemed fairly confident that she would, the Chimney Pond campground ranger post would be vacant. And he was the man to fill it. As the rock-climbing center of Baxter State Park, the Chimney Pond site needed an experienced rock climber in charge. Most of the assistant rangers had trained, as he had, at the national park ranger school, but none of the others were technically qualified, as he was. At least, that was the line he was planning to use with Haverty.

Unfortunately for him, his two previous summers at Chimney Pond had failed to provide him with the opportunity to show off his technical expertise. Despite the thousands of hikers who climbed Katahdin each season, the only mishap had occurred last year when a Boy Scout who'd become separated from his troop took the wrong trail down. Realizing his error, he had turned around and gone back the way he had come, meeting the search party almost before it set out. Which wasn't to say that Sargent hadn't proven himself in other ways: for instance, in coping diligently and effectively with the day-to-day problems that arose at the campsite. Thinking of problems, he was reminded of the sticky little problem that was plaguing him now—a prankster in the camp; someone who was appearing to campers in the middle of the night dressed up as Pamola, the malignant Indian spirit who was supposed to dwell in a cave at the summit. At least, it was Pamola whom he thought the prankster was supposed to be, with his moose antlers and eagle mask. Three nights in a row, now. It was stupid, really. Like a Halloween trick. Sargent was pretty sure the culprit was the nut case in Lean-to Number Two who had bored him for two afternoons running with his theory about how the patterns in the fissures on the headwall spelled out messages in Penobscot from the Great Spirit. Sargent hadn't found anything when he'd checked the camper's lean-to for the Pamola costume, but that didn't mean he couldn't have stashed it in his car, which was parked down at Roaring Brook Campground. Sargent didn't know quite what to do about this problem. But he was damned if he was going to ask Haverty. He'd been planning to stay up last night to catch the guy in the act, but those plans had been ixnayed by the Mrs. Richards business. It would have been a waste of time anyway, since the prankster hadn't shown up. He'd probably been kept away by the same fog that had foiled Sargent's search efforts.

Yes, the Mrs. Richards business. He thought it unlikely that she had come to any calamitous end. For Iris Richards, as for many Mainers, climbing Katahdin was an annual ritual. Though there had been many accidental deaths on the mountain, they were almost without exception due to two factors: ignorance or weather, and usually a combination of the two. Most of the deaths had taken place on the Knife

Edge, the narrow glacial arête that had been created by two glaciers biting into the opposing walls of the ridge like the blades of a knife sharpener. Despite prominent signs warning hikers not to leave the Knife Edge Trail, inexperienced hikers were sometimes seduced into thinking that the ravines that cascaded down the face of the headwall were easy shortcuts back to Chimney Pond. From the ridge, the tops of these ravines resembled trailheads, but hikers who chose to descend by these routes quickly found that they led to vertical drop-offs that were impossible to negotiate without technical equipment and expertise. In fact, as his boss was fond of saying, there were only three ways off the Knife Edge: forward, backward, and to your death. Which was a bit of an overstatement. Many stranded hikers had been plucked off the headwall, but there were others who had indeed either plunged to their deaths or died of exposure overnight. For Katahdin, with an elevation just under a mile, was subject to sudden changes in weather; in fact, the Penobscot Indians, to whom the mountain was sacred, said that Pamola cooked up its furious storms in the Great Basin to keep interlopers off his turf.

But Mrs. Richards hadn't been an inexperienced hiker. She had climbed the mountain a dozen times or more. She would have known there were no shortcuts off the Knife Edge. Nor had she been caught by the weather. The day before had been clear and warm, and though a fog had moved in around noon, it had not rained and the temperature had stayed fairly mild. If she *had* been forced to spend the night on the headwall, she wouldn't have died of exposure. There was a chance that she had fallen off. Her companion had described her as being extremely fit, but there were accidents of health that could befall a woman of her age: a mini-stroke, a dizzy spell brought on by undetected heart disease, or an episode of forgetfulness that resulted in her wandering off the trail. Thus he had made the circuit: up the Dudley Trail and across the Knife Edge. Though the chance was slim that he would see the neon-green windbreaker that

Miss Ouellette said the missing woman had probably been wearing—the headwall was buried in a sea of fog—he had hoped he might see a signal from the flashlight she had been carrying. But he had found nothing except some trash left by hikers on Baxter Peak. At Baxter Peak, he had turned south to Thoreau Spring, which Mrs. Richards had given as her first destination. It was ten by the time he got to the Baxter Peak Cutoff, where Mrs. Richards and Miss Ouellette had separated, and past eleven by the time he got back, completely exhausted, to Chimney Pond. After trying once again to make voice contact, he had radioed in his report to Haverty, and, after being instructed to get a good night's rest in preparation for a more thorough search in the morning, had collapsed into the unaccustomed luxury of the campground ranger's double bed.

Now he found himself scanning the headwall again. Picking up the field glasses with which, at intervals during the night, he had searched for a signal from Mrs. Richards' flashlight, he sat up and studied the wall of fog through the naked branches of the trees. Though it was June ninth, the trees here were just beginning to bud, in contrast to those at the Roaring Brook Campground three miles below, which were nearly fully leafed out by now. Even when the trees here were in full leaf, however, there was still a magnificent view of the headwall. How he loved this sleeping porch! Ever since he had arrived here three years ago, he'd been coveting the accommodations at the ranger's cabin. By most people's standards, they would be considered primitive—a small log cabin without even the convenience of central heating—but to him, they were the height of luxury. In addition to the sleeping porch, there was a private outhouse, a little kitchen, and, best of all, space. As assistant ranger, he was relegated to the dark, cramped crew cabin, uncomfortable enough in itself and made even worse by the fact that he had to share it. It could accommodate eleven, and often did: visiting rangers, Student Conservation Association workers, park employees who wanted to climb the mountain on their day off—a sneezing, farting, coughing, snoring mass of humanity.

Plumping up the pillows behind him, he sat up against the headboard and continued to study the wall of fog through his field glasses. Magnified by the lenses, the texture of the fog revealed itself to be brittle and porous, like the ice sheet on the surface of a lake just before ice-out. If his guess was right, it would burn off by ten. Which meant that the rescue party would be able to see something. He checked the clock: it was already ten past five. Getting up, he quickly pulled on his shirt and pants, and went outside to check the weather. Then he went back inside to radio his report to park headquarters thirty-one miles away in Millinocket. He didn't usually broadcast the weather until seven; in fact, the dispatcher didn't usually come on duty until then, but Haverty had said that a dispatcher would be coming in early to help with the rescue effort, should one be needed.

"Good morning, Betty," he said once contact had been made.

He quickly gave her the weather report. Temperature: 42 degrees; wind: calm to light; heavy fog, with a clearing trend expected by mid-morning. He had decided on a Class I ranking, which meant that the trails above the tree line would be open, and that good weather was predicted. This information would be posted at the park gates and at the ranger stations.

After giving Betty a moment to write the report down, he asked: "Any news on Mrs. Richards?"

"Negative," replied the familiar voice at the other end. "The police have been checking her house every hour throughout the night. She still hasn't come home. Or hadn't as of an hour ago, which was the last report I got."

"What about Scott, then?"

"He got back to Old Town at nine. Said he ran into her briefly at Thoreau Spring, but that's all. Haverty's mounting a search party. They're assembling at Roaring Brook now. They should be up to Chimney Pond by eight-thirty."

Eight-thirty. That gave him three hours to look for the missing woman. Technically, he should ask permission, but what if Haverty said no? He would be denied the chance of being the first to find her.

"Anything else?" asked Betty, sensing his hesitation.

"Nope, that's it," he replied. "Over and out."

After signing off, he ate a breakfast of a bagel and coffee while he drew up the poster giving the weather report and the trail-ranking for the hikers, who, judging from the thudding of the outhouse doors, were beginning to awaken from their slumbers. When the poster was finished, he hung it on the front porch next to the glass case enclosing the hikers' register.

His official duties out of the way, he filled his canteen and loaded a day pack with a thermos of coffee, a ham and cheese sandwich, and a bag of gorp, which he made himself from M&M's, raisins, and cashews. Though he expected to be back within a few hours, he had learned the hard way that it was wise to be prepared with adequate food and water in case of an unexpected delay.

Then he attached his walkie-talkie, which he was never without, to his belt, and set off for the Cathedral Trail.

The Great Basin, as it was called, was often described as looking like a giant bowl, five miles in circumference, with a piece broken out of one side. The intact sides of the bowl were represented by the headwall, which was a sheer rock face, two thousand feet high. The bottom of the bowl was occupied by Chimney Pond, a pristine mountain tarn that lay in the center like a spot of dew in the center of a leaf. Sargent thought the bowl analogy was a good one, except for the fact that it would have to be a very old bowl whose edges had been badly chipped by heavy wear, for the Knife Edge had been eaten away over the millennia by the weather to the point where it resembled not so much the blade of a knife, even a serrated one, as that of a large-toothed saw. The notches between each of the many teeth directed the rain and snowmelt downward, so that the headwall was striated with deep ravines, any one of which might conceal the body of the missing hiker.

If the Great Basin was a bowl with one side broken off, the Cathedrals, which were Sargent's immediate destination, were like three giant cairns that had been deposited at the edge of the break. So-called because of their resemblance to the buttresses of a cathedral (though he had never quite seen the similarity), the Cathedrals rose in steps along the edge of the headwall. Since the Cathedral Trail was almost entirely above the tree line, it offered the best close-ups of the rock flank of the mountain. It was also the shortest, steepest route to the summit. If he had any chance of spotting Mrs. Richards, it would be from one of these rock formations.

He walked quickly. He wanted to get up and back before the rescue party set out from Chimney Pond, and it would take him a good hour to reach the Middle Cathedral, which would afford him his first good view. He didn't want to miss out on the search and rescue operation, but he didn't want to miss out on being the first to find the missing woman, either. By now, he was convinced that Mrs. Richards was on the mountain. What else could possibly have happened to her? So far, he hadn't been able to see anything, but there were moments when the breeze would momentarily blow the mist away, creating windows through the fog. At the lower altitudes, these windows revealed only the dense spruce and fir that lined the bottom of the basin like a cushion of green, but as the trail emerged from the scrub onto the talus slope at the foot of the headwall, he began to catch glimpses of the slide of giant boulders that led to the Lower Cathedral, giving him hope that the fog would clear enough to allow him glimpses of the headwall itself once he was further along.

His arrival at the first of the giant rock buttresses yielded nothing except a dense, dank wall of mist that rose from the cloud factory below like vapor from a giant cauldron. But by the Middle Cathedral, the mist had begun to thin, and by the time he got to the Upper Cathedral he had emerged from the clouds into the brilliant sunshine of an early spring morning. As always with the weather on Katahdin, the change was sudden, dramatic, and exhilarating.

On the far side of the Upper Cathedral was a stretch of slope called the Brickyard after the rubble of sharp granite rocks that blanketed it, as if it had hailed rocks for days on end. Unlike the gray Katahdin granite of the Cathedrals, these rocks, which were found only at the higher elevations, were the pale pink of weathered brick. It was here, on the edge of the Brickyard overlooking the Great Basin, that he took a seat and waited for the fog to recede. He knew from experience that it would, just as surely as the soapsuds on the surface of a sink full of water go down when the plug is pulled. He didn't have to wait long. As he slowly ate his sandwich, savoring the warmth of the sunshine, he could see the edge of the fog bank slipping away, leaving dilatory fingers of gray clinging to the snow in the ravines. His sharp young eyes scanned the headwall, leaping from one ravine to the next, prying behind every boulder, sifting every pile of scree.

It was about three-quarters of the way across the dark, bare, inhospitable wall of granite that he saw it, wedged like a chockstone in the path of one of the longest and steepest of the ravines. It was about halfway down, which was to say about a thousand feet from the rim, and an equal distance from the foot of the headwall. A patch of fluorescent chartreuse, a color like none in nature. His heart pounding, he jumped up, and slid down the scree for a better view. Mind your footing, he warned himself. It was on terrain like this that experienced climbers hurt themselves, not on the technical routes.

About twenty yards down, he stopped and raised his field glasses. Yes, it was unmistakably her. And she was unmistakably dead, though there was nothing in particular about the position of the body to indicate that. He just knew, somehow. Something about that patch of green against the cold gray granite.

On second thought, the color *was* like something in nature, he decided. Like a pale green monarch butterfly chrysalis that hangs from the underside of a leaf, rolled up into a tight little ball.

He could already hear voices resounding beneath the clouds. The search and rescue team was assembling at Chimney Pond. But it wouldn't be needed now, he thought. At least the search part wouldn't. Unless the fog lifted, and they were able to see the body on the headwall for themselves. Wouldn't that be a disappointment—to miss his chance for glory! He prayed for the fog to hang in there a little bit longer. It would be such a feather in his cap to have found the body. It might even mean a promotion. If he hadn't screwed up, that was. According to regulations, he wasn't supposed to have gone off on his own. The rescue effort was supposed to be centrally coordinated, so that everyone knew where everyone else was and what they were doing. But he knew for a fact that other rangers had acted as he had under similar circumstances, and had been rewarded for their efforts. And it wasn't as if he'd left the others entirely in the dark; he had left a note saying where he was going and when he expected to be back.

The return trip was treacherous. The Cathedral Trail wasn't recommended for descents. It was too steep—almost vertical, in fact—and involved lowering oneself down over boulder after boulder. Moreover, the boulders were still wet from the fog. When Governor Percival Baxter had deeded the two hundred thousand acres he had pieced together over the course of a lifetime to the people of the State of Maine in the 1940s, he had stipulated that it be left "forever wild," which meant that there were to be no iron handholds or ladder rungs to aid climbers, as there were in other parks. Although Sargent heartily approved of the former governor's stipulations, there were moments like this when he wished there was something to hang onto. After slipping several times, he kept reminding himself to keep his mind on the trail rather than on the green parka. He didn't want to break a leg before he'd had a chance to prove himself.

As he descended, he considered the problem of how the rescue team was going to remove the body. It would be difficult, but at least the weather would be on their side. It was a good thing it wasn't raining. In the rain, the gullies turned into rivers. The rescue coordinator, who would in all likelihood be Haverty, would probably call in the 112th Medivac team from the Army National Guard base at Bangor to evacuate the body from Chimney Pond. By the time the rescue team got the body off the mountain, the weather should have cleared up enough for flying. The Medivac helicopter wasn't ordinarily used for transporting bodies—it was supposed to be reserved strictly for life-saving missions—but he knew that in the past the Medivac crew had picked up bodies at Chimney Pond to save tired rescue teams the exertion of hand-carrying a litter down the boulder-strewn trail to Perimeter Road at Roaring Brook Campground, and possibly risking yet another injury.

The thought struck him that he would have to report an exact location. What was the name of that gully? The biggest of the ravines, or couloirs, which was the technical term, had official names, like the Chimney (after which the pond was named) and the Waterfall, but the smaller ones carried the informal names of the rock-climbing parties that had been the first to ascend them. The Something-Baker. The first name sounded a bit like the word gully itself, which was what was confusing him. He tried to form a mental picture of the technical climbing map of the headwall in the office at the ranger's cabin. But unlike the map in his office, the map in his head had no names. Then he resorted to the alphabet. Bully, Cully, Dully, Fully, Gully, and so on. At *T*, he stopped. The Tully-Baker, that was it! As he remembered, it had a Yosemite Decimal System rating of a fairly sustained five point eight, making it one of the most difficult on the headwall.

Now that he knew the woman was dead, he started wondering about her. Why had she come back year after year? Unusual for a woman of her age. Did she have friends or family who would have to be notified? He thought of her companion, Miss Ouellette, sitting in his office in the chair under the poster of the moose, tearing the tissues clenched in her hands to shreds. Then there was the press to think about. They would already be gathering at park headquarters in Millinocket. The *Katahdin Times*, the *Bangor Daily News*, maybe even the *Portland Press Herald* and the *Boston Globe*. He could imagine Haverty being quoted on Sargent's role: " 'The body was discovered by Assistant Campground Ranger Christopher Sargent during an early morning search,' said South District Supervisor William Haverty."

At the base of the headwall, he decided that it was finally time to check in. He should have done so the minute he found the body, but he had been worried. What if Haverty got pissed off at him for taking off on his own? But it was now time to face the music. Taking a seat on a boulder, he made his call. The disapproving tone of Haverty's voice when it came in on his walkie-talkie wasn't encouraging. "We thought you'd be here," said the older man.

Uh-oh, Sargent thought, I screwed up. Before the supervisor could go on, he blurted it out: "I've located the accident victim, sir," he said. "She's on the headwall. In the Tully-Baker Gully. About a thousand feet down."

Sargent could sense that Haverty was impressed that he knew the gully's name. *This kid knows his stuff*, he could imagine the older man thinking. He assumed his most deferential tone. "I'm pretty sure she's dead, sir."

With relief, Sargent listened to the silence on the other end as Haverty turned his mind to the tricky problem of how to get the body off the headwall without breaking someone else's neck.

"I understand you've had experience in technical rescue, Sargent," he finally said. "A former member of the Dirigo team. Is that right?"

"Yessir," said Sargent, holding his breath. "Team leader, sir."

"Do you think you could help coordinate a recovery effort?"

"I think I could, sir," he said.

But as he spoke, his mind wasn't on the recovery of Mrs. Richards' body, but rather on the double bed with the fabulous view that was the most appealing perquisite of a promotion to the position of campground ranger.

·3·

CHARLOTTE GRAHAM WAS sipping a cup of coffee on the deck of her summer cottage in the coastal town of Bridge Harbor, Maine, when she got the call from Howard Tracey. Hearing the phone ring, she set down the script she was studying and hurried inside to answer it. She was hoping it would be her stepdaughter, Marsha, but instead she heard the broad vowels and measured cadences of Tracey's Downeast accent repeating her name. Her first name. After eight years, Tracey had finally gotten over the formality of calling her Miss Graham. She eagerly awaited what he had to say. Tracey would never have called just to chat, being as parsimonious in the number of words he employed as he was reluctant at dealing them out. Having retired to Maine for a two-week vacation after completing her last movie, Charlotte was now getting a little bored. Actually, more than a little bored. Being a sensible Yankee, she had told herself that she needed a vacation. She had been working very hard. Having been thrown off kilter by a recent divorce, she had turned to work to bring herself into balance again, leaving little time between projects: an adaptation of a Henry James story for public television, a made-for-TV horror film, a feature film for a French director. She wasn't complaining. Quite the contrary: she was very happy that there *was* work, the number of roles for a woman of her age being limited, though not as limited as it had been twenty years ago. But after seventy-one years, she should have known herself well enough to realize that she dealt as badly with rest, even active rest, as others her age did with activity. She had swum across her favorite lake, climbed her favorite mountain, sailed to her favorite island—her usual anodynes to a too-busy career. Under other circumstances, she would have turned around and gone home, but she had a reason for hanging around.

The year before, she'd signed a contract with a publisher for her autobiography, which was now largely completed. That is to say, she'd written the sections dealing with the beginning of her life and the end of her life, and she was stuck on the middle. It's been said that the bane of the biographer is the subject who accomplishes a great deal at the beginning of his or her life, and then lives on in obscurity. She had a similar problem, except that her period of obscurity had occurred in mid-life. Her black years, she called them: the period from her mid-thirties to her mid-forties when she'd been too old to play young women and too young to play old women. The development of television had helped, as had Broadway, which had always been her refuge when the going got tough in Hollywood, but the pickings had still been pretty slim. But her difficulty in writing about this period in her life wasn't due solely to the dearth of events; it was also due to her reluctance to revive painful memories. The lack of work had been bad enough, but her black years had also been painful on account of an event which took place during this period, and which was inextricably linked to it in her mind: the death in 1957 of her lover, the actor Linc Crawford. Linc's death was symbolic of the downward turn her life had taken.

She had thought that by staying on in Maine, she would force herself to come to grips with her mid-life chapters. Instead, she had just gotten lonely. She missed the company of her circle of friends in New York, and especially that of her stepdaughter, Marsha. Technically, she supposed, Marsha, as the daughter of her former husband, was her ex-stepdaughter, but in this case the ex applied only to Marsha's father, who had been Husband the Fourth and would probably be Husband the Last. Charlotte had no intention of severing relations with Marsha just because her father's ego hadn't been able to withstand living in Charlotte's limelight, and because Charlotte herself couldn't tolerate living in Minneapolis, which was where he spent most of his time.

Failing Marsha, however, Howard Tracey would do very nicely. She had met Tracey eight years before during the course of an investigation into the murder of a Bridge Harbor acquaintance, a botany professor who had died as a result of drinking a cup of poisoned tea. At that time, Tracey had been the police chief in Bridge Harbor. Since then, the prospect of financing college educations for his three children had forced him to seek out a more remunerative position, and he had joined the Maine state police, rising rapidly to the rank of lieutenant. She wasn't surprised at how well he had done. Underneath his country rube persona, which Charlotte suspected he cultivated out of a chameleonlike need to blend in with his surroundings, he was a very smart man.

Despite their disparate backgrounds—though he admitted to having traveled to Boston on a couple of occasions, Tracey was generally loath to leave his little corner of the Maine coast, and was about as unworldly as they come— Charlotte felt a strong kinship with this country police officer. They had a tribal bond, the tribe being that of the old-fashioned Yankee: hard-working, resourceful, persevering, and not without a fair degree of craft and cunning.

Charlotte took a seat on the couch facing the fieldstone fireplace in her living room, telephone receiver in hand. "Ayuh, Howard," she replied, mocking him gently. He always sounded to her as if he were speaking through a mouthful of pebbles, like Demosthenes practicing his orations.

"Something's come up that I think you might be interested in."

Charlotte's ears perked up. Taking into account the Yankee penchant for understatement, she interpreted this statement to mean that an event of major proportions had taken place, and moreover, that it was an event of the utmost importance to her. What on earth could it be!

"Are you free today?" he asked.

"As a bird," she replied, thinking guiltily of her autobiography, the deadline for which had already been postponed twice.

"I'll be over to pick you up in twenty minutes."

"Are you going to pay me the courtesy of telling me what this is all about? Or are you just going to sit there and let me go on wondering what it could be until you get here?"

"The latter. If I knew what it was about, I wouldn't be calling you to find out, now, would I?"

True to his word, Tracey pulled the unmarked state police car over on the gravel shoulder of the Harbor Road exactly twenty minutes later. Though he now worked at the state police barracks, which were an hour and a half away in the university town of Orono, he still lived in Bridge Harbor, which was the hamlet that Charlotte overlooked from her mountainside aerie. She was waiting for him at the foot of her driveway, sitting on a granite boulder. When it came to promptness, Charlotte was as irritatingly scrupulous as Tracey. It was an annoying (to her) habit, but she'd never been able to get over it. As a veteran of fifty-one years in front of the cameras, one of the traits she should have acquired by now was sufficient temerity to put someone out, even if it was only once in a while and for a few minutes. She took her habitual promptness as a fault of character, on a par with a childish propensity to tell the truth even when it wasn't in one's own or anyone else's best interests. (Though an unfailing desire to tell the truth was decidedly not one of her character flaws, her aptitude for dissimulation being one of the factors that had prompted her to go into acting in the first place.)

By now, she had learned to accept her promptness, along with some other undesirable character traits that she might at one time have been inclined to overlook but over the years had been made well aware of, thanks to the tireless efforts of one man or another—if not a husband or a lover, both categories being numerous enough, then a director, a co-star, or a playwright. Since each of the many men in her life had designated different areas of her character as being worthy of remediation, she supposed that she had, given the overwhelming nature of her burden, simply given up. Her long experience at being a candidate for reform had also helped her to discern a pattern in these attempts to make her over, namely that the character traits singled out as faults by a particular man often stood in direct contrast to his own, to his mind, blameless habits, i.e., being prompt was only a character flaw in the eyes of the husband who was habitually late. Had she still been married to Husband Number One, she would probably still be worrying about risking a host's disapprobation by arriving on time for an appointment. She remembered well her habit of those early years, inspired by her husband's criticisms, of walking around the block in order to arrive fifteen minutes after the appointed hour. Without the perspective of the years, she would never have realized that there were people, Howard Tracey among them, who were as concerned about promptness as she, but nevertheless led perfectly respectable lives, and were even invited back by hostesses who hadn't had time, on those occasions where the guest in question had arrived on the dot, to set out the crudités or plump the pillows.

As the car came to a halt, Tracey reached over to open the door for her. "Morning," he said. His round cheeks bulged like a chipmunk's under the brim of his tan porkpie hat, which was a decided sartorial improvement on the baseball cap he had always worn as police chief.

"*Now* are you going to let me in on what this is about?" she asked as she settled in on the front seat next to him.

Ignoring her, Tracey pulled out onto the road that skirted the harbor. The sun was burning the mist off the water, and it rose in wispy tendrils that wound around the masts of the sailboats at their moorings.

"It's about a woman named Iris Richards from Old Town," he said finally. "I think she might be an acquaintance of yours." He looked over at her inquiringly with his big, watery blue eyes.

Charlotte was convinced that much of Tracey's success as a police officer had to do with his appearance. Someone with eyes like a baby's and cheeks like a cherub's inspired one to cooperation.

She combed her memory. She had known Irises—several of them, the most memorable being "her" screenwriter during the Golden Years, Iris O'Connor. Iris O'Connor had been a genius at the kind of sophisticated comedies that had been Charlotte's bread and butter. But she had never known an Iris Richards, especially one from Old Town, Maine.

"Doesn't ring a bell?" he asked.

She shook her head. "What makes you think she might be an acquaintance of mine?"

"You'll see when we get there," he replied.

"Are we going to Old Town, then?"

Tracey nodded as he turned onto the secondary highway that led inland in the direction of the mill town that was just north of Orono on the west bank of the Penobscot River.

Though she had never been there, Charlotte was familiar with Old Town as the site of the Penobscot Indian reservation, which had been much in the news in the 1970s as a result of the land claims settlement act, which awarded the Indians millions of dollars as restitution for their loss of treaty lands.

"What's your interest in this Iris Richards?" she asked.

He looked over at her. "She's dead. Fell off the Knife Edge two weeks ago. Came to a stop a thousand feet later."

"On Mount Katahdin?" It was a statement more than a question. Anyone who had spent any time in Maine had heard of the famous trail, so-called because of its resemblance to a knife blade. It was often referred to as the most difficult nontechnical trail in the East.

"I can tell you haven't been reading the papers," he said. "It's been all over the news. There's going to be an inquiry into her death this afternoon. That's the second of our destinations. It's at one."

Charlotte picked up the folded copy of the *Bangor Daily News* that lay on the seat between them. "Does this tell about it?" she asked.

He nodded. "There's a photograph there, too."

Charlotte opened the paper to the story "Hearing to Be Held on Hiker's Death," which was at the bottom of the front page. A blurry photograph showed a handsome woman in her sixties, with a long, aristocratic face capped by an unruly head of white hair.

"Do you recognize her?" asked Tracey.

Charlotte shook her head. "There's something familiar about the lantern jaw and the deep-set eyes, but I suspect it has more to do with a vague resemblance to FDR than any previous acquaintance on my part."

She went on to read the story, which was about the hearing that was to be held before the Mount Katahdin Tragedy Board of Review, which had been set up to review the accidents that occurred from time to time on Katahdin, with an eye toward instituting policies that would help avert such tragedies in the future. Although, as the article pointed out, mountain-climbing by its very nature carried a certain amount of risk, much of which was unavoidable, and there were actually fewer accidents on Katahdin than might be expected for a mountain climbed by so many people.

But it wasn't this bureaucratic response to the accident that Charlotte was interested in; it was the accident itself, the details of which she found buried in the middle of the story, their being old news by now.

It seemed that Mrs. Richards had fallen off a narrow section of the Knife Edge into a ravine known as the Tully-Baker Gully. After slipping on the rotten granite, she had then dropped about five hundred feet before hitting a ledge and rolling another five hundred feet. The body had finally become wedged in a cleft in a ravine, where it was spotted the next morning by a park ranger. The cause of death was multiple head injuries.

Though Mrs. Richards had climbed the mountain with a companion, a woman by the name of Jeanne Ouellette, they had separated when they had reached the ridge at the top. Miss Ouellette, being the less experienced hiker, had taken an easier route to another one of Katahdin's many peaks, while Mrs. Richards had crossed over the ridge to an area of tableland on the southwest side, where she planned to stop at Thoreau Spring for lunch before climbing the mountain's highest peak, Baxter Peak. From there, her plan was to set out across the Knife Edge.

The article went on to say that although others had died in a similar way as a result of mistaking the head of the ravine for a shortcut off the Knife Edge, this was not presumed to have been the case for Mrs. Richards, who, as an experienced hiker who had climbed the mountain numerous times, would have been aware of the danger of wandering off the trail. If indeed she *had* fallen off the Knife Edge, she was the first to have done so, and one of the purposes of the inquiry was to find out why this might have occurred.

Because of a bottle of rum found in her pack, park authorities had at first thought that Mrs. Richards was intoxicated, but Miss Ouellette explained that it was an annual ritual for her employer to make an offering to the Indian god Pamola by emptying the bottle on Pamola Peak. "Mrs. Richards had read about the Penobscot Indian practice of making an offering of rum to Pamola in the book *The Maine Woods* by Henry David Thoreau," the article quoted Miss Ouellette as saying.

The article went on to say that Mrs. Richards was the president of the New England chapter of the American Thoreau Association and was founder and editor of a journal for followers of the American naturalist, entitled *The Pumpkin Paper* after a quotation from Thoreau's *Walden*:

"I would rather sit on a pumpkin and have it all to myself than be crowded on a velvet cushion."

Reading this, Charlotte felt an odd kinship with the dead woman. She herself was a closet Thoreauvian, and had been a member of the American Thoreau Association for years, though she had never attended any of the meetings.

The investigation into why Mrs. Richards might have fallen off the Knife Edge was now centering on the state of her health, the article continued, quoting the park supervisor as saying that she might have been the victim of a heart attack or a stroke. The article concluded: "The results of the autopsy conducted by State Medical Examiner Henry Clough are expected to be presented to the Baxter State Park Authority at the hearing this afternoon."

As she read this sentence, Charlotte suddenly had an intimation of why Tracey had asked her along. She was acquainted with Henry Clough as a result of the poisoning case. Though the murder rate in a rural state like Maine was only a fraction of that of any major city, Clough was nevertheless considered one of the country's ablest medical examiners. He also had a taste for the limelight, as well as a reputation for surprises, on which he seldom failed to deliver.

"I'm beginning to get the picture," Charlotte said as she refolded the paper and placed it on the seat between them.

Charlotte had originally met Tracey as the result of a best-selling book that had been written about her role in solving the murder of her co-star in a Broadway play. Tracey had read the book, which was called *Murder at the Morosco*, and, when he subsequently needed some help on the poisoning case, had called on her. Now she had the feeling that he was about to call on her again, though she had no idea what her connection with Iris Richards might be.

"Am I correct in assuming that there may be some doubt that Mrs. Richards' death was an accident?" she asked.

"Let's just say that some folks suspect otherwise."

"Like Henry Clough?"

*   *   *

As long as Charlotte had lived in Maine (which was eight years now; she had bought her summer house shortly after the earlier murder), she never tired of driving Maine's back roads. The roadside advertisements were a lesson in Yankee resourcefulness. The variety of goods that could be wheedled out of the harsh environment with the investment of only a pair of willing hands and a few basic tools was astonishing to her. Every farmstead seemed to offer something new, with the products often being displayed on stands at the roadside: jam, honey, maple syrup, pickles, relishes, pies, bread, lobster, crabmeat, canoes, picnic tables, Adirondack chairs, birdhouses, gliders, decoys, quilts, doghouses, lawn ornaments, moccasins, weather vanes. And that was to say nothing of the piles of broken and rusted junk billed as antiques that were displayed as part of the "yard sales" to which there seemed to be no conclusion as long as there was still some gullible tourist who was willing to shell out five dollars for an old horse collar that could be made into a picture frame, or a washboard that could be turned into a lamp. For the Maine native's reputation for resourcefulness also extended to a talent for fleecing the out-of-staters of as much of their hard-earned cash as possible during the transitory run of the tourist season.

Charlotte also loved the rural roads of Maine for their beauty, which was all the more apparent on a spring morning like this one. The morning sun behind the soft mist bathed the landscape in a romantic wash, gilding the stalks of the field grasses and turning the bursting buds into glowing pearls.

"I don't think I've ever seen a prettier spring than this one," said Tracey, echoing her thoughts.

She agreed, though she found any Maine spring a spectacular event. Instead of a succession of bloom—daffodils, quinces, apples, lilacs, peonies—the blossoming period was compressed by the harsh climate, so that everything seemed to explode into bloom at the same time.

Just before the city of Bangor, they left the secondary highway and took the Interstate to Old Town, which was located about ten miles upriver.

Their destination was Hilltop Farm, which was the name of Mrs. Richards' home as well as that of her business, a small wildflower nursery. After leaving the highway, they headed east on Stillwater Avenue, named after the Stillwater River, a tributary of the Penobscot, which they crossed just past a strip of gas stations and fast-food restaurants. Past a sign welcoming them to Old Town (Established 1840), the road took on the character of a village street, lined as it was with gracious old farmhouses.

At the top of the hill leading up from the river, they turned into a driveway bordered by an old stone fence onto a property that was concealed from the road by a dense stand of evergreens. Past the evergreens, the driveway opened up onto a field studded with enormous old trees, at the rear of which a rambling old farmhouse with steeply pitched gables stood against a background of towering pines. A small flock of sheep grazed in the field. In a morning filled with charming farmhouses, this was by far the most enchanting.

A blue state police cruiser was parked in front of the house, and Tracey pulled up behind it. The driver got out and came over to Tracey's window. "Right on time," the trooper said, checking his watch.

He was wearing a blue state-police uniform and the Mountie-type hat that had earned Maine state troopers the nickname "Royal boys" for their resemblance to the Royal Canadian Mounted Police.

"Ayuh," said Tracey proudly, using the Maine substitute for the affirmative, which, in order to be pronounced authentically had to be uttered with a quick little inhalation of the breath.

Tracey obviously suffered none of the insecurities about his promptness that had so plagued Charlotte.

"Is this the lady?" asked the trooper as he removed his hat.

"Ayuh," said Tracey again, with another little gasp. He nodded at Charlotte. "This is Miss Charlotte Graham," he said. "Charlotte, this here is Trooper Douglas Pyle from the Orono barracks. He's assisting me on this case."

"I see," said Charlotte. "It's a case, then," she added, raising an eyebrow in a skeptical expression that was one of her on-screen trademarks and, as she did so, mentally translating Tracey's word "fell" to describe the nature of Mrs. Richards' death to "was pushed" or possibly "was shot."

Tracey grinned, his cheeks bulging. "I'm not saying anything," he declared.

Charlotte reached across Tracey's chest to shake Pyle's hand. He was about thirty, with yellow-blond hair slicked back in the style of a movie star from her era, and a short, dark mustache.

"Good morning," Charlotte said as the young police officer returned her handshake with a pleasant grin. "I'm not sure I know what I'm doing here, but I guess I'll find out soon enough."

"Momentarily," said Pyle. Coming around to her side of the car, he opened the door for her. "Right this way," he said as Charlotte stepped out, leading her up a flower-lined flagstone path to the front door.

The door was answered by a woman in her fifties with wispy gray bangs, thick glasses, and a sallow complexion brightened by a slash of too-pink lipstick.

Charlotte studied her with interest. If, in fact, there was a case, this woman, who had been on the mountain with Mrs. Richards, was a prime witness, if not a suspect. She was tall—close to six feet—with strong, broad shoulders: a woman who was certainly capable of pushing someone off a mountain.

Tracey introduced the woman as Jeanne Ouellette, Mrs. Richards' companion, but introduced Charlotte only as his nameless assistant, knowing how she preferred her anonymity.

Nonetheless, Charlotte had the sense that the woman seemed to know who she was, seemed in fact to be sizing her up. Though Jeanne Ouellette welcomed her visitors politely, Charlotte could sense an undercurrent of fear and worry under the veneer of hospitality. What was she worried about? Charlotte wondered.

Their hostess ushered them into a hall that was presided over by a bronze bust of a young man with an intense gaze and long, curling hair whom Charlotte recognized as the young Henry David Thoreau. She then led them down the hall past a dark-walled, low-ceilinged living room furnished with antiques whose surfaces gleamed in the sunshine that pooled onto the floor.

"This is a lovely home," Charlotte said sincerely. Unlike many houses of this type, it wasn't cluttered, but had the spare simplicity that came from plain walls, wood floors, and a few very good things.

"Thank you," the companion responded with a smile. At the end of the hall, she paused in front of a low door concealed under the staircase opposite the kitchen, and turned to the police officers. "The library," she said.

"What's in there?" asked Charlotte.

Miss Ouellette cast a sidelong glance at the two men, and shrugged. "I don't know," she said, pushing her glasses nervously up over the bump on the ridge of her nose. "She never allowed me in there."

"Are you ready?" Pyle asked Charlotte as he pulled a key out of his pocket. It was strung on a long, black, silken cord.

Charlotte threw up her hands in a gesture of bewilderment. "I wish I knew what it was that I was supposed to be ready for," she said as the trooper inserted the key into the lock.

The door opened into a room with a low, beamed ceiling and a bank of windows overlooking the greenhouses at one side of the property. It was a comfortable room, with walls papered in green, and a worn and faded Oriental rug. A sofa occupied one end, and a wall of bookcases the other.

After the policemen and Charlotte entered, Pyle closed the door behind them, leaving Miss Ouellette out in the hallway.

Charlotte took in the overall effect, then shifted her attention to the details, like the well-tended tray of African violets on the coffee table and the row of photos in silver frames on the shelf under the window. The photographs were all portraits of a glamorous young woman.

Charlotte had been looking at them for several seconds before she realized with a start that they were photographs of her younger self.

"What!" she exclaimed in surprise.

It was like seeing a familiar face among the throng of shoppers in a mirror at a department store, and then realizing that it's your own. Other photographs of Charlotte as a young woman hung on the walls. The walls were covered; there were literally dozens of them.

For a moment, she just stood there, rooted by shock and confusion. The room was a shrine to Charlotte Graham! In the past, she'd sometimes received letters from fans who said they'd collected fifteen hundred photographs of her, or some such nonsense, but she had never actually set eyes on such a collection before. Moreover, that was when she was still at the peak of her stardom. She hadn't heard from that type of fan in years. She was more likely to be admired today for her age and her history, like a national landmark.

The photographs were mostly from the forties, with a few from the early fifties. Studio publicity portraits, mostly. Charlotte in a feather boa, Charlotte in a sequined evening gown, Charlotte in a mink coat. All of them with her signature scrawled across the lower right-hand corner. Then there were the movie stills, many of them showing her locked in an embrace with one leading man or another. There were several of her with Linc, who had been her leading man in some of her most popular pictures. She'd always been convinced that their romance had been plotted by the publicity department. A romance between the leading man and the leading lady made for sizzle on the screen and simoleons at the box office, the saying went.

These were some of the thoughts that passed through her mind as she took in the collection of photographs. But as her attention shifted to the bookcase at the end of the room, she realized that her first assumption had been wrong. In each of the photographs on the bookshelves she was accompanied by another woman. Some of the photographs included other people as well, but the woman was in all of them: a woman with a rich, polished look, and with a long face, a lantern jaw, and a dark cap of wavy black hair.

Charlotte was beginning to realize why she had been invited here. She glanced over at Tracey and Pyle, who stood at the door with their arms across their chests and expectant looks on their faces, and then walked over to the bookcase. It was all there—a collection of scripts in elegant leather-bound volumes with expensive gold lettering, the framed awards from the Screen Writers' Guild, the gleaming Oscar for best original screenplay, 1949. It was the memorabilia of fifteen years as a Hollywood screenwriter.

The room wasn't a shrine to Charlotte, it was a shrine to a career, a career for which Charlotte's beauty and talent had been the raw materials in the same way that the planes of a fashion model's face are for a makeup artist, or a chunk of Carrara marble was for a Renaissance sculptor.

Taking a deep breath, she crossed the room to the sofa, and sat down. Then she said, "She was Iris O'Connor, wasn't she?"

·4·

FOR A MOMENT, Charlotte just sat on the couch, trying to digest it all. She could feel Pyle's hazel eyes studying her, comparing the face of the seventy-one-year-old woman seated before him to that of the glamorous young woman in the photographs. The comparison held up pretty well, she thought. It was one of her life's little benisons that the years had been kind to her. She still looked much as she had in her youth. Her best features hadn't changed: the strong jaw line; the glossy black hair, once worn in a pageboy but now pulled back into a chignon (the gray concealed with the help of the bottle); the thick, winged eyebrows that had become a cause célèbre when she had refused to let studio makeup men pluck them to the pencil-line thinness that was in fashion when she made her first movie in 1939. She had also been blessed with good enough skin that she had never even considered a face lift. But she would never have done so even if she'd had the kind of skin that turned to crepe paper at age thirty; she wouldn't have wanted to look like an emaciated caricature of her younger self—an old woman in a Charlotte Graham mask—as some stars did who'd been lifted too many times.

God! How she hated being scrutinized like this. Looking over at Pyle, she arched an eyebrow—the same expression that was displayed in several of the photographs. It was an expression that had deflated more than one leading man, and it worked like a charm on young Pyle, who shifted his gaze to the greenhouses out on the lawn, and started twirling his hat nervously in his hands.

That problem resolved, she turned her thoughts back to Iris. It must have been—she did a quick mental calculation—thirty-eight years since she had last seen her. It was now 1990, and the last time Charlotte could remember seeing her was at Musso & Frank's Grill in 1952. Charlotte had been with Linc, who had gone there to see a screenwriter. Between six and nine in the evening, you could find any number of Hollywood's screenwriters at Musso & Frank's.

The physical differences weren't that great—Charlotte could now see the Iris of old in the wrinkled face of the newspaper photograph—but she had a hard time reconciling the witty, urbane sophisticate she'd known with a woman whose life had been dedicated to a thinker who preferred a pumpkin to a velvet cushion.

Taking their cue from Charlotte, Tracey and Pyle had seated themselves as well—Tracey on the couch next to Charlotte; Pyle on an easy chair next to the window overlooking the greenhouses.

"How on earth did she end up here?" she finally asked. It struck her that Maine was about as far away from Hollywood as you could get, in the continental United States, anyway.

"That's what we were hoping you could tell us," Tracey said. "No one here even knew she was Iris O'Connor."

"Even Miss Ouellette?" Charlotte asked, with a nod at the door.

"Even Miss Ouellette. She always kept this room locked. Miss Ouellette confessed that she had tried several times over the years to get in. 'Just curious,' she said. But she could never find the key. As it turned out, Mrs. Richards wore it around her neck. It was among the effects that were turned over to us to pass along to the next of kin."

That explained the key being on a black silk cord, thought Charlotte. "Who *is* the next of kin?" she asked.

"We don't know. Miss Ouellette said that she had no brothers or sisters, and that her parents are dead. Again, we thought you might be able to help us out. Any children that you know of?"

Charlotte shook her head. "She was married briefly, but there were no children. I'm pretty sure O'Connor was her maiden name."

"I wonder where the 'Richards' came from," said Tracey.

"I think that was her husband's name, though I couldn't say for sure. It's been a long time. He was a screenwriter who drank himself to death. It was an occupational hazard. Who's the heir?" Charlotte asked. She nodded again at the closed door. "Miss Ouellette?"

"We don't know," replied Tracey. "We haven't gotten that far yet. We're still on Step Number One: identifying the victim. In fact, we don't even know if we have a case yet."

"Maybe it would help revive my memory if you told me what you do know," she said. She looked around her at the green-wallpapered room. "Starting with how you discovered this room."

"The room part is easy," said Tracey. "When we learned that we might have a case—" He looked over at Charlotte, and grinned. "If I could arch an eyebrow, I'd do it now, Charlotte, but it's a trick I've never mastered. Anyway, when we learned we might have a case—"

"From Clough, I presume," she interjected.

Tracey nodded. "—we searched the victim's home. As I mentioned, the key to this room was found on her body." He heaved a deep sigh. "I'll tell you, Charlotte. I don't think I've ever been as dad-blamed hornswoggled as I was when I opened the door and saw all those pictures of you." He looked around the room. "I still can't believe it."

"You couldn't have been any more hornswoggled than I was."

"I guess not," said Tracey. "Anyway, as for the rest of it, I'll let Pyle here give it to you. He's from Old Town, so he knows the story firsthand."

Charlotte was impressed at the easy relationship between Tracey and Pyle, but then, Tracey was an easy man to get along with. She shifted her attention to his earnest young assistant.

"She came here in 1953," Pyle said. "She inherited this property—it's about twenty-three acres, including fifteen acres of woods—from an aunt. She'd never met the aunt. The woods out back are unique; they're one of the last stands of virgin forest in New England."

"It's one of the most substantial properties in town," added Tracey.

Charlotte nodded in acknowledgment of this obvious fact.

"She was a recluse when she first moved here," Pyle continued. "There was some talk of a drinking problem." He looked at Charlotte. "An occupational hazard, right? But if she did have a problem, she got over it."

"How do you know?" she asked.

"In a small town, you just know," Tracey explained. "Especially if every lush in town has to buy their booze at the state liquor store."

Charlotte had forgotten about Maine's state liquor stores.

"Miss Ouellette joined her in 1955, part-time at first," Pyle continued. "But as the wildflower business grew, she moved into a full-time position, and has lived here as Mrs. Richards' companion for the last thirty-three years, helping to run the nursery and the Thoreau business."

"What exactly is the Thoreau business?" Charlotte asked. "I read about the Thoreau journal in the newspaper."

"*The Pumpkin Paper*," said Pyle.

"Is there any more to it than that?" she asked.

He nodded. "Thoreau passed through Old Town on his trips upcountry," said Pyle. "The Indian guides for two of his trips—his trip to Chesuncook and his trip to the Allagash—came from Indian Island."

"Joe Aitteon and Joe Polis," she said.

"Yeah," he said, his jaw dropping in surprise. "How'd you know?"

"I was in a play once with Thoreau, or rather, with John Redfield, who played Thoreau," she replied. "So I did a lot of reading about him. I played Margaret Fuller, his editor at *The Dial*. Henry David and I spent a lot of time on stage rowing around Walden Pond."

"The title was *On Walden Pond*," said Tracey, who was one of her loyal fans. "Miss Graham was nominated for a Tony award."

Charlotte nodded. The role was one of her favorites both for the powerful woman she had played—"I wish I were a man," Margaret had said. " 'Tis an evil lot to have a man's ambition and a woman's heart"—and for the lifelong fascination with Thoreau it had inspired.

"Anyway," Pyle continued, "she became a leader in Thoreau studies, I guess you could say. She started *The Pumpkin Paper*, taught a course on Thoreau at the university, led trips upcountry that traced Thoreau's footsteps—that sort of thing. I know she had quite a following."

"In what way?" Charlotte asked.

"I only know that before I joined the state police, I was a police officer in Old Town. Not a week went by that someone didn't stop by the station to inquire how to get to Hilltop Farm."

They were interrupted by a knock. A moment later, the door opened and Miss Ouellette stuck her gray head through the opening. "How are you doing?" she asked, clearly curious, but afraid to ask outright.

Charlotte noticed that she didn't take advantage of the opportunity to look around the room, which she thought odd for someone who had presumably been excluded from it for thirty-odd years.

"We're doing fine, Miss Ouellette," said Tracey dismissively. "We're just about finished here." He checked his watch, then turned to his companions. "I don't know about you, but I'm getting hungry. How about some dinner?"

Maine was one of those places where people still referred to the midday meal as dinner, and ate accordingly.

"We just have time before the hearing," he added.

Charlotte and Pyle agreed.

"We'll be right out," Tracey said to Miss Ouellette, and her gray head withdrew from behind the door.

She was waiting for them just outside when they emerged a moment later. "Did you find anything, Lieutenant?" she asked tentatively. She had a way of hovering, like an over-sized mother hen.

"We'll get back to you when we learn more about the circumstances of Mrs. Richards' death," said Tracey as the small group made its way back down the hall. "Meanwhile, we appreciate your help."

As she and Tracey followed Pyle to the coffee shop that he had recommended for dinner, Charlotte found herself pondering the metamorphosis of the Hollywood sophisticate into the proprietor of a wildflower nursery in rural Maine. It didn't make any sense: there seemed to be no overlap between the two. They were as distinct from one another as the austere farmhouse was from the cluttered green room shut away within it. An interest in gardening or a love of the outdoors might have explained it, but the closest to gardening Charlotte could remember Iris ever getting was a story conference at the Garden of Allah, one of Hollywood's most popular watering holes. Or even a rural upbringing, but she knew for a fact that Iris had grown up in a Chicago suburb, and Pyle said she hadn't even known the aunt who left her Hilltop Farm. Not that she hadn't physically fit the part of the nurserywoman. With her tall, rawboned figure and patrician bone structure, she'd always looked as if she belonged more on a gentlewoman's farm than on a Hollywood movie set.

From Hilltop Farm, they followed Stillwater Avenue down the other side of the hill toward downtown Old Town, which lay in the river valley. The road ended a few minutes later at a stop light at the intersection with North Main Street, which ran along the river. To their left, a two-lane bridge arched over the river. Next to it was a sign that read INDIAN ISLAND, HOME OF

THE PENOBSCOTS. The picture on the sign was of an Indian in profile with two feathers hanging down over his ear and an arm pointing over the bridge. Underneath was a notice that read "Penobscot Nation High Stakes Bingo: Next Game Saturday, June 23 & Sunday June 24."

"There's Indian Island," said Tracey.

Charlotte looked over at the placid island with interest. Old Town had been so-named by the Indians, who called it that because their ancestors had inhabited this spot for ten thousand years or more. Relics of the Red Paint People, the prehistoric ancestors of the Penobscots, had been found buried in red ochre powder in graves on Indian Island. "I don't know what I expected," she said, gazing out at the steepled church and clusters of white clapboard houses. "But it wasn't this." Somehow she expected an island that had been inhabited for ten millennia or more to look more prepossessing.

"Doesn't look like an Indian reservation, that's for sure," said Tracey. "But I can't say that I've ever seen any other Indian reservations. Except in the movies," he added.

As they waited for the light to change, Charlotte studied the sign. The Indian was shadowed by a bald eagle with an outstretched wing. The Indian's outstretched arm and the wing, which merged into one, pointed to a distant, snow-capped mountain. "Is that Katahdin?" she asked.

"Ayuh," said Tracey, looking over at the sign. "It's the sacred mountain of the Penobscots. Home of Pamola, the Indian god who inhabits the summit. Part moose, part eagle, with a wicked temper. I've heard that the Penobscots won't go above the tree line for fear that he'll come after them."

"Unless they take along a bottle of rum."

"Huh?" said Tracey.

"The article said that's why Iris took along a bottle of rum. To pacify Pamola. She got the idea from Thoreau's writings."

"I must not have gotten to that part," Tracey said.

When the light changed, they turned right onto North Main past a row of old red brick mills, once the economic backbone of the city, which had been transformed into senior citizens' apartments or office buildings, or stood vacant, windows empty and roofs caving in. Beyond the mills the wide, green river flowed south to the sea under a high, light blue sky, the opposite shore fringed with willows whose leaves were still the pale green of early spring. Though its surface was smooth, the river nevertheless gave the impression of enormous power and weight. Charlotte had once read that the Penobscot drained a quarter of the state, and the river seemed to carry the authority that came from having traveled a long distance. The waters that flowed past these mills had once been snow on the summit of Mount Katahdin, and had traveled through hundreds of miles of paper-company-owned forest land before reaching Old Town, which was the first in a string of good-sized towns and cities that lined the river on its path out to Penobscot Bay.

As they approached the center of town, Pyle pulled the police cruiser to a stop in front of an unpretentious eatery called the Canoe City Coffee Shop. Old Town was also known as Canoe City after the Old Town Canoe Company, whose factory outlet store adjoined the coffee shop. Tracey pulled in behind Pyle, and a moment later they were sitting in a booth by a sunny window overlooking an old hydro-electric dam.

The menus, which were propped between the sugar bowl and the napkin holder, didn't offer any surprises. It was all hearty down-home fare: baked ziti, meat loaf, hot turkey sandwich. "Any recommendations?" Charlotte asked Pyle, who, judging from the welcome he had received, was a regular.

"Everything's good, but the hot turkey sandwich is especially good," he replied enthusiastically. "Real turkey breast, thickly cut, with homemade gravy. None of that fake pressed turkey stuff."

"A hot turkey sandwich it is," said Tracey, closing his menu.

"How about the mashed potatoes?" asked Charlotte. "Not instant, I hope."

"No way," said Pyle.

"That makes three," added Charlotte. She was a great fan of diners, of which this was the Downeast equivalent. One of the great virtues of a good diner was the ability to do simple food very well.

After they had given their orders to the blue-haired waitress, Charlotte asked Pyle what Iris had been like. She was curious how life in this small Maine river town had changed her.

"Town character's what she was," he replied. "An odd duck."

"In what way?" Charlotte asked. Pyle was clearly one of those taciturn Yankees whom you had to prod a bit to get going.

"Every way, near's I can tell. Always wore old, baggy clothes and a straw hat; walked everywhere—didn't believe in cars, or telephones, for that matter. Lived right here in town, and didn't have a telephone. Can you fathom that?" He shook his blond head in disbelief.

Not unlike Thoreau himself, Charlotte thought.

"A lot of people thought she was a mite prickly," Pyle continued. "She had strong opinions about a lot of things, and she didn't mind telling people their business—that's for sure."

"Then she made enemies," said Charlotte.

Pyle nodded. "Plenty of 'em. She was kind of a hermit, though. Miss Ouellette took care of all of her business: shopping, errands, and so on. It wasn't that she didn't get out and about—you'd always see her out walking—but she didn't mingle much, if you know what I mean."

"A hermit-about-town," said Charlotte.

"That's it," said Pyle with a smile. "A hermit-about-town."

"It's what New Yorkers used to say about Garbo," she explained. The great Swedish movie star had just died and was very much on Charlotte's mind, her death seeming to mark the end of a Hollywood era.

"Can't tell you much more than that," said Pyle.

"Now, Charlotte, why don't you tell us what you know?" Tracey asked as the waitress set the heavy Buffalo-ware platters with their hot turkey sandwiches down on the Formica table. Speedy service was another virtue of the good diner.

"She was my screenwriter," Charlotte said. "In the old days, we each had our own. She had been a novelist. Maybe you've read some of her books: *The Lonely Heart* is considered a classic; it's on every eleventh-grade English teacher's reading list."

"I've read it, but it was a long time ago," said Tracey as he tucked into his dinner. "In eleventh grade, as a matter of fact. I remember thinking that it was a girl's book. At that point, I was more into Edgar Rice Burroughs."

Charlotte gave him a look of distaste, at which he grinned and pounded his chest in an imitation of Tarzan.

"She came to Hollywood with the rest," Charlotte continued. "Faulkner, Hemingway, Fitzgerald. It was the offer they couldn't refuse; the money was too good. Many of them ended up leaving. Either they hated it or they were no good at it, usually a combination of the two. But that wasn't true of Iris."

"This is delicious, Pyle," interrupted Tracey, pointing with his fork to the food on his plate.

"What did I tell you?" the trooper replied.

"Sorry, Charlotte," Tracey said. "Didn't mean to interrupt."

"That's okay," she said. She addressed Pyle: "It is good. Perfect, as a matter of fact. Anyway," she went on, "Iris had a knack for comedy, which was odd, since her novels weren't funny. She had a light, easy touch—a way of flirting with the material. I don't think a man could have done what she did. She and I usually worked with the director Harold

Ames. As a writer, actor, director team, we were unbeatable. We had hit after hit."

"You've probably seen some of those films on television, Pyle," said Tracey. He reeled off a list of titles.

Pyle nodded in recognition.

"I owe much of my success to Iris," Charlotte said.

"Then what?" Tracey prompted.

"HUAC," she said as if it explained everything, which it did.

Pyle looked at her with a quizzical expression. "The House Committee on Un-American Activities," she said. "Otherwise known as HUAC. Self-appointed guardians of American internal security from 1947 to 1953."

"Oh," said Pyle, who still looked baffled.

"Their mission was to expose Communists, and their special target was the entertainment industry," Tracey explained.

Charlotte continued. "Iris had some friends—other screen writers, mostly—who were self-confessed Communist sympathizers, or com symps, as they were known. She had been very close to some members of the Hollywood Ten, who went to jail for their beliefs, as well as to other blacklisted writers."

"Blacklisted?" asked Pyle.

Charlotte sighed. She was feeling more and more like a time traveler these days. She realized that she would have to start from Square One.

"If a writer was called to testify before HUAC, and refused to answer the sixty-four-dollar question, as it was called, after the quiz show, which was, 'Are you now, or have you ever been, a member of the Communist Party,' his—or her—name was put on a list and he or she could expect never to work again."

"Unless he or she implicated others," interjected Tracey, who, thank God, had some acquaintance with the events of that era.

"Right. Those who were subpoenaed had the option of getting off the hook by naming names. And many of them did. Losing your swimming pool or your tennis court were powerful threats. But there were some who would rather have lost everything than turn stool pigeon." Like Linc Crawford, she thought.

"Was Iris O'Connor a Communist?" asked Pyle in the same tone of voice one would use to refer to a child molester or a rapist. It was clear which side he would have been on had he been born a generation or two earlier.

"It didn't matter. It was a witch hunt. Two hundred and fifty people were blacklisted. Thousands more were graylisted. And the FBI had dossiers on hundreds of thousands more, myself among them, I suspect."

Pyle looked contrite.

To be fair, she thought, it was probably difficult for a thirty-year-old to see the idealistic appeal of a system that in those days was still young enough not to have demonstrated its essential unworkability or revealed the evil and corruption that went along with it.

"Anyway, in answer to your question: I don't know. She wasn't a card-carrying Communist, to use McCarthy's phrase. She may have gone to a few meetings, but so did a lot of people."

"Of the Communist Party?" asked Pyle incredulously.

Charlotte tried to explain. "The line between capitalist and Communist was thinner then. No group could have been more plugged into the capitalist system than the Hollywood screenwriters. Yet a lot of them were outraged at how blacks were treated; remember, there was still segregation then." She paused for a moment to eat her dinner, which was indeed delicious, and then continued. "Then there was the Spanish Civil War."

"The Abraham Lincoln Battalion," said Tracey.

"Yes. A lot of actors and writers supported the Loyalists; some, like Hemingway (and Linc, she thought), even joined international battalions that were formed to fight Franco. Though that was all in the late thirties, the Red hunters had long memories."

"I guess I don't know much about history," Pyle apologized.

What were they teaching in school nowadays? Charlotte wondered. "Anyway, it didn't matter whether Iris was a Communist or not. It was enough to have breathed the same air as a Communist, and Iris had associated with a number of self-confessed Reds."

Thinking about those days, Charlotte remembered a story she'd once heard about someone who was subpoenaed because they'd been at the same bullfight with Picasso, an admitted Communist. It didn't matter that the person didn't know Picasso, hadn't even sat on the same side of the ring. He had been there.

"Did Iris go to jail?" asked Tracey.

"No . . ."

"What happened to her?"

"That's a good question." She was trying to remember. She had repressed a lot from that period. Part of it had to do with her own passive complicity, or what she perceived as her own passive complicity, in the witch hunt. Despite the fact that she too had associated with known Communists, one of her favorite directors among them, she had never been called upon to testify. The reason for this, she was sure, lay with her public image. It would have been impossible to convince the public that an actress who had made a career out of playing idle debutantes and sassy secretaries could ever have been a Communist. The same had been true of the war heroes; they were untouchable by virtue of their public image (except for Linc, she thought).

At the time, she had felt much as a Vietnam-era student who received a high number in the draft lottery must have felt—relieved at not having to take a stand (or rather, *the* stand). But as the hearings had dragged on, leaving a trail of blighted lives in their wake, she had begun to feel ashamed of this chapter in her life. Yes, she had joined the Committee for the First Amendment, flying to Washington with a plane load of stars to protest the first round of HUAC hearings in

1947, but the committee had folded almost as fast as it had coalesced, and other protest efforts were equally short-lived, especially after friendly witnesses starting naming names.

Iris' was one of those ruined careers that had left Charlotte with survivor's guilt. She supposed that's why she had thought so little about her over the years, despite the fact that her name still came up with some frequency in literary and cinematic circles. What *had* happened to Iris? she asked herself. As she gazed out the window at the water falling over the dam, it slowly came back to her. "She was subpoenaed," she said finally. "It was in the winter of 1952, after HUAC had reopened its investigation. I remember the date because several other people I knew got their pink slips at the same time. Her testimony was taken in executive session at a hotel in L.A."

"Executive session?" said Tracey.

"It meant that the testimony wouldn't be released. It was a deal that the lawyers were sometimes able to work out to avoid having their clients' names dragged through the mud. But it only worked for the small fry. The big fish didn't have that option."

"What happened to her after that?" asked Tracey.

"She simply disappeared. Went underground, I guess you'd say. Most of the blacklisted screenwriters went to New York; some went abroad—Paris, Mexico, Paraguay; some moved to rural areas where they could live cheaply."

"Like Old Town," said Tracey.

She nodded. "The situation was better for writers than for actors or directors because they could change their names or hire fronts and continue working. A lot of them wrote for television. People used to say that there were more aliases in television than there were fleas on Lassie."

"I like that," said Tracey with a chuckle.

Having finished their meals, they leaned back in the sunny booth and relaxed, three empty platters on the table in front of them.

"That's why the early days of television were so wonderful," Charlotte explained. "The finest screenwriting talent in the world was available at bargain basement prices."

"Is that what Iris did?" Tracey asked.

"Maybe, but I don't think so. Television was my refuge for a while too. I would have recognized her work, or have heard about her. You usually knew that a script had been written by a blacklisted screenwriter."

For a moment, the conversation lapsed as the waitress cleared their plates. "Any dessert?" she asked.

Tracey checked his watch. "I don't think we have time. The hearing starts in twenty minutes. In fact, I'd better go up and pay now," he added as he picked up the bill. "This one's on the State of Maine."

Excusing himself, he went up to the cash register.

Charlotte was still thinking about the blacklist era. "The writers who continued working were the lucky ones, even if they were only paid a pittance," she reflected to Pyle after Tracey had left. "Many of the people on the blacklist ended up killing themselves, or drinking themselves to death."

"Like Mrs. Richards almost did," he said.

Charlotte nodded. She was reminded of the bottle of rum in Iris' pack. She suspected it was more likely to have been an offering to propitiate the alcohol demon than the Indian god.

As she thought about the rum, she suddenly realized the answer to the question that was lying at the back of her mind. The link between Iris the screenwriter and Iris the nurserywoman was Thoreau's essay, *Civil Disobedience*, which had inspired the Civil Rights activists and countless others to stand up to the Government in the name of justice. Thoreau had chosen to go to jail (if only for a night) rather than pay a tax to a government that supported slavery. Iris had chosen to sacrifice a lucrative career rather than testify against her colleagues. "Under a government which imprisons any unjustly, the true place for a just man is also in prison," Thoreau wrote. Unlike the Hollywood Ten, Iris hadn't been imprisoned, but she had created her own prison of sorts in this central Maine mill town.

At first, at any rate. It appeared that it hadn't remained so, that she had, in fact, created a rich and rewarding life here. Charlotte could imagine her seeking out Thoreau's words as consolation for her lonely stand, and then, taking comfort from the solace they offered, being drawn into the simple life he espoused. Something of the same sort had also happened to Charlotte as a result of her on-stage boat rides with Henry David in *On Walden Pond*. She had taken a more moderate course in her pursuit of the simple life, her experience at living in the woods being limited to her mountainside retreat, and there was much of Thoreau she couldn't abide, starting with his admonition to "beware of any enterprises that require new clothes," clothes being one of her great passions. But she found it interesting that both she and Iris, neither of whom could claim any natural propensity for rusticity, had discovered the Philosphers' Stone in Thoreau's prescription for the simple life.

She wondered how many other Thoreauvians there were. A good many, from what Pyle had said about the pilgrims to Hilltop Farm. The only other one she had ever known was Linc, an appreciation for Thoreau being a natural for a rugged individualist with a love of the outdoors. He could cite Thoreau chapter and verse. She still remembered the marked-up Heritage Press edition of *Walden* that he'd always carried around with him. It was one of his things that she wished she could have had when he died, but it had gone to his ex-wife or his sister, like everything else. To them, she thought with some bitterness, the book had probably meant nothing.

Dismissing her morbid thoughts, she took advantage of Tracey's momentary absence to pump Pyle for information: "Lieutenant Tracey has indicated that there might be some cause to think Iris' death wasn't accidental," she said. "Do you know anything more about it?"

But Pyle wasn't biting. "Nope," he said as he drained the dregs of his coffee. "But I doubt it was really murder. The M.E. is such a publicity hound that he'd try to give that impression just to get a good turnout."

"I guess we'll find out in a few minutes," she said.

· 5 ·

THE HEARING BEFORE the Mount Katahdin Tragedy Board of Review was to be held at the Eastern Region Headquarters of the state forest service, which was located in a cluster of log cabin-type buildings on the bank of the Penobscot, overlooking the northern end of Indian Island. On the river bank itself were two airplane hangars that serviced the float planes that flew fire watches all over the state. A couple of these were anchored in the river at the seaplane base at the foot of the complex. Next to the hangars, a cluster of helicopters and a row of tank trucks stood at the ready in case of a forest fire.

After parking, Tracey and Charlotte were directed to a meeting room in one of the buildings. Pyle had gone back to the barracks. To their surprise, they found that not only was the meeting room full, a bank of television cameras was lined up at one side.

"The word must be out that Dr. Clough has a surprise in store," said Charlotte as they headed toward the few empty seats at the back.

"Thanks no doubt to Clough himself," Tracey growled.

The front of the room was occupied by a dais, on which the four members of the board sat behind a long table. They consisted of the Inland Fisheries and Wildlife Commissioner, who was the chairman; the Maine Forest Commissioner; the attorney general; and the Baxter State Park Supervisor. To stage left was a chair for the witnesses, and in front was a table for a court stenographer.

No sooner had they taken their seats than the hearing opened.

The first to speak was the chairman, who thanked the park employees and volunteers who had assisted in the recovery effort. This was followed by a brief speech in which he explained that the purpose of the hearing was not to find fault or assign blame, but to reconstruct the sequence of events that had led up to Mrs. Richards' death, with an eye toward instituting procedures that would prevent future occurrences of such a nature.

These remarks were followed by the witnesses' testimony. The first witness to take the stand was the park ranger who had discovered the body, a young man named Chris Sargent. Sargent began by pointing out Iris' route on a topographical map that was projected onto a screen at the front of the room. The map was then replaced by a slide of the Great Basin, which was a perfect bowl with walls of sheer granite, encircled by the sharp rim of the Knife Edge.

"Wow!" exclaimed Charlotte as the slide appeared on the screen. Seeing the mountain's most prominent feature for the first time, she was taken aback by its strange and magnificent perfection. It was as smooth and regular as if it had been hand-thrown by God himself on a celestial potter's wheel.

"Pretty impressive, isn't it?" said Tracey as the ranger pointed out the spot where he had located Iris' body.

"I'll say," Charlotte agreed. She could readily see why the Indians had designated it as their sacred mountain.

The ranger nodded at the projectionist, and the slide of the basin was replaced by a slide of the headwall, which was striated with the snow that still lay in its ravines.

"Here we see the headwall with the body of the victim," said the ranger. Picking up a pointer, he indicated a small patch of vivid green lodged in one of the ravines, about halfway down the headwall.

He nodded again, and the slide on the screen changed to a close-up which showed Iris' body caught in a niche, folded up almost flat, with her feet up against her head. She was wearing a neon-green rain suit, which was spattered with blood. The contents of her ash splint pack, which had been crushed, lay spread out along the path of her fall.

Above the niche, the ravine narrowed to a cleft. Below, it widened to a steep, jagged slope covered with loose granite. Charlotte wondered how the rescue team had ever gotten the body off the mountain.

At this point the park supervisor leaned into his microphone and said, "Some people have the impression that getting an accident victim off the mountain is an easy matter. They say, 'Why don't they just lug him or her on down?' " He spoke with a Downeast accent that was almost as thick as Tracey's. "Well, I think you can see from this slide that it's not that simple."

These comments were followed by the ranger's description of the evacuation itinerary, which was also illustrated with slides. It had taken the rescue team the best part of a day to evacuate the body. The task had involved lowering the body down three three-hundred-foot technical pitches to the point where a ground crew could reach it from the ledges at the back of the basin.

After Sargent had finished his presentation, the district supervisor and the leader of the rescue team described the roles they had played, from when they had first learned of the accident to when the body was flown out of Chimney Pond. Several made suggestions as to how rescue procedures could be improved, but in general they agreed that the operation had gone smoothly.

At last, it was time for the chief medical examiner, Dr. Henry Clough, to testify. A hubbub swept the room as he took a seat in the witness chair. He was carrying a canvas boat bag, which he set down at his feet.

He was a short, slight man with a long, ruddy face, a fifties-style crewcut, and a wool tartan tie. After identifying himself, he began by noting for the record that he had examined the body of the deceased at the Dow Funeral Home in

Millinocket, where it had been taken after being evacuated to the Millinocket Municipal Airport by the 112th Medivac.

He then went on to describe the victim as a white Caucasian female of about seventy years of age, weighing approximately one hundred and forty pounds, and standing five feet six inches tall. Next came the description of the injuries, which went on for some time, each contusion, laceration, and broken bone, of which there seemed to be dozens, being precisely enumerated.

At last, he signaled the projectionist for the first slide.

There was a collective gasp from the audience as the slide appeared on the screen. It was a photograph of the dead woman's head and neck, taken from the side. The body was lying on its back on a stainless steel autopsy table. The head was covered with dried blood, which had turned black. She looked as if she'd fallen headfirst into a mud puddle.

Charlotte looked for signs of the Iris she had once known, but the body was like a complete stranger's to her.

"Here you can see some of the injuries that the victim sustained in the fall," Clough said. "Basically, she was beaten to a pulp. There was a lot of bleeding; some of it's from the cuts and lacerations that occurred as a result of the fall. However," he added, "not all of it." After a brief pause, he turned to address the board directly. "It wasn't the fall that killed her."

"Are you saying that she was shot?" interjected one of the television newsmen. At this question, flashbulbs started popping, and the cameramen started jockeying for position.

"Would you like to tell us what it was that killed her?" the Fisheries and Wildlife Commissioner said tartly, obviously perturbed at the medical examiner's grandstanding.

"Certainly," Clough responded. He nodded again at the projectionist, and another slide appeared on the screen. This one showed Iris' head in the same position, but in this slide the dried blood had been washed off. The side of her head was caved in, like a jack-o'-lantern that's begun to rot.

Rising from the stand, Dr. Clough picked up the pointer and went over to the screen. "This is what killed her," he said, touching the tip to a small, neat, round hole on the side of Iris' neck. "A perforating injury to the side of the neck produced by the tip of an arrow."

For a moment, there was stunned silence as the audience took in his statement. One of the journalists finally spoke. "She was murdered with a bow and arrow?" he asked incredulously.

Tracey leaned in close to Charlotte's ear. "You'd think Clough would have had the courtesy to let the state police in on this before he blabbed to the press," he whispered, a look of consternation on his usually genial face.

Nodding affirmatively to the journalist's question, the M.E. explained that the unusual amount of blood had been caused by the arrow hitting the carotid artery. He then went on to describe the nature of the crushing injury that had occurred at the juncture of the cervical and thoracic vertebrae.

"Dr. Clough, wouldn't one of the other hikers on the Knife Edge or on Baxter Peak have noticed someone carrying a bow and a quiver full of arrows?" asked another reporter.

"That would be true of a longbow," Dr. Clough replied. "But not of a crossbow." Returning to the stand, he reached into his bag and pulled out a weapon the likes of which Charlotte had never seen. "Especially one like this," he said, holding it up. "For those of you who are unfamiliar with it, this is a pistol crossbow."

Tracey let out a long, low whistle.

"Basically, it's a cross between a bow and a pistol: a short, powerful bow mounted at right angles on the forward portion of a pistol body. Fourteen inches long, collapsible"—he demonstrated by folding the limbs up, and sliding the stock into the body—"and neatly fitted into a carryall."

"What's the range?" asked one of the board members.

"Thirty to forty yards." Pulling the weapon back out, Clough opened it up. "This one's fitted with a rear notch sight and an adjustable front pin sight," he said, pointing the sights out to his audience, "but they can also be fitted with scopes."

The journalists, no longer skeptical, were writing furiously.

Holding the weapon at arm's length by its pistol-type grip, which resembled that of a military weapon, Dr. Clough sighted a bead on an imaginary target, and pulled the trigger. "As accurate and deadly as a pistol, but with the advantage of making very little noise."

"Aren't crossbows illegal in the state of Maine?" asked one of the television journalists.

Tracey leaned over to whisper again in Charlotte's ear. "Since when does a weapon's being illegal mean that criminals don't use it?"

"Illegal to hunt with, but not to possess," Dr. Clough said. "I got this one at a local sporting goods store. The clerk described it as looking like a gun and shooting like a bow, but in my opinion, he should have said that it looks like a bow and shoots like a gun." Bending over, he reached into his bag again and pulled out an arrow, which was about eight inches long. "This is the arrow," he said, holding it up. "It's called a bolt, or a quarrel."

"Can you spell that, please?" asked one of the reporters.

"Q-u-a-r-r-e-l," he said. "Like an argument. Maybe that's where the word comes from. Anyway, this is a target bolt made from high-strength drawn aluminum alloy." He pointed to the tip. "The point has been fitted with an ordinary cartridge shell to create a blunt head."

He nodded to the projectionist, and an enlargement of the point appeared on one half of a divided screen, and a close-up of the entrance wound on the other. "As you can see, the shape of the point corresponds exactly to that of the entrance wound. Judging from the fact that the bolt didn't go all the way through the victim's neck, I'd guess that the victim was shot from some distance, let's say about forty yards."

"Would it be correct to say that the murderer would have to be a good shot?" asked one of the board members.

"I would say so, yes," Dr. Clough replied. "It requires a lot less skill to hit the bull's-eye with a crossbow than with a conventional longbow, because the speed of the bolt is much greater, but . . ."

"How great?" interrupted the chairman.

"The bolt speed of this model is two hundred and eighty feet per second."

"That's almost as fast as a bullet, isn't it?" asked the park supervisor.

"About a third of the muzzle velocity of a .38 calibre revolver, but enough to kill you nonetheless," the medical examiner replied.

"Jeezum," muttered Tracey under his breath.

"As I was saying," Dr. Clough continued, "it requires less skill to hit a target with a crossbow because the bolt speed is greater and the trajectory is flatter, but there was also a lot of wind up there. The murderer would have to have adjusted for windage, which can be done with the front sight." He demonstrated by moving the sight from side to side.

"Can we tell from which direction it was fired?" the chairman asked.

"We know from the location of the entrance wound that the weapon was fired directly from the side, but not from which side. The victim could have been looking out either to the north or to the south. I assume she was standing, since it's my understanding that the trail at that point is too narrow to sit on." He looked over at the board for confirmation.

"Unless you set astraddle it," said the park supervisor.

Dr. Clough went on. "But I would venture to guess that the murderer was facing away from Baxter Peak, where we know there were other hikers who might have seen him raise a crossbow."

For a moment there was silence as the audience studied the two photographs. Then the chairman asked, "Why wouldn't the murderer have used an ordinary arrowhead?"

"I was waiting for someone to ask that question," Dr. Clough replied with a smile. "I don't know for sure, of course. But what I surmise is this: if the victim was shot with a broadhead, as an ordinary arrowhead is called, it would have gone through her neck, and it would have stayed there."

"Making it obvious that she was murdered," commented the chairman.

The medical examiner nodded. "I think the murderer was counting on the entrance wound being overlooked among the multitude of cuts and lacerations caused by the fall," he explained.

"But he wasn't counting on you," said the chairman.

"Exactly," said Dr. Clough, humility not being his strong suit.

"Where *is* the bolt?" asked the chairman. "Was it dislodged in the fall?"

"Maybe," said Dr. Clough. "In which case, state police investigators"—he nodded vaguely in Tracey's direction—"may find it somewhere on the headwall. But I seriously doubt it."

"Why?" came a question from the audience.

Rising from the witness chair, the medical examiner picked up the pointer and went back over to the screen. "The neatness of the entrance wound," he replied, circling the pointer around the perimeter of the hole. "If the arrow had been dislodged in the fall, there would have been more tissue damage."

"What do you think happened to it, then?" the chairman asked.

The medical examiner nodded to an assistant at the back of the room, who came forward with an archery target mounted on an aluminum stand, which he set up at one side of the raised platform.

"That's another question I was waiting for someone to ask. I think the murderer rigged the crossbow like a fishing bow." Returning to his seat and reaching into his bag again, he pulled out another weapon. "This is a pistol crossbow that's been mounted with a drum reel"—he pointed to the reel mounted on the rear portion of the body—"which holds about a hundred feet of ordinary monofilament fishing line."

"The line's attached to the arrow?" asked the chairman.

Dr. Clough nodded. "In essence, it's a retrievable bullet. The line is run through a hole at the back of the bolt, and then through a second hole near the head, where it's secured." Rising again, he walked over to the lectern and showed the crossbow to the board. Then he turned to face the audience. "Now, I'm going to demonstrate." He held up an apple. "Any volunteers?"

The joke produced a hearty laugh from the audience.

"Who does this guy think he is, P. T. Barnum?" whispered Tracey, who was clearly not amused by the medical examiner's stunt.

It struck Charlotte as more than a little tasteless, especially with the slide of Iris' head still up on the screen.

When no one volunteered, he placed his foot in the cocking stirrup, grasped the string with both hands, and drew it back into the trigger mechanism. Then he loaded the bolt into the firing track. Holding his arm fully extended, he took aim through the rear sight, adjusted the bead of the front sight, and then pulled the trigger.

As the audience watched, the bolt whizzed across the stage, and struck the yellow bull's-eye. For a moment, it rested in the target, its spine vibrating from the force of the impact. Then the medical examiner began to reel it in, as if it were a trout on a hook. The bolt had been shot and retrieved as quietly as a shuttlecock sailing back and forth over a badminton net.

"Well, I'll be darned," said Tracey.

Dr. Clough had delivered, as promised.

*   *   *

Afterward, they adjourned to Tracey's office at the state police barracks. Tracey had called a meeting with Bill Haverty, the South District supervisor for the park, who attended with the Chimney Pond ranger, Chris Sargent. The purpose of the meeting was to divide up the responsibilities of the investigation. The task of searching for the bolt was assigned to Haverty, who would need to put together a technical team for the purpose. Haverty was also to provide Tracey with a list of drivers' names and license plate numbers for the cars that had been in the park on the day of the murder. This wasn't as difficult as it might have seemed. The park was accessible by road by only two entrances, a northern gate at Matagamon and a southern gate at Togue Pond, which were linked by a forty-three-mile perimeter road. As a result of the need to control access, a system had been introduced whereby rangers at the two gates filled out entrance permits for all vehicles entering the park, as well as for the occasional hiker or bicyclist. In addition to the driver's name and the vehicle's license plate number, the permits also included information on the number of people in the party, where the journey had originated, the length of stay, the purpose of the visit, and at what campground the party would be staying. Part of the permit was torn off and given to the driver, who was asked to deposit it in a box at the gatehouse when exiting. At the close of the day, the permits on file at the gatehouses were matched with the slips returned by the drivers, thus allowing park authorities to keep close tabs on who was in the park (and who was supposed to be gone, but wasn't).

Once Haverty came up with the list, Pyle would get the addresses from the state motor vehicle departments, with the goal of interviewing everyone who had been in the park on the day of the murder, paying particular attention to visitors who gave their destination as Katahdin on the hikers' registers. Perhaps one of these hikers had noticed something—or someone—unusual. Another goal of these interviews would be to look for some link to the victim. The murder was apparently premeditated, since the killer had taken along a crossbow. And although it was unlikely that anyone planning to commit murder would register at the gatehouse, criminals could sometimes be amazingly stupid, the police had noted.

On the theory that the murderer had gained access to the park via some other route, Pyle was also charged with the task of exploring the forest land along the park boundaries. He would be aided by deputies from the Piscataquis County Sheriff's Department who were familiar with the terrain. This land, which was owned mostly by the paper companies, was honeycombed with old tote roads, relics of the days when log drives on the West Branch of the Penobscot were the means by which much of the state's lumber made its way to market. The murderer might have parked on one of these roads and hiked into the park. Another task would be to check the guest registers at local motels and inns, as well as those at the sporting camps and campgrounds.

Their most immediate task, however, would be to clear up the mystery of the Pamola prankster. On this, the state police and the park authorities would work together. On several occasions, someone dressed as Pamola had appeared in the night to campers sleeping in lean-tos at Chimney Pond. After awakening the campers by shaking a rattle, he would slip away into the night as mysteriously as he had come. One of the lean-tos at which he had appeared was the one in which Mrs. Richards and Miss Ouellette had been staying. Though it was unlikely that the prankster had anything to do with the murder, apprehending him would eliminate a pesky problem for park authorities as well as a potential murder suspect.

Listening to these plans, Charlotte thought of her old friend, Tom Plummer, the author of *Murder at the Morosco*, who was fond of quoting a Latin proverb called Occam's Razor (quoting Latin proverbs being the only use to which he was able to put a degree in classics from a prestigious institute of higher learning). The proverb was *Entia non sunt multiplicanda praeter necessitatem*, which, roughly translated, meant "All unnecessary facts in the argument being analyzed should be eliminated." Or, as Thoreau would have said, "Simplify, simplify." It was in the service of Occam's Razor that Tracey had put catching Pamola at the top of his list.

"It's been a busy month of June," the district supervisor concluded, after telling them about the prankster. "I just hope it doesn't keep up like this for the rest of the summer."

"Do you have any ideas about who this mischief-maker might be?" Tracey asked.

"I'll let Sargent answer that," said Haverty. "He's just been promoted to campground ranger at Chimney Pond. He moved up from the job of assistant ranger. The former ranger just took a job at Denali."

"Congratulations," said Tracey.

"Thanks," said Sargent.

He was a wholesome-looking young man, with gold wire-rimmed glasses and a wide, eager smile.

"At first, I thought the prankster might be a camper who was staying at the campground at the time of the incidents earlier this month," Sargent replied. "He was kind of a weirdo; he had some strange notions about the Indian language. But now Pamola's back—he appeared again last night—and there's since been a complete turnaround of campers, so that theory's out."

Tracey turned to Pyle. "Make a note to get this weirdo's name from the records at park headquarters, and check him out. We want to make sure he *is* long gone, and not staying at Roaring Brook or some other campground."

"Good idea," said Sargent.

"I do have another thought," said Haverty. "I don't have any basis for it. It's just a hunch. I was going to keep it to myself . . ."

"A hunch is the best thing we've got going at the moment,"

interrupted Tracey, with an encouraging wave of his arm. "Shoot."

"Remember the Indian land-claims business?" he asked.

"How could we forget?" said Pyle. "They claimed half the City of Old Town, to say nothing of the rest of the state."

Haverty nodded, and went on. "As you probably recall, the Indians were given money to buy land in other parts of the state as restitution for the land they claimed was theirs in settled areas like Old Town. They used the money to buy land from the paper companies. One of the chunks they bought was in T3 R11, which abuts the park on the western boundary."

Charlotte had been in Maine long enough to know that T3 R11 referred to Township 3, Range 11. The designation was a way of referring to northern Maine's vast uninhabited territories, which were divided by blocks into unincorporated townships and plantations.

"I think I have a geological survey map of that quadrangle here," said Tracey. Searching through a stack of rolled-up maps in a corner, he picked one out and spread it out on the surface of his desk.

Coming around to the other side of the desk, the district supervisor pointed out the area in question. "This is the area here," he said. "The Penobscots have set this tract aside for ceremonial purposes. As you probably know, Katahdin is sacred to them."

"What does ceremonial purposes mean?" asked Charlotte.

"I'm getting to that. They put up a building there, the Katahdin Retreat Center." He pointed to a small puddle of blue. "Here, at Beaver Pond. One of the things they use it for is as the destination of the Sacred Run. Every year, the tribe makes a pilgrimage from Old Town to Katahdin. Some run; most walk or drive. They have a big potlatch supper at the end."

Pyle nodded. "It's coming up later on this summer."

"That's one of the ceremonial purposes they use it for. It

doesn't have any relevance here. I'm just mentioning it. Its other ceremonial purpose is for the vision quest. I had never heard of it either," Haverty said in response to Tracey's baffled expression. "It's a rite of passage ritual; they do it at puberty, and at other times of transition in their lives."

"The Indian equivalent of being confirmed?" asked Tracey.

"Something like that," said Haverty as he went back around the desk to resume his seat.

"What does it consist of?" asked Charlotte.

"First they undergo a purification ceremony in a sweat lodge. Then each participant goes into the woods alone to fast for three or four days. The goal is a vision of a power animal who will be their guardian spirit. The Sioux term is 'Crying for a vision.' An Indian shaman, or spiritual leader, knows where each person is, and helps them interpret their vision when they return. They have another sweat lodge ceremony at the end."

"Haverty," said Tracey, "I don't know where the hell you're going with this, but I sure know you're taking us round Robin Hood's barn to get there."

Haverty smiled. "Hold your horses. I'm getting there. Anyway, these vision quests have become popular among the New Agers out West. People pay hundreds of dollars to spend a week starving themselves in the wilderness of the Colorado Rockies or the Arizona desert."

"You've got to be kidding me!" said Tracey.

Haverty raised his hands in denial. "I'm serious. Instead of a shaman, the groups are led by vision quest guides, who are usually psychotherapists. At the end, the participants get back together and trade notes. It's sort of like a group therapy session, except that it's in the wilderness."

"How do you know all this?" asked Tracey.

"I read about it in a park management magazine. It caught my eye because of what the Penobscots are doing here. It's become something of a problem out West. There have been several deaths: one guy got lost in Death Valley, another guy had a heart attack, a woman went into diabetic shock."

"I can imagine how it might become a problem," said Tracey. "With all those half-starved people running around in the wilderness."

Haverty nodded. "Anyway, the Penobscots have been doing vision quests at the retreat center. At first, they were just for tribal members, but now they've opened the program up to outsiders. I have a photocopy of a flier for one of their courses here." He pulled a sheet of paper out of his briefcase and passed it to Tracey.

Tracey held the flier out at arm's length. "It's entitled 'The Vision Quest: Attuning to the Earth and the Self in the Wilderness,' " he announced. He then proceeded to read the copy aloud: " 'A seven-day retreat at the Katahdin Retreat Center, located on beautiful Beaver Pond in the wilderness forest of northern Maine near Mount Katahdin.' "

"Here, Chief," said Pyle, and handed Tracey his reading glasses.

Though Tracey was now a lieutenant for the state police instead of a small town police chief, everybody here still seemed to call him Chief.

"Thanks," Tracey said. He put on his glasses, and continued reading: " 'The goals of this intensive Native American course are to facilitate personal growth, to reconnect with the earth, and to uncover life's deeper meanings.' " Pausing, he looked up over the tops of his glasses for their reactions.

"Sounds like a pretty tall order for only a week," Charlotte commented.

"I'd say so," Tracey drawled. Then he turned his attention back to the flier. " 'The vision quest should not be undertaken lightly,' " he went on. " 'It involves a four-day fast which can be both difficult and confrontational.' How's it confrontational if they're all alone? I wonder. 'You must be able to carry a forty-pound pack three or four miles. Meals will be provided. Participants should provide their own camping equipment. Course fee: Twelve hundred dollars, with a nonrefundable deposit of four hundred dollars.' "

"Twelve hundred bucks and you don't even get to eat!" said Pyle.

Tracey was still studying the flier. "The vision quest guide is someone named Keith Samusit," he said. "He's described as the executive director of the Katahdin Foundation and a ceremonial leader of the Penobscot Nation."

"I know Keith," said Pyle. "We graduated from Old Town High together. I didn't know he was doing this."

The group's attention shifted to Pyle.

"Did he seem like the type to become a spiritual leader?" asked Tracey.

"Yeah," he said. "Actually, he did. He was a very nice guy. Very quiet, very serious. The kind of guy who might have become a priest. He went to the forestry school at Orono. He's the tribe forester now. Looks after the tribal timber. Lumbering provides a fair amount of income for the tribe."

Tracey looked over at the district supervisor. "Well, Haverty?" he prompted. "We're still only halfway there."

Haverty smiled at Tracey's ribbing. "Three fourths," he said. He went on. "From what I understand, opening the center to whites has caused some problems within the tribe. Samusit is promoting the vision quest as a way of disseminating Indian spiritual values. But some tribal members are accusing him of selling Native American rituals for profit."

"Isn't the tribe getting the profit?" asked Tracey.

"I would think so, but it might be worth looking into who's actually making the money from this," Haverty said.

Tracey nodded.

"I'm finally getting to it," he continued. "The first of the vision quest sessions that were open to the public was held a couple of weeks ago."

"And?" said Tracey.

"I heard from a ranger who had been talking with a camper who participated that someone dressed up in a Pamola costume had appeared to a couple of the white vision questers in the night."

"There you go," cheered Tracey, slapping the surface of his desk. "Give this man a medal for making it to the finish. Have you looked into it?"

Haverty shook his head. "No jurisdiction. Penobscot lands are under the jurisdiction of the tribal police."

"Not in the case of murder," added Tracey. "Any theories?"

Haverty nodded. "I think this guy might be trying to scare whites away from the retreat center. Or maybe he's doing it just to get attention. There's a radical element among the Penobscots who are demanding that Katahdin be returned to the Indians because of its being their sacred land."

"Do you think this guy could be the murderer?" Pyle asked his boss.

Tracey shrugged. "He's the only lead we have. Also, it makes sense that an Indian would use a bow and arrow. Maybe too much sense; it might be too obvious a choice. Unless he thought nobody would figure it out. In any case, I think we have to catch this guy. How many times has he appeared at Chimney Pond?"

"I'll defer to Sargent on that one," Haverty replied with a nod to the young ranger at his side.

"Earlier this month, it was five," said Sargent. "All between the first and third quarters of the moon. Plus two nights at the retreat center. He didn't appear on the nights it was overcast. I figure he needs the moonlight to get from wherever he comes from and back without a light."

"What about this time around?" asked Tracey.

"His first appearance this time was last night," said the young ranger. "Again, there was a half moon."

Tracey swiveled his chair around to look at the calendar on the wall behind his desk. "The third quarter is July seventh, which means we have roughly two more weeks to catch this guy." He turned back to face Haverty. "Is it possible to clear the Chimney Pond Campground?"

Haverty nodded. "Yep. We can relocate the campers to other campgrounds. They won't be happy about it, but those are the breaks."

"Good. Then we can fill the lean-tos with our own people. Nab this guy in the act. How many lean-tos are there?"

"Nine," Haverty said. "Each accommodates four people. But we don't usually have four in every one. I'd say we average between two and three."

Tracey nodded. "That means we need, say, twenty people for the lean-tos, and another half a dozen or so posted around the campsite."

"Sounds about right to me," said Haverty. "When are we going to do this?"

"As soon as possible."

· 6 ·

AFTER THE MEETING, Charlotte and Tracey set out on the task that Tracey had assigned to himself: finding out about Iris' personal life. They decided to start by going back to talk with the person who had known her best, Jeanne Ouellette. Charlotte had offered to kill time until they headed back to Bridge Harbor by taking a walk, but Tracey insisted that she come along. He wanted her help. After the Bridge Harbor murder eight years before, Charlotte had assumed the role of unofficial investigator in the perennially short-staffed Bridge Harbor Police Department, a role that was primarily confined to dropping in when she was in town and getting the scoop on local crimes before they appeared in the "Police Beat" column of the *Bridge Harbor Light*. Though there were occasionally problems to be solved, with stolen bicycles and unreturned video rentals heading the list, the vast majority of crimes fitted roughly in the driving-while-intoxicated category, the many variations of which included car crashes, joy rides, speeding, and collisions with deer, and required no investigative abilities, it being quite obvious who the drunken party was.

Since joining the state police, Tracey had had no real need for Charlotte's help, but she supposed he'd gotten used to having her around. "Won't Gaudette mind my interference?" she had asked, referring to Tracey's superior. "What he doesn't know won't hurt him," Tracey had replied. "And with so many law enforcement agencies already on the case, who's going to notice?" Then he had ticked off the agencies involved on his fingers:

"The state police, the Baxter State Park authorities, and the Piscataquis County Sheriff's Department for starters, with the probable addition of the Old Town police and the Penobscot Indian police. With five in the picture, what's one more? Besides, you're the only one who knew the victim when she was Iris O'Connor."

"I don't think that's going to matter," Charlotte had said.

"Who knows? Maybe she was killed by someone from her past who came back to redress a festering grievance," said Tracey.

"Wearing moose antlers from the costume department?"

On their second visit to Hilltop Farm, Charlotte had a better chance to notice how beautiful the property was. It was beautiful in the way she liked beautiful, with a kind of aged grace. Not falling down the way many old Maine farms were, and not overly shipshape—just a serene, understated beauty. Part of its appeal lay in its setting: it sat back from the road instead of being snuggled right up to it as most old New England farmhouses were, and it was set off by a backdrop of tall pines. But not all of the effect had to do with the setting. Had she not had the chance to compare it with the farms she had seen on the ride over, she probably wouldn't have noticed that its beauty was like that of a face that is beautiful in old age because it's been molded by a quiet intelligence. This time around she noticed details like the roof, which was shingled with wooden shakes weathered to the color of old pewter instead of the usual gray asphalt; and the long gravel driveway, laid out in such a way that its gentle curves most pleased the eye. Nor did she fail to notice this time that the apple trees, whose flower-laden limbs seemed to cascade so naturally to the ground, had been carefully pruned to achieve this effect. Even the stone fences, a cardinal feature of the Maine farmhouse, seemed different: they weren't just heaps of rocks, but had been carefully pieced together by a master stonemason. Most impressive of all were the fields of wildflowers in which the sheep grazed, fields that appeared to be natural, but in their profusion of bloom were unlike any Charlotte had seen that morning.

And now that quiet intelligence was dead. What would happen to Hilltop Farm? she wondered. She imagined that would be among the first of the questions that Tracey would want answered.

Having failed to get an answer to his knock, Tracey let out a loud "Hello!" His shout produced a reply from the direction of a long, low shed in a grove of pines to the left of the house. Following a path through an opening in the stone fence, they emerged at a grassy roadway that ran between the shed they had seen and another, similar shed before curving around toward the back of the house. A fork led off into the woods. Charlotte concluded that the sheds must once have been carriage houses, and the fork a carriage path.

Jeanne Ouellette was standing in front of one of the sheds among a collection of pots that sat in flats on the grass. Each pot held a trillium, which, with the exception of the pink lady's-slipper, was perhaps the country's most beloved wildflower. She was in the process of writing the names of the varieties and the prices on wooden tongue depressors, and then sticking them into the pots.

"Hello again," she said as they approached. She gestured at the pots at her feet. "I was just getting this shipment ready to send out." She brushed a stray lock of gray hair out of her face and pushed her glasses up her nose. Her sallow face was filled with pain and hurt and confusion. "I figured you'd be back. I just heard the news on the radio."

"We're back," said Tracey. "This is Miss Charlotte Graham," he said, introducing Charlotte, as he'd failed to do on their first visit. He didn't elaborate, obviously not wanting at this stage to get into the issue of Iris' other life.

Jeanne rubbed a muddy palm on the front of her soiled khakis. "Excuse my hands," she said as she reached over to shake hands with Charlotte. "I'm very pleased to meet you, Miss Graham."

The fact that she didn't say anything more suggested to Charlotte that she must have known about her connection with Iris' past life. Otherwise, she surely would have commented on the movie star's having shown up in her backyard.

Charlotte had stooped down for a closer look at the flowers. Many of them were in bloom—June was trillium season—and Charlotte was captivated by the star-shaped flowers. The only trilliums she was familiar with were white, but these came in pink, purple, red, yellow, green.

"They're beautiful," she said, gazing out at the plants.

She was thinking about buying a pink one for her townhouse garden in New York until she noticed the price, which was sixty dollars, from which she concluded that the wildflower business was probably more remunerative than one would have thought.

Tracey, who had also been looking at the price tags, had come to the same conclusion. "Pretty pricey, aren't they?" he said to Jeanne.

It was typical of Tracey, and of Mainers in general, to put off mentioning whatever business was at hand for as long as possible, as if coming directly to the point would be a breach of good manners.

It was a style that drove Charlotte crazy. Her approach would have been to plunge right in with the questions, such as "Where were you when Iris was killed?" and "Who stands to inherit this farm?" but she recognized that Tracey's aimless fishing expeditions often netted the bigger catch.

"For a reason," Jeanne replied. "It takes six to eight years for a trillium seed to come to flower, and we grow them from seed. We don't dig them from the wild." Holding a plant out at arm's length, she leaned back to study it. Then she rearranged the blossoms, fluffed the leaves, and set it back down.

Seeing how she fussed, Charlotte couldn't help comparing her to her own secretary, Vivian Smith, who served a similar function in her life. Vivian's style was to bully. Of the two,

Charlotte preferred bullying. This constant fussing would have driven her crazy.

The thought of Vivian reminded her of what she was supposed to be doing. Vivian had been calling daily to nag her about her autobiography. Putting her guilty thoughts out of her mind, she addressed Jeanne. "I had no idea that trilliums came in so many colors. Have you developed your own hybrids?"

"No," Jeanne replied. "These are the natural color variations. Iris didn't believe in improving on Mother Nature." Bending down, she picked up one of the flats and turned toward the shed. "I'll get you a couple of our brochures."

Charlotte was impressed at her strength. The flat probably held twenty good-sized pots and must have weighed a hundred pounds or more.

She emerged a couple of moments later with two copies of a color brochure that read "Hilltop Farm: Wholesale Nursery-Propagated Perennial Wildflowers. Specialists in Trilliums," which she gave to them.

"Would you like to sit down?" Jeanne asked after they had looked at the brochures. She nodded at a weathered picnic table in the tall grass at one end of the shed. "We can sit there, or we can go inside."

"This will do fine," said Tracey. "It's a nice day for being outdoors."

Once they were seated, Tracey finally asked his question. Remembering his impatience with Haverty, Charlotte observed that it was only other people's failure to get to the point that annoyed Tracey, never his own. "Now," he said, "why don't you tell us about that day?"

"Where do you want me to start?" Jeanne asked. She had a way of cocking her head forward attentively, as if she were waiting for directions.

"Anywhere you like," he said as he took out a notebook.

"We set out about eight on the Saddle Trail. Iris liked to get an early start. It's supposed to take two and a half hours to get to the rim, but for a couple of old ladies like us"—she attempted a smile—"it always took longer. We got to the rim a little after eleven. That's where we split up."

"Why did you split up?" asked Tracey.

"Two reasons. The first was that Iris didn't like walking with other people, generally speaking. She used to quote Thoreau, who said he had no walks to throw away on company. That was especially true of her annual pilgrimage to Katahdin; it was a sacred ritual for her."

"And the second?"

"The second was the *Diapensia lapponica*. It's an unusual alpine wildflower that grows on the Tableland. She always climbed the mountain during the second week in June so she could see it in bloom. It's especially thick around Thoreau Spring, which she liked to visit anyway. Again, it was part of her solitary ritual."

"How do you spell that?" asked Tracey.

Jeanne spelled it for him. As she stared out at the woods, her gray eyes started tearing up. "It's so odd, really."

"What's so odd?" asked Tracey.

"In Emerson's eulogy for Thoreau, he compared him to the Tyrolean youths who risked their lives to gather edelweiss from the alpine cliffs. He described how they were sometimes found dead at the foot, with the flowers in their hands. Not that Thoreau actually died like that . . . ." Her voice drifted off.

"It was a metaphor," prompted Charlotte.

Jeanne nodded, and continued. "For the pursuit of noble purity, which is what edelweiss means in German. I was just thinking how odd it was that Iris should have died at the foot of a cliff in pursuit of a rare wildflower that grows on our most inaccessible summits."

"Did you draw the same metaphor at Iris' funeral?" asked Charlotte.

"There was no funeral," Jeanne said. "She considered public ceremonies a waste of time and money. Religious ceremonies most of all."

"Getting back to your movements . . ." Tracey said. He consulted his notes. "Mrs. Richards continued over the ridge to Thoreau Spring to see this rare wildflower that grows there, *Diapensia lapponica*."

Jeanne had regained her composure. "Yes," she said. "She took the Baxter Peak Cutoff Trail, which begins about a half mile south of the head of the Saddle Slide. From there, it's a mile to the Spring."

"And you?"

"I took the Northwest Basin Trail, which goes in the opposite direction. It links up with the Hamlin Ridge Trail, which leads to Hamlin Peak. It's the long, gradual way: it follows the rim of the basin all the way back around to Chimney Pond. I have bad knees," she explained. "The steep descents bother me."

Tracey nodded in sympathy. "I have that problem myself."

"That's another reason we split up: I wasn't up to the Knife Edge."

"Did you see anyone else on the trail?"

She shook her head. "As I said, we left pretty early. The only other hikers on the trail at that hour would have been other campers from Chimney Pond, most of whom are young people who take the Cathedral Trail or the Dudley Trail, either of which is more interesting than the Saddle Trail."

"What about day hikers?" asked Tracey.

"They have to start out at Roaring Brook Campground at the foot of the mountain. It takes two and a half hours to get from there to Chimney Pond, so they don't start hitting the upper trails until about ten. Oh, I just remembered. There was one person: a man in an orange windbreaker."

"But you didn't talk to him."

"No. He was just ahead of us on the Saddle Slide for a while. You're apt to notice someone who's ahead of you on the Saddle Slide because of the chance that they'll dislodge a rock that could come bouncing down on your head, which in fact he did several times. You have to be careful to stay back."

"Any other description of this man?"

"Middle-aged. Gray hair, I think. Medium height, a bit burly. I did notice that he either had new boots, or old boots with new Vibram soles. They left sharp imprints in the mud around the brook at the foot of the slide. Not that something like that would matter . . ."

Tracey made a notation. "You never know," he said.

"You could see the inset in the arch with *Vibram* spelled out. I noticed because I had just had my own boots resoled with Vibram soles."

"When did you get back to Chimney Pond?"

"About six. I took my time, stopped for lunch. Looked at the *Diapensia* and the Lapland rosebay. The exact time would be in the hikers' register. I signed in when I got back. I was surprised that Iris hadn't returned yet; I had expected her to be back long before me."

"Did you see anyone after you separated?"

"From a distance. Nobody up close. It was still pretty early in the season. There weren't that many hikers out. Which is another reason we went at that time. Later on, it can get pretty congested up there. Also, the Hamlin Ridge Trail is kind of off the beaten track."

"I would imagine that most hikers would want to climb Baxter and go across the Knife Edge to Pamola," said Tracey.

Jeanne nodded. "Or vice versa," she said.

Tracey paused, and then looked directly at her. "Of course, you realize why we're asking you these questions," he said. "I'm sorry to have to do it, but it's part of the procedure. Now let me ask you this: Is there anyone you know of who might have wanted to kill Mrs. Richards?"

"I've been thinking about little else ever since I heard the news on the radio," she said. "She had angered a lot of people in town for one reason or another. She could be difficult at times."

"For example?"

"Oh. Well, like last winter when she raised a ruckus with the public works department about the salt they were using on the roads. She said it killed the sugar maples. But it was institutions more than individuals that she had it in for. I do have one idea, though . . ."

"I'm listening," said Tracey.

"There was a car that was hanging around here about a month ago. I used to see it parked on the other side of Stillwater Avenue. It even drove in here a couple of times." She nodded at the road that ran between the sheds. "Once I noticed the driver looking at the house through field glasses."

"Any idea who it might have been?"

"We get all kinds coming here to see Iris. People had a reverence for her. Treated her as if she was Thoreau himself. I thought it might be a Thoreauvian who was too shy to visit. But now I wonder."

"Any other description of the driver?"

She shook her head. "No. I never got a good look at him."

"How about the car?"

"I did get a good look at that. It was a Ford Bronco. Ordinarily, I don't notice models. But I remember the picture of the bucking bronco on the cover of the spare tire that was mounted on the back. It was black, with Colorado plates. They have a mountain on them."

"Colorado plates," said Tracey. "That's interesting."

"How did she respond to these admirers?" asked Charlotte.

"You never knew. Friendly one minute, unfriendly the next. Once, I remember . . ." She smiled to herself at the memory.

"Yes?" said Tracey.

Jeanne continued. "She opened the door to a young man who asked to see Iris Richards. She patted her belly and said, 'Front side.' Then she turned around, arse-to, and said, 'Back side.' Then she turned back around again and slammed the door in his face."

"Were any of these Thoreauvians regular visitors?"

"Oh, yes. A number of them. There was a young couple from a town over by Farmington—Temple, I think it was—who'd built themselves a replica of Thoreau's house at Walden Pond and were trying to live as he did."

"Must've been pretty cramped," said Charlotte.

"That's what I thought, but they didn't seem to mind. Then there was a man from Massachusetts who was writing a book about Thoreau's time in Maine. He'd come by every couple of months, and Iris would feed him information. She was the one who should've been writing that book."

"Names?" asked Tracey.

Jeanne gave him the names, and he wrote them down in his notebook.

"Then, of course, there was Mack," she went on once Tracey had finished taking notes.

"Who's Mack?"

"Mack Scott. He was a—" She groped for the right word. "I guess you'd say he was a disciple of Iris'. He was on the mountain that day, too."

"On the day she was murdered!"

"Or he was supposed to be. He was going to take the route that Thoreau had followed—that's the Abol Trail; it comes up from the south—and meet Iris at Thoreau Spring. I don't know if he actually did. He said he'd climbed the mountain enough times from the north, and wanted to try it from the other way."

"We should talk to him," said Tracey. "Where does he live?"

She paused for a moment, and then said, "He doesn't have a formal address. He lives in a trailer down by the railroad tracks. On South Water Street. You go down South Main and turn left on Sawyer. It's at the foot of Sawyer Street, on your left. Gray with maroon stripes. You can't miss it."

Tracey wrote down the directions, and then asked, "Can you tell us anything more about him?"

"He's about forty, I'd say. Blond and stocky, with a beard. The beard is red. If you're going to meet him, I'd better leave it at that. He's . . . he's a hard person to describe, kind of an eccentric."

"I have a question," interjected Charlotte. "You said that Iris didn't have a funeral because she didn't believe in them."

Jeanne nodded. "She was cremated. She didn't want a fuss made over her." She cast a glance at the gabled farmhouse. "I have her ashes inside. I'm planning to scatter them in the woods sometime. That's what she would have wanted."

"If she *had* had a funeral, who would have come?" Charlotte asked.

"Her favorite people, you mean?"

Charlotte nodded.

Jeanne thought for a moment, then said, "Her lawyer, Ellsworth Partridge. He handled all of her affairs. She was very fond of him."

"I know Ellsworth," said Tracey.

"Everybody knows Ellsworth," she replied. "He was president of the state Senate. Another would be Dave Stadtler, the publisher of the local newspaper, *The Penobscot Times.* That's where she got *The Pumpkin Paper* printed. Also, various people from the New England chapter of the Thoreau Association."

"What about this guy Mack Scott?" asked Tracey.

"Mack, of course. There were only two people whom she would regularly walk with, and he was one of them. She walked with me too, of course, but only sometimes. I wasn't a regular the way they were."

She spoke with some bitterness, obviously offended that Iris didn't treasure her company enough to consider her worthy of walking with.

"Who was the other person?" Charlotte asked.

"Keith Samusit."

She seemed almost to spit the name out, as if it pained her to voice the sounds. It was clear she didn't like this fellow.

"The Penobscot Indian?" asked Tracey.

She nodded. "He manages Hamlin's Woods. That's the woods out back." She nodded at a red pickup truck that was parked behind one of the sheds. "He happens to be here right now if you want to talk with him."

"We would indeed," said Tracey.

She nodded at the carriage path. "Just follow the path into the woods, and give a holler. It curves around in the shape of a W and comes out on the other side of the house, so you're not likely to miss him."

"Thanks," said Tracey.

At the end of the string of sheds, the carriage path abruptly entered the woods, which were like few Charlotte had ever seen. They had a fairy-tale quality, as if elves and giants dwelt there. Also, an incredible tranquility. The clear, straight trunks of the old trees soared to the sky like the pillars of an ancient cathedral, and the forest floor, clear of underbrush, was padded with a thick russet carpet of old pine needles. The cool air had the invigorating smell of pine resin, and the feathery plumes of the green pine needles seemed to charge the air with an invisible current.

They found Samusit a short distance down the carriage path. He was limbing up the small pines that had sprung up under the old growth, using a hatchet to trim away the dead branches that encircled the trunks like the spokes of layer upon layer of wheels. As he struck them, the limbs fell away with a crack in a tangled web of silvery gray. A pruner attached to a long handle for reaching the higher branches lay on the ground at his feet, and several piles of the slash that had already been pruned away stood nearby, indicating that he had been at his work for some time.

Seeing Charlotte and Tracey, he stopped what he was doing, and waited.

Keith Samusit did not fit Charlotte's idea of what an American Indian looked like. In fact, had she not known he was a Penobscot, she would have thought he was Japanese. He was a slight man, with thick black hair, and eyeglasses with narrow tortoise-shell frames. His eyes were slightly slanted, and his black eyebrows flared upwards. The color of his skin was not so much red as yellow. If evidence were ever needed that the Indians had crossed to the Americas via the Bering Strait, it could be found in the Asian features of Keith Samusit's angled face.

He was dressed in jeans and a flannel shirt, over which he wore a blue denim jacket. The only hints of the Indian in his attire were his simple leather moccasins, and a heavy silver ring with a turquoise stone.

"I heard about Iris on the news," Samusit said after Tracey had introduced himself and explained the purpose of his visit. (Tracey had also introduced Charlotte, but Samusit showed no signs of recognizing who she was.)

Tracey looked around. "Pretty nice stand of timber." Then, flinching suddenly, he swatted at a black fly, the small biting insect that was Maine's springtime scourge. "Jeezum," he said, "the flies are wicked in here."

Charlotte was swatting away as well. The flies suddenly seemed to be biting every inch of exposed flesh, and some that was unexposed as well, like that on her ankles. The viciousness of the attack made her want to cut and run. It was like walking into a hornets' nest.

"They launch their attack the minute you stop moving," said Samusit. Reaching into the pocket of his jacket, he pulled out a small container and offered it to Tracey. "Here's some fly dope," he said.

Taking the container, Tracey spread a coating of the liquid, which smelled like citronella, on his hands and neck and along his hairline, and then offered it to Charlotte.

She read the label aloud. " 'BUG AMMO. If you've got the bugs, we've got the ammo.' Well," she said, "we certainly have the bugs."

"If you don't get them, they'll get you," said Samusit. "It's war."

Charlotte followed Tracey's example, and then handed the container back. "Thanks," she said. The effect was almost instantaneous. Already, there were fewer of the awful flies.

Tracey was looking up into the tops of the trees. "I've heard that this is one of the few remaining stands of virgin forest in New England," he said, choosing the indirect approach as usual.

"That's what people say, but it's not true," Samusit replied. "There wasn't much in this area that escaped being cut, and that would be especially true of a stand so close to the river. But I estimate this land hasn't been logged since the eighteen twenties, which would still make it one of the oldest around."

Charlotte could see why Pyle thought he would have made a good priest. He had an air of gravity that men of the cloth often exhibited, as if they navigated the difficult passages of life in a ship with a deeper keel than that of ordinary men.

"That means that some of these trees are a hundred and seventy years old," said Tracey, looking up at a giant white pine with deeply fissured bark.

"At least. There are some, like the one you're looking at, that were skipped over when this stand was logged, and are probably two hundred years old. They logged differently then: it was one man, one horse, one ax; everything didn't get cut the way it does today."

"How long will a tree like this live?" asked Tracey.

"Eastern white pine will live to three hundred years or more, so that tree still has a century or more to go." He nodded at a nearby hemlock. "That hemlock is probably over two hundred years old. You can tell an old hemlock because the bark turns that cinnamon color."

"I understand that you manage this woodlot," said Tracey.

"Yeah," Samusit said. "Not that a woodlot this old requires much management." He looked around at the big old trees. "Occasionally a tree dies, and I cut it down. That's about it, except for thinning out the underbrush from time to time to give the new growth a chance."

"What about the limbing up?" said Tracey, nodding at the hatchet Samusit still held in his hand.

The Indian looked down at the hatchet as if he had forgotten it was there. "The limbing up really isn't necessary. I do it because I find it relaxing. I came here today because of Iris." Setting the hatchet down, he took a seat on a fallen log and rubbed his temples with his fingers. "What a shock," he said.

"How long had you known Mrs. Richards?" asked Tracey.

"Six or seven years. I first came here when I was a forestry student. She used to let the forestry professors bring the students here to see what an old-growth forest looked like. I noticed that the woodlot needed some work, and asked her for the job."

"And she hired you just like that?"

"Well, not just like that. She only hired me after she found out I was descended from the Indian guide who accompanied Thoreau on his trip to Chesuncook. He was my great-great-granduncle. I thought it was a dumb reason for hiring someone, but she liked the idea of the connection."

"And you became friends," prompted Tracey.

Samusit nodded. "I'm the tribe forester now, so I don't really need this job. But I've kept on doing it as a favor to Iris, and also because I like it in here." He looked again at the tall trees around him.

"I have to ask this next question of everyone who was close to her," said Tracey. "Where were you on the day she was killed?"

"I understand," Samusit said. "Though I had no reason to kill Iris. She was . . . well, I guess you could say she was like a mother to me." He fixed Tracey with a level gaze. "In answer to your question, I was cruising."

"On the coast somewhere?" asked Tracey.

"No," he said with a smile. "On fee land up by Katahdin. I should have said *timber* cruising, as opposed to sailboat cruising."

Charlotte had always been struck by the fact that inland Maine and coastal Maine were like two different states, one drawing its identity from the woods, the other from the sea. In this case, the same word had different meanings in the two cultures.

Samusit explained. "Surveying the timberland for prospective cuts. Inventorying sample stands. I'd been away for a week. When I came back, I found out that Iris was dead."

"Were you by yourself?" asked Tracey.

He nodded. "But my girlfriend could confirm when I left and when I returned. Her name is Didias Thomas, and she lives with me on Indian Island." He gave Tracey the address and telephone number.

"I heard that you're associated with a retreat center on fee land up by Katahdin," said Tracey, leading up to the Pamola issue.

"I'm associated with the Katahdin Retreat Center," he replied. "Everybody thinks it's on fee land, but it's not. It abuts fee land, but the land is actually privately owned by a foundation, the Katahdin Foundation."

"Who controls the foundation?"

"That question would be better put in the past tense," said Samusit. "The answer is, or was, Iris Richards. She was the founder and the chairman of the board, and it was her money that paid for the land and the building."

Then it was also her foundation that made the money, Charlotte thought.

Tracey looked as astonished as the fisherman whose aimless trolling has netted him a big one. Charlotte could almost see his brain analyzing the question of what this meant to the case.

For one thing, she reflected, it opened up the possibility that the Pamola business wasn't just malicious mischief perpetrated by some disaffected tribesman, but part of a deliberate campaign to harass, and possibly even kill, Iris.

"Now, why would Mrs. Richards have founded a retreat center for the Penobscot Indians?" Tracey asked.

"I had an uncle who always said, 'You can take the woods away from a Penobscot, but you can't take it out of him.' The woods are a part of our collective soul; we need the woods, we need Katahdin, and we need the Penobscot River. That's what the retreat center's for. But in answer to your question, the retreat center isn't just for the Indians. Though it's been the Indians who've used it the most. It's for anyone who's interested in the vision quest: Native Americans, whites, Thoreauvians."

"I'm listening," said Tracey.

"Do you know what a vision quest is?" he asked.

"I have a rough idea," said Tracey.

"Iris had a theory that the vision quest is expressive of a basic human need to reconnect with the wilderness, and through that connection to explore the wilderness that lies within our souls. She believed that this need expresses itself in various ways in every culture."

"I'm not sure I follow you," said Tracey, who was writing it all down.

"For instance, Iris saw Thoreau's stay at Walden Pond in terms of a vision quest: a time of living simply, away from the demands of daily life in order to get in touch with one's deeper self. Jesus' forty days in the wilderness was a vision quest; Iris' own annual pilgrimage to Katahdin . . ."

"I see," said Tracey, nodding.

"She even wrote an article about it for *The Pumpkin Paper*, in which she talked about how the erosion of the wilderness is affecting this need. That's why she founded the Center."

" 'In wildness is the preservation of the world,' " said Charlotte, quoting a well-known line from Thoreau.

"Exactly," said Keith. "In fact, that's the Center's motto."

"Speaking of vision questers . . ." said Tracey.

At last, Charlotte thought.

Tracey continued. "One of the park rangers told us that a man dressed up as Pamola appeared to a vision quester at the retreat center earlier this month. It was his theory that the man was an Indian who was trying to scare off the white vision questers. I'm interested in what you think."

"He may be right," Samusit replied. "There's a lot of opposition to the Center from Penobscots who don't want to see whites participating in Indian rituals, but there's a lot of sentiment the other way too. Many of our people realize that if we don't share our medicine, we'll lose it."

"Do you think it might be someone who's angry about what they perceive as the exploitation of Indian culture?" asked Tracey.

Samusit's dark brown eyes suddenly turned fiery. "Exploitation!" he spat. "If you're talking about exploitation, let's talk about opening up tribal lands to gambling. If high stakes Bingo in what's supposed to be the tribe's recreational facility isn't exploitation, I don't know what is."

"I wouldn't know about that," said Tracey softly.

"Right," said Samusit. "You wouldn't. Sorry."

"Do you have any idea who might be doing this?" Tracey asked again.

He shook his head, and looked down at the unfurled ferns that were pushing up through the mat of pine needles at his feet.

Charlotte had the feeling that he was lying.

"Did you know that this person dressed up as Pamola appeared to Iris at the Chimney Pond campsite on the night before she was murdered?" Tracey said.

Samusit's head jerked up in surprise.

Tracey went on. "If what you say about tribal resentment is true, she would have been a natural target. It's because of her that a lot of people—white people, that is—have been drawn to the retreat center, right?"

Samusit nodded. "Do you think there's a connection?" he asked.

"I don't know. It could have been a coincidence. But it also could have been a personal vendetta. All I know is that the Pamola prankster is our only suspect at the moment." Tracey pulled out a card and handed it to Samusit. "If you hear anything more, I'd appreciate it if you'd let me know."

Samusit tucked the card into his breast pocket, but Charlotte doubted that Tracey would be hearing from him. Despite his apparent openness to whites, he was still an Indian, and every Indian she had ever known (which was a fair number, given the Westerns she had done), had no use for white police.

The tall trunks of the trees were casting long shadows on the forest floor, and the stray shafts of sun that pierced the forest canopy were turning the hairs on the moss a golden yellow. It was getting late.

Tracey checked his watch. "Well, I guess we'd better get going," he said. They said goodbye, and turned back toward the house.

· 7 ·

IT AT FIRST seemed odd to Charlotte that of the half dozen people to whom Iris had been close, three of them—Jeanne Ouellette, Keith Samusit, and Mack Scott—had been on or in the vicinity of the mountain on the day she was killed. Thinking about it again, however, as she and Tracey headed back out of the woods, she decided that it wasn't so odd after all. Iris had apparently been something of a mentor to both Keith and Mack, and Charlotte supposed that their interest in the mountain had grown out of Iris' own. This was confirmed, at least as far as Keith was concerned, in further conversation with Jeanne, who was still labeling the trilliums when they emerged from the woods. She talked readily about Keith's relationship with Iris, but with the same tinge of hostility that Charlotte had noticed earlier. Because of Iris' deep interest in Indian culture—one of the offshoots of her devotion to Thoreau—she had served as cheerleader, sounding board, and ultimately financial backer in Keith's mission to revive Penobscot culture, and in particular, the tribe's spiritual heritage. Under Keith's leadership, the tribe had formed a men's drumming circle, one of whose goals was to revive forgotten Penobscot sacred music, a lot of which had been written down by nineteenth-century ethnologists; had revived a lapsed tradition of holding an annual Indian pageant for the performance of traditional Penobscot dances; and had launched the tradition of the annual Sacred Run to Katahdin. A retreat center for the practice of Native American religion at Katahdin, and in particular for the enactment of the pan-Indian vision quest ceremony, had been Keith's dream, and he had worked for years to bring it to fruition.

One thing was certain about the case, Charlotte thought as she and Tracey headed back to the car: the central role in the drama was not a person, but a mountain. She was reminded of what Thoreau had written in his journal about the mountain in a recurring dream of his. In his dream, he was always climbing this mountain, which was situated on the outskirts of Concord where no mountain in fact existed. His climb started out through a dark wood and then proceeded along a rocky ridge studded with stunted trees before finally emerging onto the bare and trackless rocks of the summit, which floated in the clouds. A perfectly shaped Katahdin had insinuated itself into Charlotte's imagination in a similar manner. She was sure that before this case was over, she would make her own pilgrimage to the sacred mountain, and she was eager to see how the reality squared with the mountain of her imagination.

"Where to now, Chief?" she asked as they got back into the car.

"Well," said Tracey, "I figure we might as well take a ride over to see Ellsworth Partridge. As long as we're here in Old Town. That is, if you're not in a hurry to get back." He checked his watch. "It's four twenty. He should still be at his office."

"Let's go," she said.

"I thought I might ask him who Mrs. Richards' heirs are."

"Ah," said Charlotte. "I was wondering when you were going to get around to asking Jeanne that question."

"Well, I figured she'd get around to it herself in one way or another, which she did, by mentioning that it was Ellsworth who handled Mrs. Richards' affairs. I figured that rather than asking Jeanne, we'd just go directly to the horse's mouth. Better to be indirect."

In Maine, it was always better to be indirect.

"I gather he's not in the state Senate anymore," Charlotte said.

Tracey shook his head. "He was always trying to bring the opposing sides together. He had an unusual attitude for a politician: he couldn't stand discord. Which I suppose explains why he's not in public office anymore."

"Unusual for a lawyer, too," said Charlotte.

"Not in a small town," said Tracey. "Not if you want to keep the respect of the community. Which Ellsworth Partridge has succeeded admirably in doing, as did his father before him."

The offices of Partridge & Partridge were located in the three-block section of Main Street that comprised Old Town's business district. The first floor of the three-story brick building had been given a façade of wood paneling and a fake mansard overhang to create the illusion of modernity, but it wasn't fooling anybody. Like almost everything else in town, it looked as if it dated from Old Town's heyday in the mid-nineteenth century when it was a center of the sawmill industry. A pleasant receptionist ushered them into an inner office where they were greeted by a thin, bent-over man with wavy black hair and a hunter-green bow tie that emphasized his prominent Adam's apple. He also had a jutting chin and prominent nose that gave him, along with his stooped posture and brown tweed suit, a birdlike appearance that corresponded to his name, as if he were half-poised to start pecking at a kernel on the ground. A diploma on the wall indicated that he had been graduated *summa cum laude* from Harvard Law School. He probably could have gotten a job at any of the top, big city law firms. Instead he had elected to return to the small town that he had come from, to practice law in his father's firm and to serve in public office. No wonder people respected him.

The introductions over, Partridge urged them to sit down. He hadn't inquired as to the reason for Charlotte's being

there. Mainers were too polite for that, which was one of
the pleasures of living in Maine, as well as one of the
frustrations. Charlotte had once been attending a movie
in Bridge Harbor when the screen had gone white. The
audience had sat there patiently munching on their popcorn
until Charlotte had finally gone to the back, and discovered
that the projectionist had fallen asleep. Had she not taken
the initiative, the audience probably would have sat there all
night long for fear of appearing presumptuous by getting up
to see what the matter was.

"What can I do for you?" asked Partridge, once they were
seated. Despite the peculiarity of his appearance, he had
about him an air of old world elegance like the game bird
whose name he bore, and a gracious manner that served to
put his visitors immediately at ease.

"We're here about Iris Richards," Tracey said. "As you
probably know by now, she was murdered on the Knife Edge
Trail on Mount Katahdin. Her companion, Jeanne Ouellette,
told us that you're her lawyer, and we wondered if you could
tell us about her will."

"Certainly," Partridge replied. "It's quite straightforward.
She left everything to Miss Ouellette: house, property, bank
accounts, business, and so on. The house and property make
up the bulk of the estate; what she had in liquid assets will
go to pay the estate tax."

The fact that Jeanne was Iris' heir gave her a motive,
thought Charlotte. But it wasn't much of one. She had lived
in the house for thirty-three years. Why should she all of a
sudden have done away with her employer?

"What's the value of the Hilltop Farm property?" asked
Tracey. He had taken out his notebook, and was poised to
make notes.

"It's assessed at four hundred and fifty thousand," said
Partridge. "But if you were out there, you could see for
yourself that it's unique. It's hard to put a price tag on a
property like that."

Tracey nodded, and made a notation.

"We're also interested in an organization called the Katahdin Foundation that was supposedly funded by Mrs. Richards," Tracey continued after a minute. "The foundation runs the Katahdin Retreat Center. We'd like to find out how it was set up financially. Do you know anything about it?"

"I've heard of the retreat center," Partridge said tentatively. "But I wasn't aware that Iris had anything to do with it. I thought it was a tribal endeavor." He looked puzzled, as if he were wondering why he didn't know about it, if it indeed was funded by Iris. He shrugged his thin shoulders. "Sorry."

Tracey leaned forward in his seat and looked the lawyer in the eye. "Now for the next question," he said. "It's a humdinger. Did she ever confide to you that she wasn't really Iris Richards?"

Partridge's Adam's apple took a dunking and then popped back up again, like a bobber after a fish has taken a nibble. "What!" he said.

"Her real name was Iris O'Connor," said Tracey. "She was a novelist"—he named her best-known book—"who went on to become a successful Hollywood screenwriter. She wrote the screenplays for a number of Miss Graham's movies."

Partridge looked from Tracey to Charlotte, his mouth agape.

Tracey went on to list some of Iris's better-known film credits.

"I had no idea," Partridge said at last, adding, "But I guess there's quite a bit about Iris' life that I wasn't privy to."

"She changed her name when she came here," Tracey explained. "There was a locked room in her house in which she kept the memorabilia of her other life. Miss Graham, who has a summer place in Bridge Harbor, told us who she really was. There were a number of pictures of Miss Graham in the room."

"But . . . why?" asked Partridge. "I know she came here because her aunt left her Hilltop Farm, but why erase her previous identity?"

"I think it was probably because she was blacklisted," Charlotte explained. "Maybe she wanted to write under another name—a lot of blacklisted screenwriters did that. Or maybe she just wanted to start over."

Partridge leaned back in his tobacco-brown leather swivel chair. "I'm flabbergasted, to tell you the truth. She certainly kept her two lives completely separate. Did Jeanne know?"

"She says not," said Charlotte.

Partridge gazed out the window for a minute, and then said, "This explains the literary executor. I wondered why she needed a literary executor. Not to disparage her achievements, but the articles that she wrote for *The Pumpkin Paper* were hardly literature."

Of course! thought Charlotte. The books she wrote would still be generating royalties, and would go on producing income for years to come. A film had been made just last year from one of Iris' books.

"Who is her literary executor?" Tracey asked.

"I don't know. She left a note instructing me to contact another lawyer about it." He riffled through the papers on his desk with his long, thin, curved fingers, and finally pulled out an envelope, which he passed to Tracey. "I've had this in my safe for years."

Tracey showed the envelope to Charlotte. Typed on the front was the sentence "To be opened in the event of my death." Below that, it was signed "Iris O. Richards."

Opening it, Tracey pulled out the sheet of paper inside, and read aloud: "In the event of my death, I wish my attorney, Ellsworth H. Partridge, of Partridge & Partridge, Old Town, Maine, to contact Ronald A. Polito, Esquire, of Hollywood, California, in regard to my literary estate."

"Ron Polito!" Charlotte exclaimed.

"Do you know him?" Tracey asked.

"Everybody in Hollywood knows him. He's the old man of Hollywood entertainment law." She didn't say "grand old man" because there was nothing noble about Ron Polito. He was a hired gun, the best there was. "He's the lawyer who everyone turns to when they're in a scrape."

"Is that how Iris hooked up with him?" asked Tracey.

Charlotte nodded. "I would imagine so. The biggest scrape that ever hit Hollywood: The House Committee on Un-American Activities. He represented the unfriendly witnesses." Then she added, "He represented the friendly witnesses too, for that matter."

"Whichever side you were on," said Partridge disapprovingly, as if the manner in which most lawyers operated was completely foreign to him.

Charlotte nodded. "I remember going to a party with him once. He looked around the room and said 'There isn't a person in this room whose neck I haven't saved.' Including my own, I might add. He got me out of jail once after I'd decked an obnoxious *paparazzo*."

"Seems to me I recall hearing something about that incident," said Tracey, with one of his dimpled grins.

Tracey had discovered this skeleton in Charlotte's closet when he'd run routine checks on the police records of everybody who was acquainted with the Bridge Harbor professor who'd been poisoned eight years before. He'd been ribbing her about it ever since.

"An odd choice for someone to oversee your literary affairs," said Tracey.

"Not really," Charlotte said. "A lot of people who turned to Ron when they were in trouble were so grateful to him that they ended using him for everything. I have for years. He's one of my oldest and dearest friends."

"I've been trying to get him on the phone ever since Iris died," Partridge said. "Without success. I've written too, but I haven't gotten a reply."

"He's hard to reach," said Charlotte.

"Maybe Miss Graham could get through to him for you," suggested Tracey.

"I'd be happy to try him when I get back to Bridge Harbor. I have a couple of things I want to talk with him

about anyway. I'll suggest that he give you a call as soon
as possible."

"Thank you," said Partridge.

"I'd like to know what he has to say," said Tracey. He
pulled a card out of his wallet, and handed it to the lawyer.
"I'd appreciate it if you'd give me a call after you talk
to him."

They stood up and said goodbye to Partridge.

"By the way, can you tell us how to get to Sawyer Street?"
Tracey asked as they headed for the door. "Miss Ouellette
told us that it's off of South Main, but I'm unclear how far
down it is."

"Where are you going?" asked Partridge.

"To see someone named Mack Scott. Apparently he was
a friend of Mrs. Richards. He was on the mountain with her
that day."

"Ah, Mack," said Partridge. He checked his watch. "He
should be getting home from work just about now."

"Miss Ouellette told us that he lived in a trailer on South
Water Street."

"A trailer," Partridge repeated. "Yes, I guess you could
call it that," he said with a smile, and proceeded to give
them directions.

Sawyer Street came to a dead end at South Water Street,
a narrow lane that paralleled the railroad tracks. Though the
lane had once been paved, the pavement was so broken up
that it was more like a dirt road, and what pavement was
left was scarred with deep potholes. To their right, a string
of a dozen or so modest homes overlooked the tracks, and
beyond the tracks, the river. The view to the distant south
was dominated by the giant tissue mill they had passed on
the way up, which produced a considerable share of the
nation's toilet paper. The mill lay sprawled out like some
huge and complex erector-set construction on a point that
jutted out into the river, the effluent from its smokestacks
filling the air with the foul smell that spelled j-o-b-s for the

area. At the opposite end of the street stood a ramshackle Victorian railroad station that had been converted into
a redemption center for recycled cans and bottles, while
directly ahead stood the Maine Central switching terminal,
its rows of track filled with colorful freight cars whose signs
conjured up images of distant locales: Santa Fe, Boston &
Maine, Delaware & Hudson, Wisconsin Central. One siding
held a string of flatcars stacked with pulpwood destined for
the tissue mill; another held a string of old Maine Central
boxcars, whose green-on-orange sign proclaimed, "The Pine
Tree Route."

After parking in a vacant lot, they got out of the car and
walked up the street in the direction of the railroad station.
Jeanne had said that Mack's trailer would be on their left,
but there was nothing on their left except a vacant lot filled
with rusting yellow snowplows that lay half-buried in the tall
grass. For a moment, they looked around in bewilderment.
The only trailer was an old horse trailer half-hidden in the
sumac and chokecherry at the back of the lot. Then Charlotte
noticed a board nailed to its side, with the name *SCOTT*
neatly carved on it in an italic script, and realized that it
was a horse trailer and not a house trailer to which Jeanne
had referred. She should have suspected when Jeanne had
described it as being gray and maroon. What house trailer
was ever those colors?

"Look," she said, pointing at the horse trailer. "I think
that may be Chez Scott. Gray with maroon stripes, right?"

Looking at the lot, Charlotte now noticed a shelter made
out of a tarpaulin supported by four bamboo poles of the
type used for rolling up rugs. This shaded an old picnic
table and three metal lawn chairs, and overlooked a fair-
sized vegetable garden in which a healthy crop of peas had
already climbed halfway up a wire support, and in which
the seedlings of lettuce, beets, and other vegetables were
peeking out of the rich black soil.

Tracey squinted to read the sign, and then said, "I'll be
damned. I guess it's a trailer all right. No wonder Partridge

looked so amused when we said we were looking for a trailer."

"I think I saw a path back there when we drove by," said Charlotte, nodding in the direction from which they had come.

Walking up Sawyer Street, they came to the path, which led through the scrub to the trailer. This was set parallel to South Water Street. A stack of cinder blocks propped up the front end to make the trailer level, and a set of wooden steps had been appended to the back end to make it easier to reach the gate that covered the bottom half of the rear opening. A sign painted in maroon on the side read "Heritage Farms."

Receiving no answer to his greeting, Tracey mounted the steps and pulled aside the plastic shower curtain, printed with a gold and silver shell pattern, that hung over the top half of the opening.

As he looked in, Charlotte considered what message they might leave on the pad that hung, along with a pencil, from a nail at one side of the opening, a primitive version of the telephone answering machine.

"Take a look," Tracey said as he stepped down a moment later, letting the shower curtain fall back over the opening. "It's not a bad little place."

Charlotte mounted the steps and pulled the shower curtain aside. Light from two small windows high on either side helped illuminate the interior, which was as neat as a pin. On one wall was an old metal cot with a sleeping bag and pillow on top of it and a cast-off mahogany table beside it. On the table were a frayed toothbrush and a tube of Colgate, a set of nail clippers, a tube of Chapstick, a container of fly dope, a Swiss Army knife, a water bottle, a ballpoint pen, and a pair of sunglasses. Next to the table was a small pot-bellied stove. The opposite wall was occupied by a bookshelf and a coat rack, the latter holding a canteen, an orange daypack, a green and black Buffalo plaid jacket, two pairs of blue denim overalls, and a couple of plaid flannel shirts. Two pairs of black engineer-type boots were neatly lined up underneath.

At the foot of the bed, which was to say immediately to Charlotte's left, was a white metal storage cupboard with a Formica top, above which was mounted a set of shelves. These held an assortment of canned food, mostly beans. Tacked on the wall next to the shelf was a Form 1040 from the IRS. Scrawled across it in red magic marker were the words "Does not apply." There was also a framed antique sign that read "For your good health, barrel-picking is prohibited."

"I wonder why someone would live like this?" said Tracey as Charlotte examined the interior. "Obviously, he's not your typical homeless person. At least, judging from the books."

Charlotte's first glance had taken in the poster of Walden Pond taped to the wall above the bookshelf, and she was now scanning the titles of the books: *Walden, Natural History Essays*, and *The Maine Woods*, all by Thoreau; the *Bhagavad-Gita*, one of Thoreau's favorite books; and books by Emerson and Carlyle, as well as a stack of back issues of *The Pumpkin Paper*.

"You're right," said Charlotte. "I think this is a modern-day version of Thoreau's cabin at Walden Pond." She went on to explain about Thoreau's famous experiment at living in a cabin in the woods. "His goal was to strip existence down to its bare essentials," she said as she stepped down, feeling a little as if she'd broken into somebody's house.

"Bare is right," said Tracey, who was pacing the small area of flattened grass that served as a yard. "I wonder what he does for a bathroom."

The answer to his question came from a man who had just emerged from the scrub that lined the path, pushing a shopping cart full of garbage bags. "I use the bathroom at work," he said. "I work over there," he added, nodding at the former railroad station. He parked the shopping cart. "Welcome to Heritage Farms," he said, holding out his hand. "Mack Scott. What can I do for you?"

As Jeanne had said, he was a stocky man of average height—built like a fireplug was the description that sprang to Charlotte's mind—with an unruly head of dark blond curls partly covered by a striped engineer's cap, a full red beard, clear gray eyes, and the ruddy complexion of someone who spends a lot of time out of doors. He wore blue denim overalls over a faded red plaid flannel shirt. A red bandanna was tied around his neck, and he smelled strongly of stale beer.

After Tracey had introduced himself and Charlotte (as his anonymous "assistant"), he asked, "Do you work at the redemption center, then?"

"Not at, for," he said. "I collect cans and bottles. Two garbage bags a day. I don't get any benefits, but I'm my own boss and I get to take time off whenever I want. Also, it's a short commute: seventy-five yards, to be precise. I don't make a big salary"—the teeth that smiled through his beard were straight and white—"but I don't need much, either. I live pretty simply."

"So I see," said Tracey with typical Yankee understatement.

"Is this your version of Thoreau's cabin at Walden Pond?" Charlotte asked.

"Actually, no. Thoreau's cabin was ten by fifteen; this is only six by nine. But the idea came from *Walden*." Mack raised a finger and quoted: " 'Consider first how slight a shelter is absolutely necessary.' Thoreau suggested that the kind of box that railroad workers used to use to store their tools would be quite enough."

"A tool storage box?" said Tracey.

Mack raised his finger again. " 'Every man who was hard pushed might get such a one for a dollar, and having bored a few auger holes in it to admit the air at least, get into it when it rained and at night and hook down the lid, and so in his soul be free.' "

Charlotte was reminded of the boxes she had read about that could be rented for a few hours of sleep at Japanese airports, but she would hardly think of sleeping in one as a soul-liberating experience.

"How big was this box?" asked Tracey.

"Six feet long by three feet wide," said Mack.

"Sounds more like a coffin to me."

Mack shrugged. "My box is a little bigger. But the idea's the same. I originally came down here in hopes that there might still be such a box here. The rest of the town's left over from the nineteenth century, why not a tool box? But there wasn't, so I took up residence in the horse trailer instead."

"The rent's cheap," said Tracey.

"Exactly. To quote Thoreau again: 'Many a man is harassed to death to pay the rent of a larger and more luxurious box who would not have frozen to death in a box such as this.' " He nodded toward the river. "What's more, Heritage Farms even has a river view. When the railroad yard is bare, anyway."

Tracey considered this idea for a moment, and obviously found some truth in it. "But why a horse trailer, when you have more spacious accommodations right at hand?" asked Tracey. He nodded at the Maine Central boxcars on the nearby siding, the doors of some of them standing wide open.

"Actually, I tried one of the boxcars first, but the cops told me to move along." He smiled in acknowledgment of Tracey's membership in the police fraternity. "Actually, they had no choice. The railroad had complained. They store their track equipment in those boxcars: cones, oil, salt for the tracks."

"Who owns this?" asked Tracey.

"I don't know who owns the trailer—Heritage Farms, whoever they are, must have junked it here—but the railroad owns the property. After I got kicked out of the boxcar, I got to know the trainmaster. He lets me stay here, and the police don't mind as long as I don't bother anybody."

"How long have you been here?" Tracey asked.

"In the neighborhood for close to two years. Across the street"—he nodded at the line of boxcars—"for about three months, and here at Heritage Farms for about eighteen months."

"Doesn't the noise of the trains bother you?" Tracey wondered, nodding at a locomotive that was parked on one of the nearby tracks, its headlight on and its engine thrumming in readiness for departure.

Mack shook his head. "It's not as bad as it used to be. The engineers are under orders not to keep the engines running while they're picking up cars. The residents of the senior citizens housing complex were complaining." He nodded at the buildings upriver. "But I never minded anyway." He raised a finger.

"I sense a quote coming on," said Tracey.

Mack nodded. " 'You can sleep near the railroad and never be disturbed. Nature knows very well what sounds are worth attending to, and has made up her mind not to hear the railroad whistle.' "

"Let me guess who said that," said Tracey. "Could it possibly be Thoreau?"

"You've got it," said Mack with a smile. He sniffed the air. "I don't mind the railroad, but I do think the quality of the air could be improved upon." He shrugged. "But you get used to that too."

"What do you do about food?"

"I have a little camp stove. Don't need anything more elaborate. I eat simply: rice and beans, mostly. No meat, no sugar, no coffee, no booze. I grow my own vegetables. A little fish: whatever I catch in the river. Bass, mostly."

"It's not polluted?" asked Charlotte.

"No. It used to be, but it's come back. We even get a pretty good Atlantic salmon run. It's not like the old days, when you could walk across the river on the salmon—the locals talk about just standing on the riverbank and spearing them with a pickpole—but it's not bad."

"They must be running now," said Tracey.

"They are. I had salmon last night for dinner. I discovered a nice little salmon pool on the other side of the river."

"With peas?" asked Charlotte, referring to the combination that was traditional in New England for the Fourth of July.

"Well, the peas aren't quite in yet," he said. "But I grow edible peapods, too, and they were ready. It was a pretty damned good meal."

"What do you do for entertainment?" she asked.

"I hang out with the guys in the switch shanty." He nodded at a dilapidated gray building in the middle of the rows of track. "I confess to being a bit of a F.R.N. myself, so their company suits me pretty well."

"F.R.N?" asked Tracey.

"Effing railroad nut. That's what the guys in the switch shanty call the railroad aficionados. Since this is a switching station, we get a lot of them hanging around here. Then there are the hobos and the canned heaters, some of them being one and the same."

"Canned heaters?" said Charlotte.

"The guys who eat Sterno. Put it in a sock, and squeeze it out. There's a regular gang of them who hang out on the river bank. They have a kind of camp down there." He smiled. "Of course, they can be pretty limited company."

"I would think so," said Tracey.

"Would you like to have a seat in my living room?" Mack asked. He nodded at the lawn chairs under the tarp.

Charlotte and Tracey assented, and Mack headed down a path toward the tarpaulin shelter, pushing the shopping cart in front of him.

"How did you come by your interest in Thoreau?" Charlotte asked as he led them through the milkweed and thistle.

"From my father," he said. "He used to read from Thoreau's journals every morning before he went to work."

"I used to know someone like that too," said Charlotte, reflecting on Thoreau's crazy-quilt constituency.

"One of the things I inherited from him was his old dogeared copy of *Walden*," Mack continued. "He had underlined his favorite passages. I'd read them a lot over the years, and they made a lot of sense to me too."

They had come to the tarp. Taking his hands off the bar of the shopping cart, Mack extended an arm toward the cluster of three rusted metal lawn chairs. Then he raised a finger. " 'I had three chairs in my house . . . ' " he began.

Charlotte completed the quotation for him: " 'One for solitude, two for friendship, and three for society.' "

·8·

WHEN THEY CAME to the tarpaulin shelter, Mack again parked the shopping cart. Then he took out the garbage bags and dumped their contents out onto the grass. "I have some work to do," he said, gesturing at the pile of cans and bottles. "Do you mind if I work while we talk?"

Charlotte and Tracey both shook their heads. The smell of stale beer was potent, and Charlotte realized that it wasn't Mack who had smelled of beer, but the beer cans in the garbage bags.

Mack took a seat in the chair nearest the pile and gestured for Charlotte and Tracey to sit down in the other two.

"What are you going to do with them?" Charlotte asked.

"Separate," he replied. "I get fifteen cents for wine and liquor bottles, and a nickel for everything else."

"So I guess you look for wine and liquor bottles," said Tracey.

"Not necessarily. They take up more space than cans, and they're heavier to carry. I get five bucks for a bag of cans, but I only get two for a bag of bottles." He smiled. "This business has its subtleties."

"How much do you make in a day, then?" asked Charlotte, recognizing that the usual proprieties concerning questions about income did not apply in the case of someone who considered himself irrelevant to the IRS.

"About twenty-five dollars. I usually work three days a week. If I need more, I work more. If I need less, I work less."

"Where do you find them all?" asked Tracey.

"This crop is from the town park, Indian Island, French Island, the airport, and the bars: the Shuffle Inn, the V.F.W., the American Legion. I alternate: one day I do this side of town, and the next I do the university and the fast-food places out on Stillwater Avenue."

"So Old Town is your bean field and this is your harvest," said Charlotte, referring to the honest labor by which Thoreau had earned the money he needed to support his modest lifestyle.

"This is a woman who knows her Thoreau," said Mack as he separated the cans by brand name, the Budweiser cans in one pile, the Coke cans in another. "Yes, Thoreau was determined to know beans, I'm determined to know cans."

Their conversation was interrupted by the squeal of brakes and clash of couplings from the railroad yard. For a moment they sat without speaking, waiting for the noise of the moving boxcars to stop.

"I didn't realize that you had to separate them by brand name," said Charlotte once the noise had ceased.

"Don't have to. But it makes it easier for Richie"—he nodded in the direction of the redemption center—"which in turn makes for good business relations. Since I'm one of his main suppliers, I figure it's sound business practice to keep him happy."

"Indeed," said Tracey. He leaned forward in preparation for getting down to business, his clasped hands resting between his knees. "As you may have guessed, we're here to look into the death of Mrs. Richards."

The engineer's cap that was bent over the pile of cans nodded.

"How long had you known her?" Tracey asked.

"Close to two years. I met her when I took one of her trips up the West Branch, following in Thoreau's footsteps. As I said, I was interested in Thoreau before that, but she's the one who made me into the fanatic that I am today. She's also the reason I settled down here."

"How often did you see her?" Tracey asked.

"Every other day, usually. She usually came with me when I worked her side of town. I'd stop by the farm to pick her up on my way over. She liked the idea of having a purpose to her walk. She also liked the idea of recycling. She was concerned about economy, like Thoreau."

"What did you talk about on your walks?" asked Charlotte.

"Thoreau, mostly. Or *Mister* Thoreau, as she called him. I liked her company. Also, she helped me with my work. She was terrific at spotting cans in the grass. She had a real eye for aluminum. I'm going to miss her." He corrected himself. "*Have* missed her."

"Miss Ouellette told us that you were on the mountain on the day that Mrs. Richards was murdered, and that you were planning to meet her at Thoreau Spring. We'd be interested in hearing about that," said Tracey.

Mack nodded. "I went up with her last year too. Not all the way. She liked to do the stretch to the summit by herself. This year, though, I wanted to try the route Thoreau took. She didn't want to go that way because it takes too long, and she wanted time to look at the *Diapensia*."

"But you didn't ride up there with her and Miss Ouellette." It was as much a statement as a question.

"No. I went up on Thursday. I hitchhiked—got a ride from Old Town all the way to Millinocket, then another ride from there to the park."

"Do you know the names of the people who picked you up?"

"My alibi, huh?" he said, and smiled. "The first ride was from a guy named Reggie from East Millinocket. He drove a blue Ford pickup. That's all I can tell you about him. The second ride was from a young couple from Boston. I don't know their names, but they drove a Volvo."

Tracey nodded, and wrote down the information. "Where did you stay?"

"The first night I stayed at Roaring Brook. I climbed the Saddle Trail on Friday. That's another reason I didn't want to go up with Iris and Jeanne. I'd just done that trail. The second night I stayed at Abol Campground."

"And did you meet Mrs. Richards at the Spring on Saturday?"

Mack nodded. "At about noon. But I wouldn't know the time for sure. I threw my watch away a long time ago. I'm not interested in knowing what time it is. For that matter, I'm not even interested in knowing what day it is. Or what week, month, or year it is."

Tracey looked at him skeptically. "Makes it kind of hard to keep an appointment, especially when you're meeting on a mountaintop."

Mack shrugged his broad shoulders. "It wasn't a formal thing. If we happened to bump into one another at Thoreau Spring, we'd have lunch; if not, *c'est la vie*." He considered a liquor bottle for a minute, and then tossed it to one side. "Too cruddy," he said.

"They don't accept the dirty ones?" asked Charlotte.

He shook his head. "I save them up. When I get a bunch together, I take them down to the river and rinse them out."

"What then?" asked Tracey, who was not to be distracted.

Charlotte had noticed a change in his interrogation style since he had joined the state police. He still took a while to get to the point, but once he got there, he stuck with it.

"We ate our lunches, looked at some *Diapensia* colonies. Then we just sat in the sun by the Spring for a while, watching the fog roll in over the Klondike. That's the bowl between Katahdin and the Katahdinauguoh Range."

"How long were you there?" asked Tracey.

"About forty-five minutes, I'd say. When the fog finally got to us, Iris went her way, and I went mine."

"Her way being to Baxter Peak?"

Mack nodded again.

"Which would have put her on Baxter Peak around one-thirty."

"That sounds about right," said Mack. "It's only a mile from the Spring to Baxter Peak, but since it's all uphill, I'd estimate it would take at least half an hour, and probably a little longer for someone Iris' age."

Tracey looked out at the locomotive, which was beginning to rev its engine. "If we assume that she set out on the Knife Edge right away, which I think we can, since she had already eaten, then we can figure she was killed between two and two-thirty."

"Does that square with what Clough told you?" Charlotte asked.

"Ayuh," Tracey replied. "He estimated the time of death to be between twenty-nine and thirty-four hours prior to when he examined the body."

For a moment, conversation ceased as they watched the engine pull out at the head of a string of boxcars. The train was like a sliding curtain, which, once it had been pulled aside, revealed a panorama of the wide green river, still swollen by spring runoff.

Finally Tracey looked back at Mack. "And what was your way?"

Mack tossed a couple of cans onto the Budweiser pile, then leaned back in his chair. "My way was back down. The same way I had come up, via the Abol Trail."

"You didn't go to the top?" asked Tracey.

Mack shook his head.

"Why not?"

"Thoreau didn't make it to the top, and I was following in his footsteps. I wanted to do it just the way he had. Actually, he didn't even make it to Thoreau Spring, but I made an exception to meet Iris."

"Did Iris mention meeting anyone on the trail?"

Mack stared out at a pile of scrap metal next to the tracks, thinking. "Now that you mention it, she did. She told me that she'd gotten into an argument with some guy over the *Diapensia*."

Tracey's interest was piqued. "What kind of an argument?"

"He had been stomping on it, and apparently she gave him what for. Iris had a temper. She said he was a member of some club. What was it? The High something." Bending over, he picked up a bottle of Jim Beam. "They climb the highest mountain in every state."

"You mean, they collect mountains?" asked Charlotte.

He tossed the bottle onto the fifteen-cent pile. "Yeah. Of course, Iris went on about that too. The Highpointers—that was it."

Tracey wrote down the information. "And how about you?" he asked. "Did you meet anyone else on the trail? Or see anything unusual?"

Mack shook his head. "Of course I saw other people on the trail," he replied. "But nobody who stands out in my mind."

"Jeanne told us that there was a man hiking just ahead of her and Iris on the Saddle Slide who was wearing an orange windbreaker. You didn't see him by any chance, did you?"

Mack thought for a moment, and then shook his head.

"From what Jeanne says, you were one of Iris' best friends," Tracey continued, suddenly shifting the direction of the questioning.

"I guess you could say that, but that's not saying much," Mack replied. "She wasn't very good at friendship. She was like Thoreau in that respect; she held people to such high standards that few could measure up."

"And you measured up?" asked Tracey.

Mack leaned back in the lawn chair and shook his head. "No. She only accepted me because I was beyond the pale." He smiled. "As far as she was concerned, there was no point in even attempting to apply any civilized standards to me. Just a bum, you know."

"But she was good friends with Jeanne," offered Tracey.

Mack shrugged. "She liked to think that Jeanne was her best friend. But Jeanne's loyalty to Iris wasn't based on friendship."

"Why not?"

"Iris took advantage of Jeanne. Bullied her, if you ask me. Do this, do that. Jeanne waited on her hand and foot. Every day, from dawn to dusk. She never had a moment to herself. But she did it all, uncomplainingly."

"Why?" asked Tracey.

"Security," he replied simply. "She grew up right here on South Water Street." He nodded down the street at the forlorn row of run-down houses overlooking the tracks. "As you can see for yourselves, it ain't exactly the Garden District."

"The wrong side of the tracks," said Tracey.

"Sort of." He smiled again. "Since the river's on the other side, there isn't really a right side. Anyway, there were seven children in a teeny-tiny little matchbox of a house, and not a pot to piss in. Working for Iris, she got to live in the nicest house in town."

"Did she know that she stood to inherit it?" Having found a ready source of information, Tracey was milking it for all it was worth.

"Sure. She not only knew, she was counting on it."

"And how did Jeanne feel about Iris' relationship with Keith Samusit?"

"That's a good question. To put it in a single word: threatened. She was afraid that Keith was going to supplant her in Iris' affections."

"Did she have reason to feel that way?"

"Sure did. There were some people who thought their relationship was"—he paused to search for the right word— "unnatural. I don't think there was anything unnatural about it. It was simply that of a lonely old woman and a young man who made her feel youthful again."

"Youthful, in what way?"

"There was a sexual element, but only in a minor way. She was always more"—he hesitated—"I wouldn't say flirtatious because it's a word that wouldn't apply to Iris—but she was definitely more *lively* when he was around. But it was really more of an intellectual thing. They shared this feeling for the importance of the vision quest, and they shared the retreat center."

"Jeanne felt excluded."

"She *was* excluded. As Keith and Iris became closer, Keith started taking over a lot of the jobs that Jeanne used to do. Running Iris' errands, answering her mail, getting involved in her business and personal affairs. A lot of this was ostensibly in connection with the retreat center, but the net effect was to push Jeanne out."

"I can see why she wouldn't like him," Charlotte commented.

"It went further than that," he said. "She was worried that Iris would leave him Hilltop Farm."

Charlotte's jaw dropped.

"You mean change her will?" Tracey said.

He nodded. "I don't know if she would have carried through. It would have been a terrible insult to Jeanne. But she had talked about it."

So the distrust of Keith that Charlotte had picked up on in their conversation with Jeanne hadn't been just in her imagination.

"Do you know about the Indian land-claims settlement act?" Mack asked.

Tracey nodded.

"Then you know the Penobscots claim to have been defrauded of hundreds of thousands of acres, including most of Old Town. Of course they were compensated by the settlement act, but Iris sometimes spoke idealistically of giving Hamlin's Woods back to the tribe."

The mention of Hamlin's Woods reminded Charlotte of the black fly attack. The bites on her ankles had now swelled into painful, itching red welts. She bent over to scratch, but it did little to help.

"Like Thoreau, she was an advocate of the Indians," Mack continued. "She felt it would be fitting for one of the region's oldest stands of forest to be returned to the tribe. But even if she had carried through, Jeanne needn't have worried. Iris would have changed her mind again."

"She was fickle, you mean?" asked Charlotte.

"Not so much fickle as hard to get along with. She'd have a disagreement with someone, and that was that." He drew his forefinger across his neck in a slicing motion. "She'd never have anything to do with them again."

"That didn't seem to be the case with Miss Ouellette," said Tracey.

"Jeanne was the exception. Which is why I said she needn't have worried. She always managed to grovel herself back into Iris' good graces. But there weren't many people willing to demean themselves to the extent that she was."

"Iris must have had enemies, then."

"By the dozens. There was hardly anybody in town she hadn't pissed off at one time or another. She was always spoiling for a fight. It was as if she didn't feel fully alive unless she had a windmill to tilt at."

"Any of them have any knowledge of crossbows?" asked Tracey.

"That I can't help you with," Mack said as he continued to sort the bottles and cans. The original pile, now reduced by almost half, was surrounded by half a dozen satellite piles. "Any suspects yet?"

Tracey shook his head. After a few more minutes of conversation, he thanked Mack for his help and they left.

"It takes all kinds," Tracey said, as they headed back to the car.

On their way back to Bridge Harbor, Charlotte and Tracey congratulated themselves on how much progress they had made. When they started out, they hadn't even known for sure if they had a case. (Tracey was still angry with Clough for having kept the state police in the dark.) But by late afternoon, they already had one major suspect and a couple of minor ones. Setting aside the minor suspects (the Pamola prankster, Keith Samusit, and the mysterious man in the orange windbreaker) for the time being, they concentrated on the major one, Jeanne Ouellette. Her presence on the mountain combined with the fact that Iris might have been planning to disinherit her put her in the Number One spot. She had lived at Hilltop Farm for thirty-three years; to lose it now would most certainly be a motive worth killing for. As a bonus, she would be getting rid of a bully of an employer. A pistol crossbow seemed like an unlikely choice of weapon for a woman, but she certainly appeared capable of using one. Charlotte remembered how easily she had hoisted the flat of heavy pots. Though she claimed to have been on Hamlin Peak at the time of the murder, she could easily have been lying. Tracey made a note to find out what she had been wearing, and to ask the other hikers who had signed out for Hamlin Peak if they had seen her. Though Jeanne said she hadn't seen anyone, it would only take one other person to confirm her alibi. He also made a note to find out if she'd had any training in archery.

The first thing Charlotte did upon arriving back at her cottage was to put some calamine lotion on the black fly bites on her ankles. Then she fixed herself a Manhattan, sat down on one of the green Adirondack chairs on her deck, and looked out at dusk descending on the harbor. Though it was June twenty-first, many of the trees still weren't fully leafed out, and she had a better view than she would have later on. But there wasn't much to look at, at least as far as the harbor was concerned. The season in Bridge Harbor didn't really get going until after the Fourth of July, and there were still fewer boats than usual at their moorings. Putting her feet up on the railing, she settled in to ponder the events of the day.

Iris' connection with Ron Polito had led her reluctantly back to the subject she'd been trying to avoid by taking Tracey up on his invitation: her black years. Charlotte hadn't been blacklisted, but she might as well have been. Iris had been put out of work because of her politics; Charlotte had been put out of work because of her age. There had been a couple of good roles, but that was it. The only parts that had come her way with any degree of regularity during that time had been TV parts, and there hadn't even been many of those. Others might have taken solace at such a time in family, but she had no family. She had sacrificed everything to her career, and then her career had turned to ashes. She had eventually made a comeback, but it had been a lurching one. A series of small comebacks was more like it (a critic had once written that her career had been recycled more times than a soda pop bottle). Her black period had profoundly affected her self-confidence. She had always prided herself on her ability to cope with whatever hand life chose to deal her, and she had coped with her black years, but only barely. She supposed those years explained why she was such a glutton for work now. She had no standards: she would take anything. Friends often asked her why she wasn't more discriminating. An actress of her stature could pick and choose, they said. They hadn't sat around for ten years waiting for the phone to ring.

But at least she had still had a career, however diminished it might have been. What must it have been like for Iris? To be sitting on top of the world one minute—a job you love, lots of money, a sophisticated lifestyle—and the next minute, nothing. All because you refused to become a stool pigeon. She could see why it would drive someone to the woods.

She checked her watch: eight here, five in Hollywood. Finishing her drink, she went inside to call Ron Polito. As she had anticipated, he wasn't available, but she left a message with his secretary, who promised he would return her call before the evening was out.

*   *   *

Iris wasn't the only one who had been driven to the woods, Charlotte thought as she dressed for dinner. She, too, had sought refuge in nature. She had bought her cabin on the mountainside long after her black period had come to an end, but that experience had no doubt provided some of the motivation for wanting a retreat from the world. She had lived here now for seven summers, and had grown to love it with a passion. It had been built by an artist in the late nineteenth century out of native cedar, and she loved the way its mossy roof and hand-hewn siding blended into the mountainside as if it had always been there. Like Thoreau, she loved the solitude and the natural rhythms of the day, but she was far from the ascetic that he had been. A dinner of a baked potato and steamed string beans was not for her. She liked food, and a lot of it. The problem was that she had never learned to cook, at least to cook to her own satisfaction. Nor was there even much of a kitchen in her cabin, the reason being that the original owner had eaten his meals at the inn at the foot of the mountain. After dinner, he would make his way back up the mountain by lantern light, on a footpath he had carved out of the mountainside expressly for that purpose. He had taken his meals at the inn for sixty-five seasons, living well into his nineties. Charlotte hoped that she would do as well. When the real estate agent had told her the story of the artist, she was sold. The combination of rustic solitude and the promise of a five-course meal at the foot of the mountain was too good to pass up. And although there was now a road, Charlotte often took the path back up from the inn after dining, albeit with a flashlight instead of a lantern. The gracious old inn, with its guests who came back year after year—some of them old enough to make Charlotte feel like a youngster—was to Charlotte what the Emersons' dining room had been for Thoreau, a refuge from the tyranny of too much solitude.

Twenty minutes later, she was dining on an appetizer of hearts of palm at her table by the window overlooking the harbor when the manager came over to tell her that she had a telephone call.

She took the call at the manager's desk in the lobby, where there was an enormous fireplace in which a fire was always burning. As she suspected, it was Ron Polito. She had left him her number at home and the number here.

"What can I do for you?" he asked after they had exchanged pleasantries. The deep voice on the other end of the phone had lost some of its robustness; was quavery, even. Charlotte wondered if he was ill.

"I didn't call about me," she said. "I called about another one of the old dinosaurs."

"Which dinosaur is that?" he asked.

"Iris O'Connor."

"Oh," he replied.

"Did you know she was dead?" Charlotte said.

Ron didn't seem surprised. The members of their former circle were dying off at such a rapid clip that the news of an old friend's death no longer carried the same emotional punch that it had even a few years ago.

Charlotte proceeded to tell him the story of Iris' murder, and her own subsequent discovery that Iris Richards was really Iris O'Connor. She also told him about Iris' note directing Partridge to contact him in the event of her death. "He's been trying to reach you for a couple of weeks now."

"I've been incommunicado," he said.

"I told him I'd use my influence to get you to call him."

"I'll give him a call tomorrow."

"Do you know who the heir to her literary estate is?"

"Yes. I do. The file's back at the office, and I'm not there right now. But I remember the name."

"Who needs the file when you're Ron Polito," she said. Ron's memory was legendary. Years after a case, he could recite all the facts, right down to the date of a particular event.

He chuckled, and then replied, "Until about a year ago, the beneficiary was the Henry David Thoreau Museum. It was her pet charity of the moment. She was head of the committee that raised the money to get it started."

Charlotte struggled to hear over the clinking of crockery and the murmur of conversation from the nearby dining room. "And now?" she prompted.

"About a year ago, she changed the beneficiary to an organization called the Katahdin Foundation," he continued. "I helped her set it up about three years ago. She used money that she had in bank accounts out here to fund it. Which is why she had me set it up, rather than her lawyer in Maine."

This was getting interesting, Charlotte thought. "I see," she said. "If her lawyer in Maine had set it up, she would have been forced to reveal how much money she had, which in turn would have put her identity as a nurserywoman with a modest income into question."

"More or less. What's your interest in this, if I may ask?"

"Just sticking my nose into places where it probably doesn't belong."

"As in *Murder at the Morosco*?"

"Sort of. I'm a friend of the state police lieutenant who's been assigned to the case. And, of course, I have a personal tie to the victim, seeing as how she was my screenwriter for ten years. What about the literary executor?"

"Ah, the literary executor," he said. "He's a young man by the name of Keith Samusit. A Penobscot Indian, from what I understand. He's also the executive director of the foundation."

Charlotte nearly dropped the telephone receiver on the desk. "Well, that puts a new wrinkle in the case." There were now two major suspects, both of them standing to gain significantly from Iris' death. "How much is her literary estate worth?"

"A lot. Her books are all still in print, so they're still generating royalties. *The Lonely Heart* is still selling two hundred and fifty thousand copies a year, world-wide. Someone once called Iris the world's most widely read, least prolific author. But that's not really true."

"Why not?"

"Because she never stopped writing; she just stopped publishing. She's got half a dozen novels stashed away in a safe at my office. This Indian is going to be surprised to learn just how rich his organization's going to be."

Charlotte was puzzled. "Why didn't she want to publish them?"

"She had some highfalutin reason based on Thoreau; something about avoiding the necessity of selling baskets instead of figuring out how to sell more of them. But I suspect it was just plain orneriness. Why should she deal with publishers if she didn't have to?"

"Didn't she care what happened to them after her death?"

"Nope. She wanted me to agent them. But apart from that, she didn't care. She said this guy Samusit could do anything he wanted with them. If they're marketed right, they could be a literary sensation. Her books have never gone out of style; they're classics."

"Does Keith know the Katahdin Foundation is the heir?"

"Yes. Iris told me that she had told him. He was the only person apart from her companion, Jeanne Ouellette, who knew who she really was."

The fact that Jeanne knew about Iris' past life didn't surprise Charlotte. She had already figured that out from Jeanne's lack of interest in the locked room, and from her reaction when they'd been introduced.

Ron continued. "They were both sworn to secrecy, of course."

"With the penalty for revealing her identity being that they would be disinherited?"

"Presumably," he said.

"Well, I guess this puts Keith at the top of our list of suspects. But why kill her now? Why not wait until she died a natural death?" She was speaking as much to herself as to him.

"I know the answer to that question."

"Yes?" she prompted.

"Iris would change the beneficiary of her literary estate every year or two. She'd become enamored of some charitable organization, but then there would be a falling out, and she'd change her will."

"Unlike Keith, however, the others didn't know they were her beneficiaries."

"Not that I know of," he said, and proceeded to name some of Keith's predecessors, which, in addition to the Henry David Thoreau Museum, included the Thoreau Alliance, Save Walden Pond, the Friends of Baxter State Park, and the Maine Nature Conservancy.

"Did Keith know she had frequently changed beneficiaries?"

"Not through me," he said. "I keep my work confidential. At least as long as the client's still alive."

"I know," she said. Another of Ron's virtues was that he could be depended upon to keep his mouth shut.

"But Iris may have told him, directly or indirectly. If he was at all close to her, which I presume he was, it wouldn't be hard to figure out that her allegiances tended to fray after a while." He continued. "I'll have a better idea of the value of the literary estate once I start shopping her manuscripts, but I would guess it's at least a million."

"That's not exactly chicken feed," said Charlotte.

"No, it's not," Ron agreed. "It's certainly reason enough to put this guy Samusit at the top of your list. Though he's not the direct beneficiary he'll be able to write himself a very nice salary as executive director. But . . ."

"But what?" Charlotte interjected.

"I think I may have another suspect for you."

"Who?" How could Ron Polito have a suspect in a murder that had taken place three thousand miles away? But she didn't doubt him.

"Are you coming out here any time soon?" he asked, knowing that her refusal to live on the West Coast meant frequent cross-country trips.

"On Tuesday, as a matter of fact. I'm meeting with someone about a project. Turning right around and coming back."

"I think you'd better drop by and see me. Will you have time?"

"I'll make time," she said. After saying goodbye, she pressed the button on the telephone base, and then looked up at the manager, who was busy with some papers behind the desk. "Mind if I make a call to Orono?"

"Not at all, Miss Graham," he replied.

He shouldn't mind—she was one of his best customers, she thought as she dialed Tracey. After dropping Charlotte off, he'd grabbed a quick bite to eat at home, and then had gone right back to Orono. When he was on a case, he worked all the time, a fact that didn't rest well with his family.

"Hello, Charlotte," he said, picking up the phone right away. "Where are you calling from? I just tried you at home. I was about to try you at the inn."

"That's where I am," she said, looking out at the fire.

"How's that for detection?"

"It doesn't take much detective ability to figure out that a woman who can't cook is at a restaurant during the dinner hour."

"Especially on a Thursday night," he added. "How's the spread?"

The Thursday night buffet at the inn was legendary, and the event, which was followed by dancing on the patio, was a social must for the residents of the summer colony.

"Great, as usual," she said. "Listen, I have some news for you. I just talked with Ron Polito. He says that Iris' literary estate could be worth a million or more. Guess who the beneficiary is?"

"You've got me," said Tracey.

"Keith Samusit."

Tracey let out a long, low whistle.

"Or rather, the Katahdin Foundation, of which Keith is the executive director. What's more, he knew who Iris really was. The question is, was he on Katahdin on the day Iris was murdered, or could he have been?"

"We know he was in the vicinity," Tracey said. "We can start by checking the entrance permits."

"What were you calling me about?" she asked.

"We're going to try to snag the Pamola prankster. Are you interested in heading up to Katahdin country?"

"Sure," she said. She had an appointment to keep with the mountain.

·9·

CHARLOTTE'S FIRST GLIMPSE of the legendary mountain came two days later on the way to Baxter State Park. Actually, on a clear day she could make out Katahdin from some of the mountaintops near her cottage on the coast. But from a hundred and fifty miles away, it was little more than a blip on the horizon. Charlotte and Tracey had driven those hundred and fifty miles earlier that morning, and arrived in Millinocket around noon. After eating at a luncheonette, they had set off for Roaring Brook Campground, which was the location of the trailhead for the trail up to Chimney Pond. They had expected to be disappointed in their wish for a view of the mountain: it was notorious for not emerging from the clouds for days on end, and the morning had been overcast. In fact, it had been raining for two days. But when they came out of the luncheonette they could see patches of blue, and by the time they rounded a bend just outside of town, there it was, its summit clad in a gleaming veil of fresh snow. To be sure, there were higher mountains, but at first glance Katahdin impressed Charlotte as being special for a quality, which for lack of a better phrase, she could only think of as mountainous. It truly was a mountain of the imagination.

Its uniqueness had to do with its unusual formation. An isolated gray granite monolith, it rose abruptly from the surrounding wilderness to a height of a mile. There were no competing peaks or foothills to detract from its solitary dignity, no trees growing on its rocky summit to dim its shining splendor. It was there, seeming to embody all of man's noblest virtues: serenity, strength, aspiration.

"It kind of takes your breath away, doesn't it?" said Tracey, as he peered up over the dashboard to get a better look.

Charlotte nodded. She couldn't take her eyes off of it. Katahdin was also unusual in not being a pointed mountain: it didn't jut harshly into the sky, but sat there square and rugged, the serene monarch of all it surveyed.

"I bet I've seen Katahdin a couple of dozen times over the years, and it always seems new to me," Tracey said. "The season, the weather, the time of day—it always looks different, but it's always fascinating."

"Who would ever have expected to find it capped with snow at the end of June?" Charlotte commented.

"It won't last," said Tracey. "But meanwhile it looks mighty pretty."

As they continued along the winding road, the mountain would disappear, then reappear to rivet their attention once again.

"When was the last time you climbed it?" Charlotte asked. From this vantage point, it seemed so immense that she found it hard to imagine that anyone had ever actually reached the top.

"The last time was about ten years ago. I went with my son's Boy Scout troop. I've climbed it seven or eight times, I reckon. A lot of people do it every year. Always seemed like a nice idea, I just never got around to it."

"It looks as if it would be a pretty tough climb."

"Depends," he replied. "It's not so bad if you start out from Chimney Pond. But if you start out from down at the bottom, it's a killer. Nothing like the view from up top, though. You must be able to see a hundred lakes."

"Do you think you'll do it again?"

"I wouldn't mind," he replied as the mountain came into view once again. "But I don't know if I'm up to it anymore."

"Maybe you'll have the chance to find out before we're finished," she said.

"Maybe," he agreed.

Tracey had spent the entire previous day working with Haverty and Sargent on the plan to catch the man who had been masquerading as Pamola. The campers with reservations at the Chimney Pond Campground had been relocated to other campsites to make room for the park employees and state police who would be posing as campers. Each of these pseudo-campers, whose numbers also included Charlotte and Tracey, would be equipped with a walkie-talkie, with which they could buzz troopers stationed at the ranger's cabin. When the Pamola masquerader appeared, the police would pounce on him, and take him into custody. Or such was the plan, anyway. With two major suspects now on hand, it seemed more unlikely than it had two days ago that the prankster had anything to do with Iris' murder, but apprehending him would get one problem out of the way. Occam's Razor, again. As far as the success of the venture went, the great unknown was the weather. So far, he had only appeared on moonlit nights, presumably because he needed moonlight to find his way without a flashlight. The weather in the area had been overcast for three days, and Tracey had been worried that the trend would continue. If the weather kept him underground, all their efforts would come to naught. The reappearance of the sun, however, validated the prediction of a clearing trend by mid-morning on which they had based their plans. Presumably he would be eager to get out again after having been cooped up since Thursday.

The other great unknown was the prankster's choice of venue. If he chose to appear to one of the vision questers at the retreat center rather than to one of the campers at Chimney Pond, they would be out of luck. They were prepared to try again the next night on the theory that he would alternate between the two locations as he had in the past, but there was a limit to how long they could tie up the time of so many people.

All these thoughts went through Charlotte's mind as they were driving through the tunnel of trees on the narrow perimeter road that led to the campground at Roaring Brook. Arriving at about one, they parked the car and then headed out on the trail. As they set forth, it struck Charlotte that any reasonable person would have experienced some degree of trepidation at the prospect of coming face to face with someone posing as an evil Indian god at a campground lean-to in the middle of the night. But that wasn't a concern of hers, at least at the moment. Maybe that would come later. Right now she was worried about just getting to Chimney Pond. The campground was a two-and-a-half-hour hike from the base of the mountain. Charlotte was in good shape for a woman of her age as a result of the long walks she was fond of taking around Manhattan. But except for Murray Hill, and a few of the island's other modest elevations, her walks were all on level ground. Nor was she accustomed to carrying a backpack; a Bloomingdale's shopping bag was about as much as she ever toted around. But she was eager to test her mettle. If she made it, she fully expected to be obnoxiously proud of herself.

The Chimney Pond trail wasn't steep, but it was all uphill, relentlessly uphill. Charlotte had probably stopped twenty times along the way to catch her breath, take off another layer of clothing, and give her neck and back a break from the weight of her backpack and her feet a break from her new hiking boots. New everything, in fact. Climbing mountains was not a sport she had been equipped for. With the exception of the camps on movie sets in various exotic locations, which were so luxurious as to hardly deserve the name, the last time she had camped out was in Girl Scouts. She was traveling light—a sleeping bag (good to zero degrees Centigrade), a foam rubber mat, a mess kit, a battery-operated lantern, a butane camp stove, a change of clothes, a few toiletries, and an assortment of freeze-dried foods—but the hike was a strain nonetheless. There had even been moments when she'd considered turning back. But the thought of Tracey waiting for her at Chimney Pond kept her going. He would be alarmed if she didn't show up. Though they had planned to hike together, he had left her behind shortly after they had set out. She had urged him to go on ahead when it became obvious that she wasn't going to be able to keep up.

Whatever doubts she may have entertained about the wisdom of her hiking venture were dispelled, however, about three-quarters of the way up. Following a side path marked by a "scenic view" sign, she emerged from the trees into a sandy, boulder-strewn clearing that gave her her first clear view of the spectacular scenery. Before her a sea of dark green evergreens stretched away to the mountain, at the foot of which lay the Great Basin, like a gigantic, terrible crater at the mountain's heart. Clouds played over the vertical walls of dark gray granite, which were still streaked with white from the previous night's snowfall. She could have been in Alaska, she thought as she took a seat on one of the boulders. After resting for a few minutes in this beautiful spot, she continued on. If anything, the trail got steeper as she went along, but she found it easier going, a feeling that she ascribed partly to the anticipation of the glorious scenery up ahead, partly to relief at being so close to the end, and partly to the fact that she'd become more accustomed to the pack. She had discovered that you had to carry your weight differently, leaning more forward than usual. She had also discovered that she had to be careful of her footing. God help her if she tripped; she'd be flat on her face in a second.

Four hours and fifteen hundred feet after setting out, she glimpsed a log cabin through the trees. She had made it! A moment later, she had arrived at the campground, which was as unique as the magnificent mountain at whose heart it lay. It was set in a grassy glade of birches and scrub spruce overlooking a pristine mountain tarn. All around, the perpendicular cliffs of the headwall soared into the clouds. The sight of the headwall reminded her of the slides at the hearing, and she searched in vain to pick out the ravine in which Iris' body had been found. As her eyes scanned the rocky crags, she thought again of Pamola. This natural amphitheater was said to be the home of the evil spirit, and she could easily imagine him swooping down from the mountain's fastnesses. Which brought her back to her reason for being here. Following the arrow on a sign, she headed down the path toward the ranger's cabin.

Arriving at the cabin a few minutes later, she was greeted by Chris Sargent, the young ranger who'd accompanied Haverty to the meeting at Tracey's office. He was a genial and fit-looking young man with a natural authority that was unusual for someone his age.

"Lieutenant Tracey wanted me to ask you something," Sargent said after she had signed in at the hiker's register (noting that she'd arrived a full hour after her traveling companion).

"What's that?" she asked.

"Pamola has always appeared to older females and, with the exception of Mrs. Richards and Miss Ouellette, to older females camping alone. We have two other women who will be camping together, both of them park employees, but you're going to be our only solitary female camper."

Charlotte completed the thought for him: "And he wants me to be the decoy. Tell me," she said, "did he just decide this, or is this something that he decided to keep from me until I got up here?" She had expected to be a decoy in the general sense, as were the other pseudo-campers, but she hadn't expected to be the bait in the trap.

"He just decided," Chris said, smiling. "He didn't realize until he got here that Pamola had always appeared to female campers. He said he thought you'd be up for it. What do you say?"

What had she gotten herself into? But after making it up to Chimney Pond with a loaded backpack, she was ready for anything. "I guess it's okay. I presume somebody's going to be keeping an eye on me."

"Lieutenant Tracey and Trooper Pyle will be staying in the next lean-to. Pyle arrived last night. We've had people arriving at various times, as if they were bona fide campers. You'll be in number nine, which is the most isolated."

"Is that the one that Iris was in?" she asked.

He nodded. "It's just off the Saddle Trail, which we think is the way he gets here. Campers who've seen him have noticed that he heads off in that direction. But we have no idea where he goes from there."

"What about my walkie-talkie?" she asked.

"I'll give it to you now. C'mon inside," he said, leading the way into the office. "In case he's watching with binoculars." Inside, he disappeared into a back room with a sleeping porch that looked out at the headwall.

"I like your digs," said Charlotte when he returned.

"Yeah," he said. "I do too. It's a big improvement over the crew cabin, which is where I used to sleep." He handed her the walkie-talkie. "Keep it out of sight, just in case he's watching."

Charlotte pushed the button on the side, and the walkie-talkie on Sargent's belt emitted an electronic squawk.

"We're connected," he said with a smile. "The signal is five beeps, very fast." He demonstrated with his own walkie-talkie. "Someone will get to you in two seconds. Everyone here will be one of us."

"How many will there be?" she asked.

"Eighteen. There are still a few real campers here, but they'll be gone by sundown." Excusing himself, he went into the back again, and emerged a minute later with a revolver. "Tracey wanted you to have this too."

She took the gun. It was a .38 Special service revolver.

"Do you know how to use it?"

"I think so," she said, testing its heft in her hand. She had appeared in enough thrillers to have a pretty good idea of how it worked.

"Let's see you aim at that," he said, indicating a poster of a moose that hung on the far wall. "Don't pull the trigger," he warned her. "It's loaded."

Charlotte raised the gun and took aim at the moose.

"Very good. I don't think you'll need it. But if Pamola takes out a pistol crossbow, you have Tracey's permission to let him have it."

"I should hope so," she said.

"I think there's a pretty good chance we'll see him tonight. The weather's clear, and he hasn't been here in a while. He usually appears between two and three, but don't bother to wait up. Just go to sleep as you usually would."

"That won't be any problem. The hike up was a killer."

"Carrying a loaded pack takes some getting used to," Chris sympathized, then continued filling her in. "He announces himself with a rattle. He stands in front of the lean-to and shakes the rattle very quietly. It's an eerie sound," he added.

So far, Charlotte had taken a pretty whimsical attitude toward the whole affair, but she was beginning to get apprehensive. "Is Lieutenant Tracey at his lean-to now?" she asked. She suspected she'd feel more comfortable once she'd gone over the game plan with him.

"I would guess so. You're supposed to be acting like real campers. There's no problem with your talking to him, but you should make it look as if you just struck up an acquaintance. On the way to the latrines, or something."

"Speaking of the latrines . . ." she said.

"I'll show you where they are. Also, where to hang up your food so the bears can't get at it. We've been fortunate in not having much of a bear problem at this campground, but it's because we've been very careful."

"Everything I have's in foil bags," she said.

"Which reminds me, the garbage gets packed out. We have a carry-in, carry-out policy. The water in the pond is only for drinking; there's no washing up. You can throw your gray water out behind your lean-to. Any questions?"

Charlotte shook her head.

"Well, if you think of any, I'll be here."

The lean-to that Sargent showed her to stood near a brook on the west side of the campsite, just off the Saddle Trail. Of the nine lean-tos, it was the farthest from the ranger's cabin. In front was a yard consisting of a patch of earth worn bare by the feet of previous campers and studded with boulders that served the function of stools. A twisting, rocky path led down to the pond. After unpacking, Charlotte went down to the pond to fill a pot with water for her dinner. Squatting at the water's edge, she looked out at the view. The sun was going down behind the Saddle, and its rays tinted Pamola Peak an apricot yellow and bathed the headwall in a golden glow. By some quirk of the local wind patterns, the surface of the pond was unruffled despite a stiff breeze, and the changing patterns of the clouds and the colored shadows on the cliffs were reflected in it as clearly as if it were a mirror. On the opposite shore, the trunks of a grove of white birches gleamed like polished silver in the twilight. The water itself was a peculiar pearly-green, like an exquisite celadon glaze. Charlotte had noticed this same color at lakes in the Alps. Maybe it was caused by the lack of vegetation; her trail guide had said nothing grew in the pond because of the deep penetration of ice in winter. In any case, it was a perfect paradise: still and clear and quiet, except for the occasional warble of a songbird—and the eerie roar of the wind. The wind had come up quite suddenly shortly after Charlotte's arrival, and blew unceasingly, sounding at one minute like a high-pitched hum and the next like the dull roar of distant surf.

Returning to her lean-to, she proceeded to set up her camp stove. Despite the somewhat complicated directions, this presented no difficulties, but getting it lighted did. She hadn't counted on the wind when she'd packed only one box of matches. Every time she lit a match, the wind would blow it out. She tried to find a more sheltered spot, to no avail.

She was just about through her box when Tracey came to her rescue with a cigarette lighter. Within minutes, the blue flame under her little kettle was burning merrily away.

After he had gotten the stove going, Tracey joined her on the raised sill of her lean-to to watch the colors on the headwall change from gold to pink to rose to purple as the sun withdrew over the western ridge of the mountain.

"Can I interest you in some chicken curry?" she asked once the water was boiling. She held up her foil packet. "It says it feeds two."

"I wouldn't count on it. I just had beef stroganoff, which also said it fed two, but I managed to polish it off quite nicely all by myself. I will take a cup of coffee, though. Once you've mixed up your dinner, that is."

"Sure," said Charlotte. "How about European-style cappuccino," she said, holding up another packet. "I got a little carried away in the camping supply store," she confessed. "I even have chocolate mousse for dessert."

"Chocolate mousse?"

"Add water and stir. It's my style of cooking. Want some?"

Tracey looked tentative. "I'll give it a try."

"What have you been doing?" asked Charlotte as she stirred the freeze-dried chicken curry into the boiling water.

Tracey tossed a peanut in the direction of a bold little chipmunk perched on a nearby rock. "Getting organized. Without being too obvious about it. There are four trails leading out of here, and we'll have people on all of them. Though he may not use a trail."

"If he's smart, he won't."

"It's pretty tough going if you don't. There's so much blow-down around that it's next to impossible to get through. I also went over the hikers' register for June ninth."

"Find anything?"

Tracey shook his head. "Nothing that jumped out at me. We'll go over it in more detail later; match the names up with the names on the entrance permits. At least there weren't that many: only twenty-three."

"That's good," Charlotte said. She poured some hot water into Tracey's cup and then added the contents of the cappuccino packet. The enticing smell of mocha filled the cool air.

"The search and rescue team was out looking for the bolt on the headwall this morning," Tracey continued. "They didn't find anything."

"Which means that Clough must have been right about the retrievable bolt."

"I reckon," said Tracey. He whistled and then tossed out another peanut. The chipmunk scampered over, took the peanut in its mouth, then raced back to the safety of his rock.

"Brazen little beggar," said Tracey as he took the cup of cappuccino.

"They're probably used to campers." Sitting back down, Charlotte took the first bite of her dinner. The sauce wasn't bad, but what was supposed to be chicken tasted like wedges of damp cardboard.

Tracey peered at her over his cup, his blue eyes dancing. "Leaves something to be desired, does it?" he said in response to her grimace.

"This may be the way I like to cook, but it's not the way I like to eat." She looked at him accusingly. "What's this about making me the decoy?" she teased. "Haven't you got any girl rangers?"

"Yes," he said. "But they're just that—girls. Pamola has a taste for older women." He grinned. "For that, I can't say I really blame him. I was pretty sure you'd go for it. Nervous?" he asked.

"A little. Like before a big scene. Actually, the thought of someone dressed up as Pamola doesn't scare me," she said. "But the thought of the pistol crossbow does. Where's your lean-to?" she asked.

"Over there," he said, nodding at the roof of a lean-to about fifty yards in front of her own. It could just be seen through the trees. "But I'm not going to be there. Pyle will be, but not me."

"Where the hell are you going to be?" she protested. "You'd better be somewhere close by. You're supposed to be protecting me."

His gaze fell on a boulder the size of a small car that was nestled in the underbrush just in front of her lean-to. "In the puckerbrush right behind that rock," he said. "Armed and ready. Just in case Pamola decides to get notional."

"If Pamola decides to get notional, as you put it, you'd better damned well be armed and ready," she said. "And a crack shot, besides."

"Don't worry," he said. "He'll be dead and done for."

After Tracey had returned to his lean-to, Charlotte did her washing up, which wasn't all that easy without a sink, and then unrolled her sleeping bag. The wind had picked up, and she set up her bed at the rear of the lean-to to be as far out of it as possible, and to be as far away as possible from her expected visitor. The noises of the campsite—the banging of the latrine door, the occasional peal of laughter, the clinking of pots and pans—were dying down as the sun descended behind the mountain. The campsite was retiring for the evening. Charlotte thought of Tracey, and wondered if he had already taken up residence in the underbrush behind the rock. After one last visit to the latrine—she didn't want to have to get up in the middle of the night—she set the alarm on her watch for one A.M. Despite what Sargent had said about going to sleep as usual, she didn't want to be caught off guard. Then she took off her boots and climbed into her sleeping bag, fully clothed. It wasn't the most comfortable bed she had ever slept in, but it wasn't as bad as she had expected, either. Her inflatable pillow was actually quite comfortable, as long as she avoided the revolver underneath. Most of all, it was warm. Once the sun went down, it had become quite cold, and she was happy to be snuggled into her down-filled bag. For reading material she had brought along *The Maine Woods*. Switching on her lantern, she started reading about Thoreau's trip up the West Branch to Katahdin, but found her eyelids getting heavy at about the same time that Thoreau found himself in the cauldron of clouds enveloping the summit.

Setting down the book, she turned out her lantern. No sooner had she done so than she heard a rustling in the underbrush behind the lean-to. Was it Tracey, taking his place? But he was supposed to be sleeping behind the rock in front of her lean-to, not to the rear of it. Maybe it was the prankster, paying an early visit. As the rustling came closer, she groped for the revolver, and then lay there, her ears straining. Even closer now. Finally, she decided to get up. Crawling on her knees to the edge of the platform, with the revolver in one hand, she peered around the side wall of the lean-to.

Standing in the underbrush, chomping away as placidly as a cow, was a mother moose, and at her side was a big-eared, long-legged calf, still wearing the woolly coat of the newborn.

It wasn't the first time she had seen a moose. She had seen several from the Interstate, and one up close: an enormous bull moose standing full square in the middle of a dirt road. Rather then getting out of the way, he had proceeded to trot slowly in front of her car for the best part of half a mile, as if he had wanted to see her safely home. But she had never failed to be astonished at how big they were, and amused by the ungainly appearance created by their oversized heads and long, spindly legs.

Sensing her, the moose turned her head and cocked her ears. Charlotte stayed stock-still, having heard that one should beware of a female with a calf. But the moose must have been as used to campers as the chipmunk had been, because she calmly turned back to her dinner, nipping the branch of a sapling with her protruding upper lip and then yanking her head backward and stripping off the leaves. She finished by biting off the tasty bud at the end, and then moved on, leaving a bare branch in place on the tree. When her calf got too far away, she would grunt, and the calf would come running back.

Charlotte was turning around when she noticed a familiar round face watching the moose from behind the boulder in the underbrush. She climbed back into her sleeping bag, reassured that she was in good hands.

The soft beeping of her watch awakened her at one. The wind had picked up, and it now sounded less like a whine or a hum than the plaintive wailing of a chorus of spirits. She was reminded again of Pamola, the evil spirit of the night wind. The walls of the lean-to offered scant protection. The wind rushed through the chinking as if it wasn't there. The open side of the structure formed a frame for the night scene, in which the ghostly shapes of the birches swayed in the wind like emissaries from the underworld. Somewhere a saw-whet owl let out its peculiar, beeping cry, like the warning beep of a construction vehicle that is backing up. With a shiver, she snuggled back down into her sleeping bag to await Pamola's arrival. The plank floor now felt as hard as a rock to her stiffening muscles, and she tossed and turned for several minutes before realizing that her foam mat had migrated across the floor of the lean-to. Moving it back into place, however, would require getting out of her sleeping bag, which she wasn't eager to do. She could tell from the feel of the air on her cheek that it was cold—she would guess the temperature had dropped to somewhere around freezing—and the wind made it feel even colder. No, she definitely did not want to get out of her sleeping bag. But there was also the matter of her bladder, which was pressing uncomfortably against her lower abdomen. What to do? If she got up, would she alarm Tracey unnecessarily? Or, more importantly, would she risk scaring off Pamola? Deciding that there was no point in jeopardizing the whole operation on account of a foam rubber pad and a full bladder, she pulled up the hood of her sleeping bag and waited.

Lulled by the roar of the wind, she found herself transported to that state between waking and sleeping where thoughts seem to float up like bubbles from the unconscious and then pop on the conscious surface of the mind. That's why she didn't recognize the sound at first. It was a soft, monotonous, susurrant sound: *shh-shh, shh-shh, shh-shh,* like the pounding of the blood in her ears. It was only when the rhythm grew faster and the volume louder that she realized it was the shaking of a rattle. Reaching for the walkie-talkie next to her sleeping bag, she pushed the button five times in rapid succession. Then she groped for the gun under her pillow. She had just laid her hand on it when he appeared in front of her lean-to.

She had been expecting something on the order of a gorilla costume, something silly and frivolous. The Pamola prankster, they had called him, as if he were playing an innocent game. But he was more like a demon from your worst nightmare. He stood in the center of the open side of her lean-to wearing a gigantic birdlike mask with freakish, staring eyes whose whites gleamed in the moonlight, and a rack of moose antlers that must have been five feet across. His chest was bare and hairless, and painted with a chevron design of black and yellow stripes. Around his neck he wore a collar embroidered with a geometric design that matched the cuffs on his wrists, and a small triangular medicine bag made of beaded leather. His loins were covered with a leather breechcloth, and his shoulders with a long cape made of some rough black fur, maybe bear.

He was all the world's most frightening gods—Pluto, Osiris, Shiva—rolled into one. He was all the bad things you had ever done, all the bad people you had ever known, all the bad memories tucked away at the back of your mind. Mesmerized by the repetitive shaking of the rattle, she sat up and watched, one hand still on the gun. Then she heard a chilling, high-pitched whine. At first she thought it was the saw-whet again. But then she realized that it had emerged from the throat of the beast: a tremolo of utter despair. His cry was followed by a quick, shrill, shriek of fear, which, she realized only after uttering it, had come from her own throat. And then he was gone.

"Halt!" Tracey shouted. Then he fired two warning shots, and took off into the underbrush after Pamola.

"I blew it," she said for the tenth time. "I'm really sorry. I just plain blew it." She was standing outside the ranger's cabin an hour later with Tracey, Haverty, and Sargent. The others had all gone back to bed.

"No, you didn't," Tracey said. "You did exactly what you were supposed to do. You were supposed to be a camper who was frightened by Pamola, and that's exactly what you were. You played your role perfectly."

"We're the ones who blew it," Haverty said. He shook his head. "We had the people; we had the moonlight. I just don't understand how he got past us. It was as if he just vaporized. The guy must be one hell of a hunter: he didn't make a sound going through the woods."

"He was probably wearing moccasins," said Charlotte.

"Even so," Haverty said. "We'll look for his trail in the morning. At least we know for sure now that he headed off in the direction of the Saddle Trail. We've got a ranger here who's an expert tracker. Maybe he'll be able to figure out where he went from here."

"Maybe he really is Pamola," said Tracey, "and he just flew away to his cave up on the mountain." He looked up at the Knife Edge, where the moon rested on the edge of the black silhouette of the headwall like a juggler's ball on an outstretched arm.

"The old ranger who used to live here told me that Pamola lived in a hole just below Pamola Peak," said Haverty. "He said he would come out on moonlit nights to roll the moon across the Knife Edge. See how it seems to be hung up there?" He nodded at the headwall.

They looked up at the moon, which did indeed seem to be stuck on one of the peaks on the Knife Edge.

"He used to say that the moon needed help getting over South Peak," Haverty continued, "and that's where Pamola would come in." He shook his head at the memory. "He had a lot of stories about Pamola. And if you spend enough time here, you start believing some of 'em."

Haverty talked for a few minutes more about the old ranger's Pamola stories, and then excused himself to go to bed.

After yet another apology, Charlotte too said good night, and headed off in the direction of her lean-to. Though she carried a flashlight, she didn't need it. The glowing disc that Pamola was pushing over the hump of South Peak shed light enough for her to see.

Back at lean-to number nine, she slid her foam mat back into place, climbed into her sleeping bag, and fell immediately to sleep.

· IO ·

THE BIRDS WOKE her at five A.M. They sang with the abandon of birds in early spring, joyous and exultant. Charlotte recognized some of them from their songs—the Swainson's thrush, the white-throated sparrow, the chickadee, the winter wren—but there were others whose songs were unfamiliar. The bass note in this symphony was sounded by the thumping of the latrine door. The campsite was coming awake. She opened her eyes to the sight of the tips of the spruces and the new leaves on the birches bathed in the golden glow of first light. It was absolutely lovely, utterly still and clear. She couldn't remember the last time she had been up this early. She breathed in the fresh air, and took note of the cloud of condensation as she exhaled. It was cold, but she felt as snug as a baby in a bunting in her warm sleeping bag. And despite the interruptions of the night before, she felt rested and relaxed.

After her own trip to the latrine, she went down to the pond to fetch some water. Then she lit her little stove, and set the water to boil for her breakfast. Once the water had come to a boil, she stirred in the contents of a packet of blueberry pancake mix. Then she set her skillet on the stove, and within a few minutes she was dining on a delicious blueberry pancake breakfast. She had always maintained that her idea of roughing it was to go from a four-star hotel to a three-star. But to her surprise, she was finding that she actually *liked* camping out. Of course, it had only been one night. She hadn't even had to cope yet with the fact that there were no bathing facilities. But she was ready for more. In fact, she was falling in love with the mountain. Though this visit would be cut short—Pamola wasn't likely to come back for another night of being shot at—she vowed to return. After breakfast, she fetched some more water and washed up her dishes. Afterward, she went around to the back of the lean-to to dump out her gray water, as the ranger had instructed. She was just turning back when she spotted an odd shape in the underbrush. Leaning over, she pushed the branches aside to get a better look.

It was a rattle: Pamola's rattle—a round, smooth, cocoa-colored gourd with a shellacked surface. A peeled stick had been stuck into the gourd for a handle, and lashed to it with leather strips. Etched into its hard, shiny surface, like a petroglyph on the wall of a cave dwelling, was a primitive line drawing of a small, short-legged animal.

After putting the rattle in a plastic Ziploc bag that she'd brought along for garbage (being careful not to get her fingerprints on it), Charlotte turned it in to Tracey, whom she found at the ranger's cabin. She then volunteered her help, and was assigned the task of looking over the entrance permits for the vehicles that had been in the park on the day of the murder. The entrance permits for the entire month were being held for Tracey at park headquarters in Millinocket. Pyle would later track down the people who had been in the park on the day of the murder through their vehicle registrations, and canvass them by telephone. Knowing this task was on Pyle's agenda, Charlotte was a bit baffled as to what it was she was supposed to be looking for. And when she'd asked Tracey, he had thrown up his hands. The real purpose of her assignment, she suspected, was to keep her occupied while Tracey spent the morning going through the guest registers at the local motels. Pyle, meanwhile, had taken the rattle back to Orono to check it for fingerprints. Having driven up with Tracey, Charlotte had no choice but to wait until he was finished, and she might as well be doing something to further the cause, however humble.

At least, that's how Tracey viewed it, she suspected. Being a provident Yankee, he was always looking to put free time to good use, and it didn't matter much to him whether it was his or hers.

By seven-thirty, Charlotte and Tracey had set off back down the Chimney Pond trail to the parking lot at Roaring Brook Campground, following in the footsteps of the park employees and police officers who had already decamped after the abortive attempt to catch the prankster. Charlotte wasn't looking forward to the hike down. Her muscles were still sore from the hike up the day before. But it turned out not to be too bad. The weather was beautiful—sunny, and much warmer than the day before, and the descent was much easier than the climb up, which gave her a chance to enjoy the scenery. But the trail was just as long, and it was two hours later before they reached the trailhead. From there, it was a short ride into park headquarters in Millinocket. After Tracey informed the clerk behind the desk that they had spent the night on the mountain (for which Charlotte was grateful, feeling as grubby as she did), he introduced her as his assistant, and explained that she would be looking through the entrance permits. Then he headed out to check the motel guest registers.

She spent the next several hours sitting at a table in an unoccupied conference room, sorting through the pile of permits. Her first step was to cull the permits for the vehicles that had been in the park at the time of the murder from the total pile for the month. This reduced the number from about five thousand to about five hundred. That done, she started going through them. First she eliminated the permits with more than one person in the party, on the theory that whoever murdered Iris was acting alone, thereby reducing the number to about a hundred and twenty. Next, she eliminated the permits for those who had been in the park for more than two days at the time of the murder, on the theory that the murderer had come to the park for the express purpose of murdering Iris, and wouldn't have come early to take in the scenery. This left fewer than a hundred. Finally, she eliminated women, on the theory that a woman was an unlikely murderer because of the type of weapon that was used. Of these, there was only a handful, which left her with roughly ninety permits. All of the criteria she had chosen for her elimination process were assumptions—the murderer might very well have been a woman who had entered the park with a group a week ahead of the murder—but she had to start somewhere.

Then she started going through the permits, one by one. What was there to learn from a name and a license plate number? she asked herself. About a third of the way through, she found out. She wondered why she hadn't noticed it on her earlier runs through: a car from Iowa with a vanity license plate that read KLIMBIN. The date on which the driver had entered and exited the park was June ninth, the day of Iris' murder. She would bet anyone twenty to one that the driver was the man with whom Iris had gotten into the argument over the *Diapensia*, the one who was a member of the Highpointers Club. She looked again at the permit. Under the heading "Purpose of Visit" was written "To climb Mount Katahdin." Why else would someone come all the way from Iowa except to climb Katahdin? She decided to call him. Iowa wasn't a populous state. Chances were that he lived in a city, and there were only two that she could think of: Des Moines and Cedar Rapids. Also, it was an unusual name, Scandinavian sounding: Haakon Hilmers. If indeed he did live in one of those cities, she should be able to get his phone number through Information. If not, Tracey could always track him down later through his vehicle registration.

Going back out to the lobby, she asked one of the clerks if she could use the phone to make a long distance call. "Of course," the clerk replied. "Mr. Haverty told us that you could have free use of the facilities." The clerk then led Charlotte to an office cubicle, where she looked up the area codes for Iowa in the telephone book. There were three: Des Moines, Cedar Rapids, and Council Bluffs. This was going to be a piece of cake.

Luck was with her. She found him on the first try, in Des Moines. As expected, there was only one listing for a Haakon Hilmers. Hoping that he wasn't still off climbing mountains somewhere, she dialed the number.

A woman's voice answered. When Charlotte asked for Mr. Hilmers, she was asked to hold. A moment later, a man's voice came on the line. "Hilmers here."

Charlotte said hello, and then asked, "Is this the Haakon Hilmers who climbed Mount Katahdin a couple of weeks ago?"

"The very same," he said. "It was a peak experience."

Charlotte laughed politely. She hated bad puns, but she also wanted to get some information out of this man. She went on. "Are you a member of an organization called the Highpointers Club of America?"

"Yep. Got my pin for thirty high points last year. Must have something to do with being from the only state in the union that's so flat it doesn't even have an official high point." He chuckled. "The closest thing we have is a manure pile. What can I do you for?"

Charlotte explained how she had tracked him down through the Baxter State Park entrance permit. Then she started to describe Iris.

"Go no further," Hilmers interrupted. "I remember her perfectly."

Then she proceeded to tell him about Iris' murder. "Apparently, you were one of the last people to see her alive."

"I was?" he said, seemingly dumbfounded.

Charlotte continued. "She told the hiker with whom she ate lunch that she'd just gotten into an argument with somebody from the Highpointers Club. Unless there was another Highpointer climbing Katahdin that day, that person must have been you."

"Are you with the police or something?" he asked.

"I'm working on the investigation," she replied, dodging the question. "Is that right?" she pressed. "About the argument?"

"That's right," he said genially. "Am I a suspect or something?"

"Not at all." Actually, the idea of the Highpointer being the murderer hadn't occurred to her, though it was possible. People had been killed over more trivial disputes. "We just wanted to know about the events of that day."

"Sure," he said, getting into the spirit of her inquiry. "You mean where I first saw her and that kind of thing?"

"Exactly," said Charlotte.

"I first saw her on the Saddle Slide. I was ahead of her and the woman who was hiking with her. We were the only ones on the trail. You tend to notice other people on that trail because of the chance of dislodging a rock that might roll down and bonk them on the head."

"Excuse me," Charlotte interrupted. "Were you by any chance wearing an orange windbreaker and new hiking boots with Vibram soles?"

"I was," he said. "How did you know?"

"Mrs. Richards' hiking companion mentioned seeing someone on the Saddle Slide in an orange windbreaker, and she had noticed the imprint of the Vibram logo in the mud by the brook at the foot of the slide."

"Very observant. That was me. I didn't talk with them, at that point. Mrs. Richards caught up with me later on the Tableland. She was alone; I guess her hiking companion had gone the other way. That's where we got into the fight. I don't like to speak ill of the dead, but she was a royal bitch."

For a few minutes, Charlotte listened to Hilmers' blow by blow account of the altercation. Then she asked, "What happened then?"

"I continued on to Baxter. Had to bag my peak, you know. That was the sixth peak I bagged on that trip. I ran into her again on the way down to Thoreau Spring. She was coming up; I presume she must have cut over to Thoreau Spring before heading up to Baxter Peak."

"Did you talk with her?" Charlotte asked.

"No. We just exchanged dirty looks."

"She was still alone?"

"Yes," he said.

"Is there anyone else you encountered on the trail that day who stands out in your mind?" she asked. "Anyone or anything? You never know what might turn out to be important."

"There weren't many hikers out; it was still pretty early in the season. But I do remember two fellows in particular. I ran into them where the Abol Trail emerges onto the Tableland. It's about a half mile below the Spring."

"What was unusual about them?"

"Two things. The first was that the one guy was extremely good-looking. Tall—about six four, I'd say—broad shoulders, rugged-looking. He looked a lot like Linc Crawford, the movie star. You're probably too young to remember him. He did a lot of cowboy movies."

"I remember him well," Charlotte said. "I always thought he was a very underrated actor," she added, feeling as always that she had to defend Linc from the accusation of being only a cowboy actor.

"Me too. I was a big fan of his. Do you remember his last movie, *Red Rocks*? What a performance."

"Yes," said Charlotte. Linc had always run down his films—justifiably so, in many cases—but he had been proud of that one. It had earned him a posthumous Oscar for best actor, which Charlotte had accepted for him.

"I remember when he died," Hilmers continued. "What a tragedy to have died at the peak of his career like that."

It wasn't the peak; it was more like the downhill side, but Charlotte didn't bother correcting him. For a moment, there was silence on the line as the memories of Linc's death flooded her thoughts.

It was odd that she could no longer picture Linc's face in her mind, though she could remember other things about him in great detail: his hands, curiously graceful for such a rough man; the set of his shoulders. Fortunately, she could always look at one of his movies, and often did.

Then Hilmers spoke. "Anyway, that was the first thing. The second was that they looked like they were having words. I don't know what about. I wasn't close enough to overhear. Maybe it was about the *Diapensia*. I'm not big on the names of flowers, but that's one I'll never forget."

"What did the other guy look like?"

"Medium height, stocky, a red beard. He was wearing an engineer's cap—the blue- and white-striped kind—and a green and black plaid jacket."

That sounded like Mack, Charlotte thought, remembering the plaid jacket she had seen hanging in the horse trailer. He would have been descending the Abol Trail at about that time. They would have to ask him about the other man when they got back, though he hadn't mentioned talking to anyone else.

"Can't think of anyone else. Sorry I can't be of more help."

"You have been a help. If you do think of anything else, I'd appreciate it if you'd call Lieutenant Howard Tracey at this number," she said, and gave him Tracey's number. "Good luck with your peak bagging," she added.

"Good luck with your investigation," he replied. By way of a valediction, he urged her to "Keep on climbin'."

She had just turned back to the stack of entrance permits when she was interrupted by a familiar voice. "How're you doing?" it said. Then Tracey's round face peered around the edge of the divider.

"I might have something." She explained about the KLIMBIN license plate, and told him what Hilmers had said about seeing Mack.

"How'd you get his number?"

"I just called Information for Des Moines, and hit it right off the bat. If he hadn't turned up in Des Moines, I would have tried Cedar Rapids and Council Bluffs. How about you?" she asked.

"I'm impressed. Maybe we should hire you. I didn't turn up anything. Nor did the tracker; he tracked Pamola to the Saddle Slide, and then lost his trail. Hard to track someone when there's only bare rock underfoot. What do you say to a little grub?"

Charlotte suddenly realized that she hadn't eaten lunch. "Sure," she said, happy to pack it in.

Twenty minutes later they were sitting at an oak dining table in the rustic dining hall of the Big Moose Inn, awaiting two orders of prime rib of beef with Yorkshire pudding. The dining hall was presided over by a large and slightly moth-eaten moose head, with a gigantic rack of antlers that reminded Charlotte uncomfortably of her nocturnal visitor. Though the inn was eight miles out of town on the road to the park, Tracey had been told by Haverty that it was the only decent place in town to eat, apart from a pizza parlor in Millinocket's Little Italy section, which stretched to all of three buildings. Judging by how crowded it was, the Big Moose Inn looked to be a popular spot. Most of the other diners were part of a raucous and sunburned group of white-water rafters who'd just completed a trip down the West Branch and seemed to think they had accomplished something worthy of celebration. Just the night before, Charlotte had been reading about Thoreau's trip up the West Branch, in which a bateauman had poled Thoreau's bateau *up* the rapids, a feat that Thoreau had considered astounding. As Charlotte looked at the rafters, she found herself pondering the social significance of the fact that it was no longer going *up* the river that held allure for adventurers, but going *down* it, and thought it must say something about the slackening moral fiber of the country. Especially when the reward for the modern-day adventurers wasn't the ascent of the state's biggest mountain, but a drunken beer blast.

But she wasn't complaining. She was happy to be here. After her foil packet of chicken curry, prime rib with Yorkshire pudding was going to taste pretty good. And who was she to cast stones? she thought as she sucked on the whiskey-soaked cherry of her second Manhattan, her sore muscles no longer seeming quite as sore as they had a short while ago.

She and Tracey were trying to talk about Pamola over the noise.

"Where would he have gone from there?" she asked, referring to the Saddle Slide, where the tracker had lost Pamola's trail. Her map of Katahdin was spread out on the table between them.

Tracey shrugged. "He might've gone down the other side, and followed the Perimeter Road north, then cut over to one of the old logging roads on the western boundary. Or he might have wickie-upped on the mountain, and be waiting until everybody's gone home to come back down."

"Wickie-upped?" said Charlotte, who still wasn't familiar with all of Tracey's Downeast expressions.

"Bedded down on the trail," he said. "I guess it must be an Indian word."

Charlotte nodded and studied his possible routes on the map.

Looking up at the moose head over the mantel as she put the map away, she observed to Tracey how difficult it must have been for him to make his way up the flank of a mile-high mountain at night wearing a headdress of moose antlers.

"Oh, I forgot to tell you," Tracey said. "One of Haverty's men found the antlers this morning. They were hidden in the woods off the Saddle Slide in a burlap bag. He was probably planning to come back for them."

"Are you going to test them for fingerprints?"

He nodded. "I picked them up at park headquarters when I came back for you. Of course, if this guy's prints aren't on file anywhere, neither the rattle nor the headdress are going to do us any good."

They were interrupted by the arrival of the proprietor, an amiable young man who introduced himself as Bruce the Moose. He brought their salads, and with them the message that there was a telephone call for Lieutenant Tracey.

Tracey took the call at a telephone table under the stairs leading to the second-floor rooms. From where she was sitting, Charlotte could see him holding a hand to one ear in an effort to drown out the reveling of the rafters.

He was back in a minute. "That was Gaudette," he said, referring to his supervisor. "He just got a call from the Indian police. They've got a body in a shallow grave at the retreat center."

"A body!" she exclaimed.

"A detective from the Indian police is on his way up now from Indian Island with an assistant to take a look. He's made arrangements for us all to fly in. We're supposed to meet him at the Katahdin Air Service in an hour."

Charlotte moved the Pamola prankster up on her suspect list, and Jeanne down. Unless Jeanne had some connection to the retreat center, this removed her from the top spot. As it did Keith, who wouldn't have sullied his own nest.

"Another crossbow murder?"

"I don't know. I couldn't hear much." He frowned at the noisy group of rafters. "But I don't think he knew much more than that anyway. The grave is on the north shore of Little Beaver Pond."

Pulling out her map again, Charlotte spread it out between them. "Here it is," she said, pointing at a small drop of blue just east of Beaver Pond, and just west of the park boundary.

"The only alternative to flying in is to drive on a logging road twenty miles up the West Branch to a sporting camp named Big Eddy"—he pointed to a site near the Ripogenus Dam—"and hike in three or four miles from there."

"Where are you headed?" asked Bruce as he served their main course. He was a lithe and fit young man, distinctly un-mooselike, and clearly curious about the business that had brought the state police to his neck of the woods.

"Beaver Pond," said Tracey.

"The Katahdin Retreat Center?" he asked.

Tracey nodded. "We're supposed to fly in from the Katahdin Air Service. Do you know where it is?"

Bruce nodded at the door. "Out the door and across the road. On the shore of Ambejejus Lake. It will take you exactly two minutes. On foot. Longer if you have to get in the car and drive."

Tracey smiled his Cheshire cat grin. "Which means we'll have plenty of time to enjoy this delicious meal," he said, studying with relish the pink slab of roast beef and the mound of Yorkshire pudding on his plate.

"Please do," said Bruce graciously.

Charlotte was glad to be sharing her time with somebody who had his priorities straight, which meant that food came first. She also was glad Maine was still the kind of place where people had their dinner at midday.

After dinner they headed across the road to the Katahdin Air Service. While Tracey checked in at the office, a small log cabin with a sign out front advertising scenic rides, Charlotte studied their itinerary on the map. As a child, she'd had an uncle who went fly fishing in Maine every spring, and the long Indian names brought back memories of his stories about the Maine woods, which in turn brought back memories of happy family gatherings. Ambejejus was near the beginning of the string of lakes, falls, and deadwaters that made up the West Branch of the Penobscot. Her uncle used to entertain the children by reciting them in fixed order: Pemadumcook, Ambejejus, Passamagamet, Debsconeag, Pockwockamus, Aboljacarmegus, Nesowadnehunk, Amberjackmockamus, Ripogenus, Chesuncook. In a Maine wilderness version of Peter Piper, she would occupy herself for hours on end trying to meet his challenge of doing the same without tripping on her tongue. She could still recite them today, though her memory had been refreshed by the previous night's reading of Thoreau's account of the same trip.

When Tracey emerged from the office they boarded the red and white float plane that was waiting at the dock. A second plane was awaiting the arrival of the Indian detective and his assistant. Once the pilot—a bearded bear of a man who occupied more than his share of the tiny space—had gotten them loaded on and buckled in, they took off with a roar across the lake, and then rose slowly into the air. Charlotte was amazed to see that what appeared from the ground to be a wilderness lake was actually surrounded by dozens of small cabins—what the Mainers called "camps"—tucked away into the woods. But the signs of habitation became less commonplace as they traveled up the West Branch, and by the time they turned north toward Beaver Pond at Big Amberjackmockamus Falls, there was nothing but dark green forest interrupted only by an occasional tote road and the patches of lighter green where the forest had been clear cut by the lumber companies. Looming over all was the majestic presence of Katahdin. A few minutes later, they had skidded to a stop in the small bowl of dark blue that was Beaver Pond. The plane ferried them over to the west shore, and they disembarked at the dock, where another float plane was anchored. The retreat center sat at the head of a meadow that sloped down to the lake, a ski-chalet-style building made of giant peeled logs.

Their introduction to the retreat center came in the form of another vicious black fly attack. The flies moved in the moment the propellers stopped whirring. This time, Charlotte was prepared. "Good job," said Tracey appreciatively as she produced a container of Bug Ammo. She had bought it on the way up to Katahdin after a sign warning tourists not to "pet the black flies or ride the mosquitoes" reminded her of their experience in Hamlin's Woods. But, oddly enough, she hadn't needed it on Katahdin. She suspected that the black fly season on the mountain came a little later on account of the altitude.

By the time they had finished anointing themselves, the second float plane could be seen heaving into view above the tips of the pines. A few minutes later, it had discharged its cargo of passengers: the detective from the Indian police, whose name was Bill St. Louis, and his young assistant. Both looked as much French as they did Indian, and probably were.

After introductions, the four of them headed up toward the retreat center. When they were halfway there, Keith emerged and headed down to greet them. This time, no introductions were necessary: Keith already knew the police officers. As he himself explained, on an island with only six hundred residents, everybody knew everybody else.

Once the greetings were dispensed with, Keith addressed the little group in a quiet but commanding voice; it was clear that he was accustomed to being in charge.

"As you already know, one of our vision questers discovered a shallow grave near Little Beaver Pond this morning. I called Lieutenant St. Louis, and he in turn called the state police because of the possible link with the murder on Katahdin. As you'll see, it looks like a fresh grave."

"Do you have any idea who the body might belong to?" asked St. Louis. He was a tall, thin man whose quiet demeanor and soft voice seemed at odds with his choice of profession.

Keith shook his head. "No. When I found out about the grave, I immediately went to check on our vision questers. A vision quest is a solo fasting ceremony that's conducted in the wilderness. Each of the vision questers is on his own, but I know where they all are."

"And they're all here?" asked Tracey.

He nodded. "We have fourteen in the seven-day Native American course right now. They're scattered around at various locations in the woods."

"Do they know we're here?" Tracey asked.

"No. They probably heard the planes, but that wouldn't mean anything to them. They didn't even know that I was checking up on them. I didn't see any point in interrupting their journeys until we know what's going on."

"What about the vision quester who found the grave?" asked Tracey.

"Eagle Woman," said Keith.

"That's her name?" said Tracey.

Keith nodded. "Each of the vision questers picks a name to use during the quest," he explained. "She was very upset about it. She thought about dropping out, but then decided to continue. The vision quest ends this afternoon anyway. She's moved her power place to the other side of Little Beaver Pond."

"What's a power place?" asked Tracey.

"Each of the vision questers chooses a site that speaks to them; it's where they carry out their vision quest." Keith paused for a minute, then asked: "Any other questions?"

"Not at the moment," said Tracey, speaking for them all.

"Then we'll head over there," said Keith. "The site's about a half mile from here, on the north shore of Little Beaver Pond. I'd appreciate it if you wouldn't talk while we walk. Voices carry easily over the pond, and I wouldn't want to disturb the vision questers."

After stopping at a tool shed to pick up a shovel, Keith headed off into the woods, with the others stretched out Indian file behind him along a trail that followed the shore of the pond.

With conversation ruled out, Charlotte found herself observing the way the Indians moved, especially Keith. They moved lightly and gracefully, with knees bent and torsos hunched over, touching down with the balls of their feet first, and then lowering their heels, without making a sound.

Fascinated, she tried to imitate them, but found that she couldn't keep her balance. Where had they learned to walk like that? she wondered, and concluded that it must be in their blood. As Keith had said, you could take the woods away from an Indian, but you couldn't take it out of him.

After a few minutes, they came to the end of Beaver Pond, whose shore had been denuded of trees by the industrious beavers for their lodges. Several of these lodges were visible in the shallow water. Beyond the pond, the trail followed a stream for a short distance before reaching Little Beaver Pond.

At Little Beaver Pond, they followed a trail along the shore for a short distance before turning into the woods, which consisted mostly of birch and scrub spruce. Once they left the shore, there was no trail, but Keith seemed to know where he was going.

A few minutes later they emerged at a fern-fringed forest dell, in the middle of which stood a freshly dug shallow grave. A cross made of two sticks lashed together with a leather shoestring was stuck in the middle.

Why the cross? Charlotte wondered. If a murderer had wanted to conceal a body, he wouldn't have marked it with a cross.

Keith held up the shovel. "Who wants to do the honors?"

St. Louis nodded at his burly assistant, who was the obvious choice on account of his broad back and strong shoulders. He took the shovel and began to dig energetically.

After a few minutes, the shovel struck something hard, which the next shovelful revealed to be a loose-leaf notebook. Reaching over, Tracey lifted it off the shovel and brushed the dirt off the cover. " 'Psychology 101,' " he read. " 'Jonathan Norwood, Harkness Hall.' "

"Let me see," said Keith, reaching out a hand.

Charlotte noticed how delicate and hairless his fingers were.

"Jonathan Norwood was a vision quester in the last session," he explained. "He went home a week ago last Tuesday." His flared eyebrows were drawn together in perplexity. "His power place was right up there." He nodded at a shelf of granite just above them. "His name was Molting Snake."

"Look at this," said St. Louis' assistant. His shovel had turned up a stack of envelopes fastened together with a rubber band. "Bank statements. Columbia Bank and Trust. Jonathan Norwood again."

As the little group looked on, the digging continued to turn up other artifacts from the life of Jonathan Norwood: a freshman beanie, a high-school yearbook, several photograph albums, even some grade-school report cards.

"What's the story on him?" Tracey asked as he leafed through the yearbook, which was from a high school in Massachusetts.

"He was a very unhappy person," Keith replied. "In and out of college. Couldn't get his life together. He lived with his mother, worked at a job he hated. He said he had come on the vision quest in hopes of gathering the courage to find a new direction for his life."

"Hence the name Molting Snake," said Tracey.

Keith nodded.

"Here's an appointment book," said St. Louis, bending over to pick it out of the pile of upturned earth.

"And what was he doing here?" asked Tracey. "Burying his past?"

"It certainly looks that way, doesn't it?"

· II ·

HALF AN HOUR later, they were back at the retreat center, feeling a bit silly about the whole incident. "I guess everybody around here is a little spooked," said Tracey, in an attempt to lighten the atmosphere. After saying goodbye, St. Louis and his assistant took the waiting float plane back to Ambejejus Lake. Since the other plane had been called back to service some other customers, and the one that was already there was Keith's, Charlotte and Tracey had to wait until St. Louis' plane returned. This meant that they were temporarily stranded with Keith and his girlfriend, Didias. Charlotte wasn't unhappy about the delay. She wanted more time to talk with Keith, who was back at the top of the suspect list now that the dead body had turned out to be a false alarm. After they had seen the plane off, Keith explained that he and Didias would have to excuse themselves: they had to get the sweat lodge ready for the vision questers who were due back later that afternoon.

Keith had expressed relief that the grave had contained only the mementoes of a vision quester past; a body wouldn't have been good for business, he said. Charlotte was also glad there was no second body, except for the fact that it put them back where they had started, with Iris murdered and an unknown prankster prowling the park. Keith didn't know anything about the former (or so he said), but Charlotte suspected he might know something about the latter, and she decided to take advantage of the wait by asking him about it.

"What do you have to do?" she asked him, in reference to the sweat lodge ceremony. "Maybe we can help."

"We can use all the hands we can get," Keith replied. "It's up that path there." He pointed to a wide swath that had been cut through the meadow grass to the right of the retreat center.

With that, they set out, Tracey walking with Keith and Charlotte with Didias. If Keith looked Japanese and St. Louis looked French, Didias looked like Pocahontas. She was a beautiful young woman, with long, shiny black hair held back by a porcupine quill ornament, and high, wide cheekbones.

Meeting her, Charlotte remembered that they still had to check out Keith's alibi. But it would be better to wait until Keith wasn't around, she decided. Also, it was more a matter of routine than anything else; all Didias could do was confirm that he hadn't been with her, which didn't mean much.

"Didias," Charlotte repeated. She turned to her companion. "I've never heard that name before. Is it a Penobscot name?"

She smiled. She had small, perfect white teeth. "A nickname, really. It means blue jay. It's a name that's traditionally given to a young woman by her beloved." She looked lovingly over at Keith, who was chatting with Tracey. "My real name is Mary. Keith is big on unearthing forgotten Penobscot traditions."

"Isn't that good?" asked Charlotte. Looking at Keith, she was struck again by the difference between the way he and Tracey walked.

"Very good," Didias agreed. "If it weren't for him, a lot of the old ways would have died out. He's committed to Black Elk's vision of the red road. He was a Sioux spiritual leader whose teachings are considered by many to be the Native American Bible," she explained. "He believed in the unity of mankind."

They had passed the retreat center, and were now entering the woods on the hillside behind it.

"Keith is always quoting him," Didias continued. " 'And I saw that the sacred hoop of my people was one of many hoops that made one circle, wide as daylight and as starlight, and in the center grew one mighty flowering tree to shelter all the children of one mother and one father.' "

"Then his belief in Black Elk's vision is why he wants to perpetuate Native American traditions among whites?" said Charlotte.

Didias nodded. "A lot of Penobscots don't approve. They want to keep our traditions to ourselves."

They walked for a moment in silence; then Charlotte said, "It would seem to me that since a lot of Maine Indians have a fair amount of white blood, to deny their traditions to whites would be hypocritical." As always, she wasn't unwilling to put in her two cents.

"Exactly," Didias concurred. "Nobody's full-blooded anymore. Nobody was full-blooded a hundred years ago. Even Chief Orono, who died in 1801, was three-quarters French," she said, naming the chief after whom the town was named.

They had arrived at a clearing, in the middle of which stood an enormous woodpile that had been stacked in a square, like a Lincoln log construction. On top of the woodpile was a pile of rocks. On the far side was a level area on which an altar had been laid out. This consisted of a pole from which hung streamers of various colors, and, at the foot of the pole, a large rock crystal. The sweat lodge skeleton stood beyond the altar. It was a wigwamlike structure, about six feet high at its peak and about ten feet in diameter, made of bent saplings that had been lashed together. These were supported around the middle by a girdle of more poles.

Keith had stopped at the woodpile and was explaining the ceremony to Tracey. "The grandfathers, as we call the rocks, are heated to red-hot in the fire, and then they're brought into the lodge and put into the fire pit," he said. "Then water is poured on them to make steam."

"It's the Indian equivalent of the Finnish sauna, but with a spiritual element," Didias interjected.

"Each sweat lodge is consecrated to a particular purpose," Keith went on to explain. "In the ceremony that will be held this evening, the vision questers will be calling on the spirits to help them interpret the meaning of the visions that came to them during their quests."

"Very interesting," said Tracey.

"What would you like us to do?" Charlotte asked.

"Lieutenant Tracey can take the wheelbarrow and gather some more rocks, and you can help me with the blankets," he replied. "The rocks have to be a certain size," he said to Tracey. "Didias will show you. She's going to collect some more kindling."

Tracey picked up the handles of the wheelbarrow. "Let's go," he said to Didias. Then they disappeared back down the path.

After Tracey and Didias had gone, Keith led Charlotte around the altar to a pile of Indian blankets on a pallet behind the sweat lodge, which was protected from the weather by a sheet of plastic.

"You never cross the spirit path," Keith said, explaining the reason for their roundabout route. "It goes from the fire to the altar to the lodge." Removing the plastic sheet, he took off the first blanket and opened it up. "You just drape them over the poles like this."

Charlotte opened up another blanket and draped it over the lodge so that it lay flat on the wooden skeleton, and then smoothed it out. She was glad she was dressed in old clothes because the blankets were dirty and musty-smelling from being stored outdoors.

"I was surprised at how fast you got here," said Keith as they worked. "And pleased. I was eager to find out what was going on."

"We were here already," said Charlotte, glad that he had provided the cue for steering the conversation to Pamola. "We set a trap for Pamola last night at Chimney Pond Campground, for which I was the decoy. All we caught was his rattle, which he dropped when he left."

"His rattle?" said Keith, looking up from his work with interest.

She nodded. "It was made out of a gourd, and it had a drawing on it of a small animal. One of the rangers said it was an otter. Lieutenant Tracey's going to have it tested for fingerprints along with the moose headdress, which one of the rangers found in the woods off the Saddle Slide."

Keith stopped what he was doing and sat down on a nearby stump, with his hands clasped together and his head bent down in thought.

"Do you know who the rattle belongs to?" Charlotte asked.

He sat silently for a minute before replying. "As a matter of fact, I do. I wasn't going to say anything. I figured the Pamola issue was a tribal matter. But if the police are testing the rattle and the moose headdress for fingerprints, they're going to find out anyway."

At last! A real lead, Charlotte thought, mentally congratulating herself for being correct in her suspicion that Keith knew who the Pamola prankster was. "Then this person has a police record?" she said.

He nodded. "He's been arrested in connection with Indian protests out West." Standing up, he resumed laying the blankets on the sweat lodge. "He used to be active in the American Indian Movement. His name is Lorne Coley. Coley is a corruption of the Indian word for otter."

"Hence the drawing on the rattle," said Charlotte. "Do all Indian names have meanings?" she asked, curious. "Like yours, for instance?"

"A lot of them, yes. Samusit means 'one who walks along the edge of something, a line walker.' I like to think that the line I walk is the line between Indian culture and white culture."

Charlotte laid a blanket on the last uncovered space. The skeleton was beginning to look like a wigwam.

Keith continued. "Lorne's grandfather was a carnival sideshow Indian. He'd dress up in Indian costumes and dance.

One of his costumes was the Pamola costume. I saw him in it when I was a kid. By then, he wasn't doing carnivals anymore. He was dancing for handouts downtown."

"He was that poor?" said Charlotte.

He shook his head. "He was a drunk," he said, "trying to squeeze drinking money out of the whites. It used to disgust me."

"Why's Coley dressing up as Pamola?" she asked as she smoothed out a moth-eaten trapper's blanket. They were now on the second layer.

"Part spite, part craziness. He's one of those people that Black Elk, the Sioux spiritual leader, called Blue Men. People who are motivated by jealousy and greed. He calls himself a Penobscot Indian *medeoulin*, or shaman."

"What qualifies one to be a shaman?"

Keith shrugged. "Your guess is as good as mine."

"Then he's a self-proclaimed shaman."

"You could say that. He leads his own vision quests, conducts healing ceremonies. He's very jealous of all this." He waved a slim-fingered hand at the retreat center, whose shallow-sloped roof could just be seen above the trees below. "It challenges his authority."

"Another shaman on his turf," Charlotte commented.

Keith bristled. "I would never call myself a shaman. To be a shaman, you have to have supernatural powers. I call myself a ceremonial leader."

Charlotte apologized.

"That's okay," he said. "It's just that it's a touchy issue with me. Given all the phony shamans that are running around these days."

Didias had reappeared, carrying an armload of kindling that she added to a stack next to the woodpile. "Who're you talking about, the male shamanist pig?"

Keith smiled. "That's what Didias calls him. One of the perquisites of being a spiritual leader is that women throw themselves at you."

"I hope not," Didias said, smiling at Keith.

He corrected himself. "At least, they throw themselves at Coley. Not all women. He specializes in old ladies. His amorous exploits have caused a lot of discord among the older members of the tribe."

"Are you friendly with him?" Charlotte asked.

"I used to be. We were both Pure Men. The Pure Men are young male members of the tribe who are honored for their fleetness of foot; in the old days, they would run down and kill the deer or moose. They were called Pure Men because they had to stay pure in order to maintain their endurance."

Which meant that Coley would be more capable than most of making the grueling hike over the mountain. But Keith also had been a Pure Man, she thought, reminded of how gracefully he had moved through the woods. And he had more of a motive, like a literary estate worth a million dollars. "And today?" she asked.

"Today, it's strictly a social honor. The Pure Men lead the Sacred Run. As soon as a Pure Man is outstripped by a younger candidate, that person takes his place. I was the one who replaced Lorne."

Not only had Keith challenged Coley's role as shaman, he had also replaced him as a Pure Man, Charlotte thought. No wonder Coley was jealous. "But you're not friends anymore?"

He shook his head. "I stopped hanging around with him when he started drinking heavily." He sighed. "It's a problem with our people, as I'm sure you know. He stopped drinking some time ago, but sometimes alcoholics act crazier after they stop drinking than they did before."

"Crazy enough to murder Iris?"

"I don't know," he said, opening up yet another blanket to spread on the lodge. "I've been thinking about little else since I spoke with you the other day. Didias, can you tell us if any light's getting in?"

Didias crawled into the lodge and reported that the southeast side near the bottom needed more blankets. Then she crawled back out and went off into the woods again to fetch more kindling.

"Lieutenant Tracey and I were trying to figure out his route. How would he have gotten here, or to Chimney Pond?"

"I have a theory about that, too," Keith said. "Our tribal lands used to be divided up into family hunting ranges; families would go year after year to the same area. The otter family's range was northwest of Katahdin in an area called the Klondike. Lorne's great uncle used to hunt moose there."

Charlotte remembered Mack talking about watching the fog roll in over the Klondike when he and Iris had been eating lunch at Thoreau Spring.

"He's the one who named it because of its resemblance to the Canadian Klondike. Do you know anything about the Klondike?"

She shook her head.

"It's a bowl of spruce that lies between Katahdin to the east and Barren, O-J-I, Coe and the Brothers to the west. It's been called the most inaccessible area in the state. There are no trails into it. The only way in is over the surrounding ranges, or through a narrow defile to the north."

"And you think he used the Klondike as his staging area?" She wondered if a former alcoholic—even one who had been a Pure Man—could have made such a grueling trek, and then dismissed her doubts, remembering all the times she had been astounded at the physical stamina of alcoholic co-stars.

He nodded. "His great uncle had a camp there."

Reaching into the pocket of her jacket, Charlotte pulled out her trusty pocket map and opened it up against the side of the sweat lodge.

"Here it is," Keith said, pointing to an area dotted with the blue plant-like markings that were the symbol for bog. "His great uncle's camp was at Klondike Pond, which is here." He indicated a slice of blue on the east wall. "I think that's where he stays."

"Right between here and Chimney Pond," she said. "But if there aren't any trails, how would he get in and out?"

"His great uncle could have told him. But he's a good woodsman in his own right. It would be difficult—it's all dense, thickly matted stunted spruce that's very difficult to get through—but it could be done. There are a lot of old logging roads in here"—he pointed to the northwest—"where he could park."

"That's what the rangers said, too," she told him.

"Once he got out of the Klondike, he could take the Perimeter Road to the Kidney Pond Campground," he continued. "From Kidney Pond, there's a trail that leads into here. It would be a long haul, but you could do it in a night."

"And to Chimney Pond?" she asked.

"Chimney Pond wouldn't be that hard. It's much closer." Again he pointed out the route on the map. "He'd just climb up this gulley to the Northwest Plateau, follow the Northwest Basin trail to the top of the Saddle Slide, and then take the Saddle Trail down to the campground."

"A ranger who's an expert tracker tracked him up the Saddle Trail, but lost his trail at the Saddle Slide."

"There you go," he said. "I'd venture to say that if you looked along the line of *krumholz* on the west slope of the Northwest Plateau . . ."

"*Krumholz?*" asked Charlotte.

"It's a German word for that stunted spruce that I was talking about. It's also called elfinwood. The trees might be over a century old, but they're only a few feet high, and very dense from being flattened by the wind and snow."

"I forgot," said Charlotte, who had been wondering how Keith knew all of this. "You're a forester."

"In places, you can walk right on top of it," offered Didias, who had reappeared with another armload of kindling.

"Anyway, if your tracker looked along the line of *krumholz* on the west slope of the Northwest Plateau, I'd venture to say that he'd find an entry point somewhere just to the east of Klondike Pond."

Tracey had appeared at the head of the path with a wheelbarrow-load of rocks. "Hello, there," he said as he paused to wipe the sweat from his brow. "I've been out gathering our grandfathers. What have you folks been up to?"

Charlotte pondered what to say, and decided to leave it until later.

"Thanks," said Keith. "We're ready to light the fire now. It takes about an hour to heat the grandfathers, which will give the vision questers plenty of time to get back here. The fire is the signal that the quest is at an end. Would you like to join us for the sweat?"

"Maybe next time," said Tracey. "We have to get back. But thank you."

They all helped pile the grandfathers on the top of the woodpile, and the kindling on top of that. Then Keith touched a match to a pile of shredded birch bark at the base of the woodpile. Within minutes, huge orange flames were darting into the cloudless blue sky.

"Some Native Americans make a practice of reading the flames," Keith said. "I can't do that. But I can tell that this is a fire with a lot of energy. I think it's going to be a good sweat."

As they stood there and watched, the heat of the flames burning their faces, they heard the hum of an engine. Turning, they saw the float plane returning over the forest to the south.

"Here's our ride," said Tracey.

Charlotte walked next to Keith as they headed back down the path toward the retreat center. As they arrived at the bottom, he turned to her and said, "You know, the Penobscots have a saying: 'The fox is smart, but he gets caught in the trap just the same.' "

Charlotte looked at him, an eyebrow arched quizzically.

He explained. "If Lorne's the one who killed Iris, you'll catch him."

After saying goodbye, Charlotte and Tracey headed down
to the dock. A few minutes later, they were airborne. As they
looked back, they saw a dense pillar of black smoke rising
out of the forest.

As the plane headed back toward Ambejejus, Charlotte
was struck by an idea. The Klondike might be inaccessible on foot, or nearly so. But that wouldn't necessarily
be true by air. It probably depended on wind speed and
direction, but she guessed it would be possible to land a
float plane there. On their walk down to the dock she had
filled Tracey in on what Keith had told her. He, in turn,
had told her that Didias had confirmed Keith's alibi, for
what that was worth. Now Charlotte turned to the back of
the plane, where Tracey was sitting (having been gentleman
enough to give her the seat with the view), and suggested
that they try to land on Klondike Pond. Tracey considered
her suggestion for a moment and then leaned forward to talk
to the pilot, who was the same bear of a man they had flown
out with.

"Do you know a place called the Klondike?" he asked.

The pilot looked puzzled. "Nope," he said. "Can't say
that I do."

"It's a basin surrounded by mountains to the west of
Katahdin."

"Oh! I know where you mean," he said, nodding in recognition. "We fly over there on sightseeing trips. I didn't
know what it was called."

"Do you know the pond there, Klondike Pond?"

The pilot nodded again.

"Do you think you could land there?"

"You mean today?"

Tracey nodded.

He considered the request. "It might be tricky. It's a
small pond, and it's tucked right up into the slope of the
plateau. But it's pretty quiet today. I'd be willing to give it
a try."

"We're game if you're game," Tracey said, whereupon the pilot rounded a mountaintop to their left and headed the plane back toward the north.

"That's Daicey Pond down there," the pilot said, indicating a collection of little cabins, looking like Monopoly pieces, that were clustered around one end of a lake. "It's one of the park campgrounds," he said.

Locating Daicey Pond on her map, Charlotte was able to follow their route as they crossed the Perimeter Road, followed the Appalachian Trail along Katahdin Stream, and then flew through a narrow pass between two mountains to emerge in the bowl of the Klondike. It was a deep depression, surrounded by mountains. Except for the fact that it was covered by a dense carpet of evergreens, it reminded Charlotte of the giant Meteor Crater in Arizona.

"Supposedly, there's an old plane wreck down there," said the pilot, looking down into the bowl. "But nobody's ever found it."

From the bottom of the bowl, they followed a stream up the side. Just as it seemed they were about to crash into the slope of the Northwest Plateau the pilot suddenly set the plane down on a tiny pond, as softly as if it were a leaf falling on a puddle.

"How do you like that for flying?" said the pilot proudly, once they had come to a gentle stop.

"Pretty impressive," said Tracey with a grin.

"Now, do you mind if I ask you one question?" asked the pilot, turning around to talk to his backseat passenger.

"Fire away," he said.

"What are you folks looking for here?"

"A camp, probably. Failing that, any evidence that somebody's been here recently."

"A log-cabin kind of camp or a tent-kind of camp, or what?"

Tracey shrugged. "We're not sure."

"Is it possible to just kind of taxi around?" asked Charlotte.

"Sure," said the pilot, turning back to his controls. "We can circumnavigate the pond. It will take two and a half minutes."

Tracey moved over to Charlotte's side for a better view as the plane started moving slowly along the south shore, which was lined by a dense growth of scrub spruce.

"Doesn't look like very good fishing," said Tracey as he looked out at the clear green water, which was as devoid of vegetation as Chimney Pond had been.

"The fishing's nonexistent," said the pilot. "Fish don't live above a certain altitude. And this pond has the highest altitude in the state. I forget who told me that, but it appears to be true."

At the eastern end, which was bordered by scree from a slide that had come down off the Northwest Plateau, the pilot turned the plane around and started heading down the opposite shore.

"I'll tell you something else about this pond," the pilot went on. "It can't be seen from any trail in the park. It's a real secret little place, the way it's tucked into the back side of the plateau."

Which also meant that the light from a campfire wouldn't be visible, thought Charlotte. Or, for that matter, the smoke from a campfire.

They were about three-quarters of the way down the north shore when Charlotte glimpsed the outline of a building through the trees. "Wait a minute," she said, but the plane had already passed by.

"Did you see something?" asked the pilot.

"I don't know," she replied. "I think so. Can we go back?"

"I don't see why not." He maneuvered the plane in a U-turn, went back to a spot at about the halfway point, and then continued down the north shore of the pond again, this time more slowly.

"There it is," she said, pointing. "It's a cabin. Do you see it?"

"I see it," said Tracey. "I also see a path through the underbrush from the shore." He addressed the pilot: "Do you think you can put in here? There's a good-sized log that you might be able to pull up to."

"Don't see why not," said the pilot, turning the plane toward shore. At the shore, he sidled it up to the log and then dropped anchor. Charlotte and Tracey got out, stepping first onto the pontoon, and then onto the log.

The cabin was small, constructed of peeled spruce chinked with clay and moss. In size it resembled Thoreau's house at Walden Pond, which was to say about ten by fifteen, though Thoreau's house had been sided not with logs but with boards that he'd scrounged from an Irishman's shanty. The cabin appeared to be quite old: the roof was caved in on one side, and the plank door hung from one hinge. The roof and walls were green with moss and lichens, giving the structure a kind of protective coloration. It was a wonder that Charlotte had seen it at all. The clearing in front bore the remains of a campfire: a heap of charred wood surrounded by a circle of blackened rocks. An old iron pot hung from a stick that was supported by two forked branches stuck into the ground on either side. Charlotte peered into the pot. The rusty water at the bottom was coated with a scum of tree pollen and brown needles. To one side of the campfire was a pile of old cans and bottles. A rusted barrel hoop hung from a tree limb. Tracey picked up an old bottle that was caked with dirt. "My wife collects these," he explained, sticking it into the pocket of his windbreaker. "They look pretty good once they've been cleaned up."

Though it didn't appear as if anyone was home (if they had been, they would have hightailed it when they heard the plane anyway) Tracey nevertheless approached the door with caution, pushing it open with his hand while standing to one side. The rusty hinge screeched in the silence. "Hello," he called. When there was no answer, he stepped in over the weeds growing on the rotting sill. Charlotte was right behind him.

The interior was dark—there was only one small window, on the west side—and it smelled damp and musty. Once Charlotte's eyes had adjusted, she could see that there was a crude bunk on one side, which was covered by a pile of dirty rags and an old army blanket, and a workbench under the window on the other. Under the workbench were some snowshoes, and an old toboggan. A line had been strung across the room, hanging from which were the dried bodies of a dozen or so muskrats with grinning skulls, dried-up eyeballs, and ratlike tails. Twin pyramids of empty whiskey bottles, some of them appearing quite old, had been stacked against the end wall on either side of a small, rusted-out, pot-bellied wood stove.

"Mack Scott should come out here," said Tracey, nodding at the whiskey bottles. "I'll bet there's a day's wages for him right there." Turning to the workbench, he started pawing through the collection of junk. Every Mainer had a streak of the scavenger in him, and Tracey was no exception.

"I don't see any sign of a Pamola costume," Charlotte said. No sooner had she spoken, however, than she did see it, hanging behind a curtain in a closet area at the back corner. "I take it back," she added.

Going over to the closet, she pulled the curtain aside. The mask sat on the top shelf, and the cape hung on a hook. The collar and cuffs were also there, on the floor. Picking them up, she marveled at the exquisite workmanship of the beautiful old embroidery.

"I guess we found Pamola all right," said Tracey, who had turned back to the heap of rusted tools on the workbench. "I'll bet this cabin is fifty or sixty years old, and nobody's ever thrown anything away."

"Or cleaned," added Charlotte. It was filthy.

But Tracey hadn't heard her. He was standing at the workbench, staring at something in the pile of old junk. Charlotte went over and scanned the pile: there were dirty rags, oil cans, coils of wire, assorted tools.

Then she saw it, lying next to a rusted leg trap. It was a pistol crossbow that had been rigged for fishing. Not a high-tech pistol crossbow like the one Clough had used in his demonstration, but a crude, handmade version.

"Very clever," Tracey said. He picked it up to study its construction, being careful not to get his fingerprints on it.

The body was made of wood painted in a green and brown camouflage design; it almost looked like a toy. It had been fitted with a trigger and trigger latch, a crossbow assembly, and the sights. The fishing rig wasn't a drum reel, but a coiled length of line that hung from a bracket.

"Look at this," said Tracey, pointing to a small beaded bag that hung from the trigger guard. He opened it up. "There's some sort of claw inside."

Charlotte was still looking at the stuff on the workbench. "Here are the bolts," she said.

Instead of aluminum alloy, the bolts were made of simple wood doweling. Some had been fitted with cartridge tips, others were awaiting theirs; half a dozen hollowed-out cartridges lay on the workbench nearby.

"I think we've found our man," said Tracey.

When they got back to the Katahdin Air Service office, Tracey called Pyle to ask him to check the fingerprints on the rattle and the headdress against those of a Lorne Coley of Indian Island. Pyle was waiting for them when they returned to Orono to tell them that the fingerprints had checked out. He hadn't even needed to consult the FBI's fingerprint identification system. Coley's prints were on file at the Penobscot County Jail, where he'd done time on several occasions for being drunk and disorderly, resisting arrest, and reckless driving. "Like eating pie," Pyle had said of the task of matching up the prints. Pyle also confirmed that Coley had a Federal record, having been arrested several times in connection with American Indian Movement demonstrations—including once with Marlon Brando, a supporter of

Indian causes, in a demonstration at Wounded Knee. He'd also been among the Red Power militants who had occupied Alcatraz Island in 1969.

After listening to Pyle's report, Tracey called Bill St. Louis to tell him that they wanted to talk with Coley, and to ask for his help in locating him. As a state police officer, Tracey had to be sensitive about treading on the turf of other police departments. Fifteen minutes later he and Charlotte were crossing the bridge onto Indian Island. Coming off the bridge, they passed a quaint old church—the oldest Catholic church in North America, Tracey told her—and continued along a winding country lane lined with lilacs in full bloom—the French influence again, Charlotte assumed—and the small clapboard-sided houses that were typical of the island. After a short distance, they made a right-hand turn past a moccasin shop. This brought them out at what appeared to be the downtown section of the island: a string of modern buildings that included the Indian Island School and the Penobscot Nation Community Center. The police station stood across the street from the largest of these buildings, the Sockalexis Memorial Arena, whose parking lot was filled with cars and a row of perhaps twenty buses.

"High stakes Bingo," Tracey explained, nodding at the arena. "They get fifteen hundred to two thousand players." He went on to explain that the arena was named after the tribe's two most famous members: Andrew Sockalexis, who was a marathon runner in the 1912 Olympic games at Stockholm, and his cousin Louis, a star of the Cleveland Spiders baseball team, which later changed its name to the Indians in his honor. Originally built for ice hockey, the arena was now used for the much more lucrative sport of high stakes Bingo, the reservation being exempt from state laws that prohibited high stakes gambling.

St. Louis was waiting for them in the lobby of the tribal police station.

When they asked directions to Coley's house, which was in a suburb of the main village called Oak Hill, St. Louis replied that he probably wouldn't be home. "If I know Lorne," he said, "we'll find him across the street. C'mon, I'll take you over there."

A few minutes later they entered the huge, smoke-filled arena, which was packed with hundreds of tables of Bingo players, most of them women and all of them eagerly watching the television monitors to see what number the Bingo machine would spit out next. Charlotte didn't know what she had been expecting, but it wasn't this little slice of Las Vegas on the shores of the Penobscot. A sign advertised The Drifters, who had apparently performed earlier in the day, and the sound system blared a Drifters recording of "Up On The Roof."

Charlotte wondered how they would ever find Coley in this crowd, but St. Louis knew exactly where he would be: sitting with a bunch of old Penobscot women at one of the tables at the back that were reserved for walk-ins. He was a middle-aged man who looked like central casting's idea of an Indian, of the bad-guy variety. He had dark, pockmarked skin; shoulder-length black hair combed back over a thinning spot; a thin, straggly mustache and a wispy Vandyke beard; and a nose that looked as if it had been in one too many fights at the Shuffle Inn. He wore a T-shirt with a picture of a medicine shield on it.

Charlotte didn't recognize Coley's face, since it had been concealed by the mask, but she did recognize his physique, with its thin legs and protruding belly, across which the light blue fabric of the T-shirt was tightly stretched. Though he scrutinized her closely, she couldn't tell if he recognized her or not. She didn't think so.

Coley sat in front of his Bingo card, which was ringed by a collection of trinkets: a red rabbit's foot, a miniature troll figure with shocking pink hair, and the beaded medicine bag.

Several of the other people at the table had similar collections, from which Charlotte concluded that they must be good luck charms.

St. Louis looked down at Coley's Bingo card, on which only a few of the twenty-five numbers were colored in. "Winning anything?" asked the Indian detective as the caller called out number O-63.

Coley looked up at the lighted board to confirm the number, and then down at his card. Then he picked up his dauber and colored in the number. Finally he looked up at St. Louis. "Naw," he said. "I never win."

What was the point of being a male shamanist pig, Charlotte wondered, if you couldn't even use your supernatural skills to help turn up the right ball in the Bingo machine? Even with the help of the trinkets.

Coley set down his dauber, and then looked up at them and smiled. It was a warm but reluctant, almost shy, smile. He had a narrow mouth and small teeth, which were very white.

Charlotte could see why the old ladies might like him.

Coley pulled a cigarette out of a packet labeled "Native Blend" and lit it with a cigarette lighter. "What can I do for you?" he asked as he leaned back and drew on his cigarette, the corners of his eyes squinting in distrust.

"This here is Lieutenant Howard Tracey from the state police," St. Louis said. "He'd like you to come across the street to the station for a little chat. You've played your package out," he added, "so let's go."

Charlotte could see from the tense set of Tracey's shoulders that he was nervous. There was always the chance that Coley might bolt.

But he needn't have worried. Coley crumpled up his Bingo card and tossed it onto the table. "Same old story," he said to his tablemates. "They ain't got nobody else to pick on, so they pick on an Indian."

The women nodded in agreement, and cast dirty looks at Tracey.

Then Coley got up and followed St. Louis out as the caller called out another number, and several shouts of "Bingo!" resounded throughout the hall.

· 12 ·

COLEY ADMITTED TO being Pamola. As they suspected, he had parked on one of the old logging roads on the northwest boundary of the park, and bushwhacked in to the Perimeter Road. To reach the Klondike, he had followed the route that his great uncle had used, down a slide on the eastern slope of Mount Coe. To get from there to Chimney Pond he had taken the route that Keith had described, and to get to the retreat center he had taken the trail from Daicey Pond. His motive had been the revenge of Pamola. Or so he said.

"Pamola don't like people trespassing on his territory," he stated, and proceeded to tell an involved story about a Penobscot who had once been forced by bad weather to spend a night on the summit of Katahdin, and had been terrorized all night long by the malevolent spirit. From the disparaging things he had to say about the retreat center, however, it was clear that his real motive was jealousy. He was one of Black Elk's Blue Men, just as Keith had said. He was probably a coward as well, Charlotte guessed, which was why he had appeared only to women. She didn't doubt that he believed what he said about Pamola. What she did doubt was his mental capacity. There were holes in his logic, gaps in his narrative. She couldn't tell if that was just the way he was, or if his brain had been pickled by alcohol.

"What about you?" Tracey asked. "Aren't you afraid of trespassing on Pamola's territory? I thought the Penobscots were afraid to go above the tree line for fear of Pamola's wrath."

"That there's just superstition," Coley replied, which Charlotte thought an odd remark for an Indian shaman to make.

Then Tracey got to the sixty-four-dollar question: "What about Mrs. Richards? Did Pamola take revenge on Mrs. Richards, too?"

"Who's she?" he asked.

"The woman who was murdered on the Knife Edge."

"Oh. I heard about that on the radio." He looked up at them. "You think Pamola killed her?" he asked, as if he were actually considering whether or not that was possible.

"No. We think you killed her," said Tracey.

Coley stared down at the toes of his beat-up running shoes for a minute, and then looked back up at his questioner. Finally he repeated Tracey's accusation. "You think I kilt her," he said, nodding his head.

Tracey stared him down.

"What makes you think that?" Coley asked. He spat out his consonants like a Frenchman, and Charlotte wondered if it was the historical contact with the French that had resulted in his peculiar accent or if it was the remnants of the lost Penobscot language.

"The fact that we found a fishing crossbow of the type she was killed with at your camp at Klondike Pond," Tracey replied.

Coley stared up at them, and drew on his cigarette. "When was she kilt?" he asked thoughtfully, as if he himself were the detective.

"On Saturday, June ninth, around two. Where were you then?"

"Playing high stakes Bingo. I play every time. I can name a dozen people who saw me. Ask any of 'em. In fact, I think I may still have my ticket stub at home." He began to get up. "Can I go now?"

"What time does Bingo start?" Tracey asked.

"The regular games start at noon," replied the Indian detective. "But he could have arrived at any time." He turned to look down at Coley, who was the only one who was seated. "What time did you get here?" he asked.

"About two," he replied. "I missed the first four games. It took me four hours to get out to the Perimeter Road, another hour to get to my car, and two hours to get back here. I left the camp at six-thirty, and still didn't get back to the island till nearly two."

"No way he could have done it," St. Louis said. "Unless he was flying."

"My powers don't extend to flying," said Coley, chuckling good-naturedly now that he knew he was off the hook.

"If you were here, that means that somebody else used your crossbow to kill Mrs. Richards, or one just like it," Tracey said.

"I don't have no crossbow," he said.

"You don't?" said Tracey.

Coley shook his head.

"It had an Indian charm on it."

"That may be, but it still ain't mine," said Coley.

"Then somebody must have put it there. Does anybody else use your camp?"

He shook his head again.

They had caught a fox, but not the right one. But at least they had the Pamola issue out of the way, Charlotte thought, reminded again of Occam's Razor. Now they could get back to the murder.

"Now can I be excused?" asked Coley sarcastically.

St. Louis' comment that Coley couldn't have made it back to Indian Island in time for Bingo "unless he was flying" had put an idea into Charlotte's head. She and Tracey had landed a float plane on Klondike Pond. Why couldn't someone else have done the same thing? She wasn't thinking of Coley— he wouldn't have had access to a float plane, that she knew of—but of Keith Samusit. It was his float plane that had been anchored at the retreat center. He presumably used it to survey tribal lands for timber. She remembered the float planes that had been lined up in the river at the regional headquarters of the state forest service, which were probably used for the same purpose. Knowing that Coley was using the Klondike Pond camp as the staging area for his nocturnal ramblings, Keith might have killed Iris and planted the murder weapon at the camp with the intention of framing Coley. Their pilot had told them that he personally flew eight or ten sightseeing flights a day over the mountain. And the Katahdin Air Service was just one of several flying services in the area. Who would have noticed one more plane? Especially when the pond couldn't even be seen from the park trails. Then there was the fact that it was Keith who had directed them to the camp, perhaps with the aim of casting suspicion on Coley. If Coley were to be believed, he was already a sort of general scapegoat. What was a murder on top of everything else? Moreover, there would be the attraction for Keith of killing two birds with one stone: not only would he be pinning Iris' murder on someone else, he would also be getting rid of a rival for his authority as ceremonial leader.

On the ride back to the barracks, Charlotte discussed her theory with Tracey. The problem was: How to prove it? They could check with the float plane services in the area to see if any pilots had noticed a plane at Klondike Pond. They could—and would—test the crossbow for fingerprints. (They would also pass the bolts along to Clough, so that he could match the tips up with the entrance wound in Iris' neck.) But Keith was not stupid: if it was his intention to frame Coley, he would have been careful not to leave any fingerprints.

It was past seven by the time they got back to Orono, but Pyle was waiting for them with more news. It was his first murder investigation, and he was all eagerness. He would have worked around the clock had Tracey asked him to. Charlotte could tell from the grin on his young face that he had turned up something significant. It was about time, too. It seemed to Charlotte that they'd wandered off track in their pursuit of Pamola, Occam's Razor or no. They were like hikers who are tramping happily along, only to be brought up short when they suddenly notice that the edge of the path is no longer marked by cairns, the trees are devoid of blazes. The Pamola issue had been a false trail, and they now had to do what any hiker would do under similar circumstances: go back to the last trail marker and set off again from there, this time with a keener eye for their direction. Not that the trail in an investigation was always clearly marked. Especially once you were underway, when it tended to branch off into a maze of narrow, interlocking paths, like a network of capillaries, which, if you were lucky, would eventually all merge, and, if you had the good sense to follow along, bring you out at the heart of the matter. But they weren't even underway yet. They were still at the beginning, where their route should have been straight, wide, and clearly marked.

Charlotte was hoping that Pyle would provide them with the next trail marker now. He had certainly set the stage. Sitting on Tracey's desk was a plateful of crackers and cheese, and three mugs of steaming hot coffee.

"Did I ever tell you what a valuable employee you are?" said Tracey as he picked up his coffee mug.

"Not nearly often enough, Chief," said Pyle.

Charlotte picked up her mug gratefully. It had been a long day, and she welcomed the lift the caffeine would bring.

"Okay, Pyle," said Tracey, once they were settled in. "What have you got?"

"Two things. Both concerning the weapon."

"Shoot."

"Do you remember asking me to check with sporting goods stores to see if any clerks had noticed anyone who looked suspicious buying a pistol crossbow, or anyone who didn't look like the typical crossbow customer?"

Tracey nodded.

"I got a bite from a store in Augusta. They remembered one guy very clearly. The clerk said he had a crew cut, a plaid tie, thick eyeglasses. He remembered that the guy had paid with a credit card, and even found the credit card receipt for me. Guess who he was?"

Tracey grinned. "He wouldn't have anything to do with the state medical examiner's office, would he?"

"Henry Clough himself," said Pyle. "I have to admit that he doesn't look like your usual crossbow customer. Otherwise, we struck out there."

So much for trail markers, thought Charlotte.

"I thought you said you had something," Tracey teased.

"I do. It's about Jeanne Ouellette. She attended Orono on a scholarship," he said. "Graduated in 1954. Guess what kind of scholarship it was?"

"You're making me play a lot of guessing games," Tracey said impatiently.

"An *archery* scholarship."

"You're joking!"

Pyle smiled and held up his hand. "I swear it's the God's honest truth. She was the women's state archery champion for seven years running. Three years in high school and four in college."

"Well, I'll be doggoned," said Tracey.

"It makes sense," said Pyle. "Old Town is known for its archery program. Old Town archers always win the state meets. Its archery program and its canoes. It's the city's Indian heritage, I guess."

"I knew about the canoes, of course," said Tracey. "But not about the archery. Is it still true, I wonder?"

"I expect so. It was when I went to Old Town High. I think my archery coach is still there. His name was Pete Roy. Take a look at these," he added, passing Tracey some papers. "They sent them over from the *Penobscot Times*."

Charlotte stood up to look. They were copies of old newspaper articles about the young Jeanne's archery achievements. One showed her in a Robin Hood-style hat shooting out the flame of a candle; another showed her shattering an aspirin tablet at twenty-five paces.

"Look at this one, Chief," said Pyle. "She's shooting the arrow through a phonograph record that's been tossed into the air."

"And it isn't a forty-five, either," said Tracey, referring to the big spindle holes in the old records.

The fact that Jeanne had been an archery champion sounded promising, but Charlotte suspected it was one of those chimerical leads that would evaporate under scrutiny. For one thing, her archery achievements had taken place over thirty years ago, and Charlotte doubted she had kept up her skills. For another, there was the matter of the camp. How would she have known about it? And, even if she had, getting there and back would have been a grueling trek for a woman of her age. From what Keith had said, it would be hard enough for a skilled woodsman who was a former long-distance runner.

"Do you think she did it, Chief?" Pyle asked earnestly. "It doesn't look good for her, does it?"

"Nope, it doesn't," Tracey agreed, but not enthusiastically. He was obviously entertaining doubts of a similar nature to Charlotte's.

"It's gonna hurt her dad real bad if she turns out to be the murderer."

"Let's not go jumping to conclusions," said Tracey.

"You know her father?" asked Charlotte, who was always fascinated by the way people in small towns all seemed to be connected.

"Yep," Pyle said. "He lives down to the Bickmore Manor, the senior citizens apartment house on South Main. He's buddies with my grandfather. They play gin rummy together. I often see Miss Ouellette there when I visit him."

Tracey cleared his throat. "Getting back to the subject . . ."

Pyle returned his attention to his boss.

"I want you to contact this guy Roy at the high school, and find out if he knows anything about crossbows. Or if he knows of anyone who *does* know something about crossbows. We want to find out where this weapon might have come from."

Pyle nodded.

"Have you got the addresses for the hikers who were signed out to the various peaks on Katahdin yet?"

"I'm still working on it. It takes a while to get addresses for that many people from the state motor vehicle agencies. I've got the names from the registers at all three campgrounds. There were eleven signed out for Hamlin Peak, twenty-two for Pamola, and twenty-four for Baxter."

"Fifty-seven in all," said Tracey. "That's a manageable number. I want you to interview every one of them. Most of them will be from Maine anyway. How many were signed out for the Knife Edge?"

"I forget exactly. Twenty-something."

Tracey nodded. "You're going to ask them if they saw Mrs. Richards. And then you're going to ask them if they saw Miss Ouellette. If they think they might have seen either one of them, get them to look at a photo."

"Right," said Pyle, rising to leave.

"And don't forget to check the times."

Pyle nodded.

In the excitement of the stakeout at Chimney Pond and the subsequent discovery of the grave at the retreat center, the fact that Charlotte would be leaving for California in less than forty-eight hours had temporarily escaped her attention. Now that she was back in Bridge Harbor, however, she found herself overwhelmed by all the things she had to accomplish before she left. At the top of her list was a call to Ron Polito to set up an appointment. Another item that had temporarily slipped her mind was his odd statement that he had a murder suspect in mind for her. Who on earth could it be? She would have dismissed such an unlikely statement had it come from anyone else, but she knew better than to take anything that Ron said lightly.

By now, it was nearly six in California, but Charlotte

suspected that Ron's dedicated secretary would still be at her desk, as indeed she was. When Charlotte asked for an appointment, the secretary told her that Ron had ordered her not to disturb him, but that she knew he would make an exception to see Charlotte. He was staying at a bungalow at the Chateau Marmont Hotel.

The bungalows on the grounds of the Chateau Marmont were where Hollywood went when it wanted to hole up and get some work done, or get out of the public eye. They were the Camp David of Hollywood. "He's going to be there through the end of the week," his secretary said. "I'm not supposed to tell anyone where he is, except for you and a couple of others."

The legendary hideaway on Sunset Boulevard was one place in Hollywood where Charlotte had always felt right at home. It had been an instant success when it was built in 1929, and it was where Charlotte had set up housekeeping when she came to Hollywood ten years later. Its suites, which were equipped with kitchens, were large, homey, and self-sufficient. She had also spent quite a bit of time there in the fifties. One of the Marmont's features was an elevator in the basement garage, which meant that the guests didn't have to pass the front desk to get to their rooms—a great advantage in a town in which privacy was hard to come by. "If you must get into trouble, do it at the Marmont," was the famous advice of the chief of her studio to his stable of stars, and Charlotte had gotten into plenty there, most of it with a cowboy actor by the name of Linc Crawford. It was, in fact, where Linc had died, in 1957. In a sixth-floor suite, on April twenty-sixth, of a heart attack. Charlotte hadn't set foot in the place since. In fact, she had been going out of her way to avoid even driving by it for thirty-three years.

But maybe it was time to confront those old memories, and in doing so, lay them to rest. For someone who was supposed to be working on the chapter of her life in which the Marmont had played such a big role, there couldn't be a better—or a worse—place to visit.

*   *   *

Charlotte's taxi pulled up to the ersatz Loire Valley chateau at the end of Sunset Strip at three on Tuesday afternoon. Perhaps the Marmont had always appealed to her because of its incongruity: the cream-colored stucco monstrosity seemed to rise out of the tattoo parlors and rock and roll clubs of the Strip with the same gloomy magnificence as the Potala Palace rising out of the slums of Lhasa. But it actually felt more like a citadel than a palace. And indeed, that's what it was: an oasis of Old World civility in a desert of southern California sleaze. Part of its charm, however, had always been that it hadn't totally escaped the influence of its surroundings. Despite its grandiosity, its ambience had always been a little down-at-the heel. Even more so in recent years, when even people who preferred their hotels on the seedy side complained about the faulty plumbing, fraying upholstery, and peeling paint. In fact, the Marmont had been about to cross the subtle line between funky and finished when it was pulled back from the brink by a New York hotelier who promised to fix it up without tampering with its faded Sunset Boulevard glamor. Charlotte hoped so. Despite the fact that she hadn't set foot in it in years, she felt the kind of fondness for the Marmont that one feels for an old friend with whom one has shared the good times, and the bad. Their careers had paralleled one another's: the onset of the venerable old hotel's bad times had corresponded with that of Charlotte's own; likewise, the hotel's career and her own were now in the ascendant. Like the Marmont, Charlotte herself had come to be viewed as something of an architectural monument to the Golden Age of Hollywood.

Over the years, a few of the bungalows on the grounds of the hotel had been sold off to private owners, and Ron Polito had owned one of these for as long as Charlotte could remember. Though he sometimes used it for work, as he was apparently now doing, it had more often been employed as a safe house for clients who found it advantageous to make themselves temporarily scarce. Charlotte herself had stayed in Ron's bungalow in the aftermath of her highly publicized divorce from her third husband in the forties. Thus she had no trouble finding it again. Like the Marmont's other bungalows, it was tucked into the hillside overlooking the smog-shrouded city, with its own private garden and its own private entrance and car port.

As she approached the front door, she paused simply to smell. If the aroma could have been bottled, it would have had a base of eucalyptus, and high notes of jasmine, honeysuckle, and old roses. The smell was overpowering in its lushness and seductiveness, and a far cry from the fresh, clean, almost clinical smell of the Maine woods. A bougainvillea vine thick with carmine blooms hung romantically over the edge of the roof above the door. No wonder so many people—herself among them—had been tempted to misbehave at the Marmont!

It was Ron himself who answered the door, and she tried to conceal her shock at the sight of him. The years had been good to her—she still looked much as she had forty years ago (thanks to a good complexion)—and, although she knew it was illogical, she expected the same to be true of others, especially in Hollywood, where cultivation of a youthful appearance was a pursuit on which so much time and money were expended. Thus, she was always surprised to meet someone who hadn't aged gracefully.

It wasn't so much that he looked that different. He still had the face of a basset hound, with long, fleshy jowls and sad brown eyes, from which hung deep folds of skin. But he had lost his imposing physical presence. A tall man with broad shoulders, he had once shared with many of the stars he represented the ability to take up even more space in the eye of the beholder than he occupied in physical fact. But he was now a star that had imploded upon itself—passive and shrunken, its brilliance dimmed.

Clearly delighted at her visit, he greeted her warmly and ushered her into the living room, which hadn't changed in forty years. The mismatched lamps and the rattan furniture, with its gray and magenta floral-patterned upholstery, unleashed a flood of memories, chief among them her humiliation at having been stupid enough to marry a man like her third husband.

"The last time I was here was just after I announced that I was divorcing Gary," she said as she took off her jacket.

"I remember," he said. "Hasn't changed much, has it?"

She looked around at the room, which was scattered with legal papers, but otherwise looked exactly the same. "No," she agreed.

"I was going to redecorate, but when I mentioned it to one of my clients, he begged me not to," he said. "Before I knew it, I was besieged with phone calls from clients urging me not to touch a thing." He shrugged. "So I didn't. I guess this place holds a lot of memories for a lot of people."

"If walls could talk . . ."

He smiled. "Have a seat," he said, gesturing to one of the rattan chairs in front of a fireplace in which a wood fire was burning away despite outdoor temperatures in the sixties. "Can I get you a drink? You drink Manhattans—straight up, if I remember right."

"Of course you remember right. Some things never change. Your memory and Chateau Marmont being two of them."

He smiled again. "Nice to see you, Charlotte. Did I say that already?"

Charlotte smiled back. "Make it a double," she said. Her nerves were frazzled from the trip. Her plans to recover from the frenetic pace of the preceding days with an in-flight snooze had been foiled by the combination of a garrulous agent for a seatmate and an unexpected layover in Chicago.

Moments later, they were comfortably ensconced in the rattan armchairs in front of the fireplace, a bowl of salted peanuts nestled among the legal papers on the coffee table between them.

Charlotte took a sip of her drink, and felt a blessed peace settle over her. Ron's presence had always had this effect on her. He was an unwavering ally—sometimes a ruthless ally, as well—in a town where unwavering allies were often hard to come by.

To her astonishment, she felt the sting of hot tears welling up in her eyes, and she wiped them away. "Sorry," she said. "It's being here, I guess. I haven't been here in years. It's a relic of the old days in the midst of a city that I hardly recognize any more. I won't say *good* old days."

"Some of them were good, Charlotte," he protested. "A damned sight more than just some, for that matter."

"That's true," she said, but she didn't want to think about the good ones, for fear that she would start bawling. She had never been one to dwell in the past, and now she blinked away her tears.

"You're looking very well, Charlotte," he said.

"Thank you." She wanted to be polite and return his compliment, but there was no point in lying to someone who knew her well enough to see right through her, acting abilities or no.

For a few seconds there was an awkward silence. Then Ron waved his drink in a gesture of understanding. "I've lost a hundred and six pounds since last fall. Probably more by now. I've stopped getting on the scales." He nodded at the fire. "I get cold easily. I hope you're not too warm."

The room was stifling, but she shook her head. "What's wrong?"

"Prostate cancer. They say I've got a fifty-fifty chance. But I'm pretty sure I'm on my way out." He smiled ruefully. "Another old dinosaur about to turn up its heels." He paused to light a cigarette, which he held in an ivory cigarette holder.

"Oh, Ron," she said. "I'm sorry." But she could see that it was true. His leathery skin, cadaverous-looking even in health, had gone black under the eyes. "If there's anything I can do . . ."

"No," he said. "I'm pretending that it's not happening. As you can see," he added, waving at the array of papers

on the coffee table, the gold cuff links in his French cuffs
flashing. It was typical of Ron that even while relaxing, he
was a model of sartorial elegance.

"Speaking of business . . ." Charlotte began.

Ron lifted a manicured finger. Then he went over to the
phone, and dialed his office. Charlotte heard him ask his
secretary to have a courier bring the Iris O'Connor file over
to the bungalow immediately.

She raised an inquiring eyebrow as he hung up the phone.

"I have something you might be interested in seeing. The
courier will be here in twenty minutes. Why don't you take
a walk around the grounds? I have to take a little nap. I'm
not very strong these days."

He went over to a rattan chaise in the corner, and lay down
on his back, his big hands folded over his chest. Within
minutes, his now-gaunt features had gone slack in sleep.

While he slept, Charlotte finished her drink, and then
quietly slipped out, closing the door behind her.

Not willing to even venture a guess at what kind of
a rabbit Ron was going to pull out of his hat, Charlotte
spent the time wandering around the grounds, reliving her
memories: ordering up from Greenblatt's during her first
weeks in Hollywood (the suites were all equipped with
kitchens, but she couldn't cook any more then than she
could now); visiting here from the East when she was married to her second husband; honeymooning here after her
marriage to her third husband; and then, only six months
later, staying at the bungalow after the announcement that
she was seeking a divorce. And later, the secret trysts with
Linc, in the romance that had captivated a nation. Nobody
recognized her now. Nor did she recognize anyone else,
though she knew some of them must be famous: men in
ponytails and jeans and young women dressed as if they
were soliciting on Eleventh Avenue. The hotel may have
been back in, but it was on cruder, harsher terms than in
the glamorous, leisured days of the past. Even the light in

the lobby seemed more glaring, and modern. The golden, dusty ambience of old Hollywood was still to be found, but it wasn't in the computerized records at the front desk or the hip soiree on the lawn, but in the hush of the thick-walled halls, the feather-duster palm trees swaying languidly in the breeze, and the homey comfort of the bungalows.

As she came around the side of Ron's bungalow a few minutes later, she saw a young man coming up the walk with a file folder in hand, and she hastened her step. She got to the door just as he was leaving.

"Perfect timing," Ron said, closing the door behind the courier.

"Did you get your catnap?" asked Charlotte.

"Mmmm." He nodded. "Feel as good as new," he said cheerfully, adding, "For about forty-five minutes, that is."

She looked at him with sympathy, then nodded at the folder. "So what have we got?"

"Iris may have forsaken her old life, but she wasn't incognizant of her place in history," he said. "Ever since she left Hollywood, she's had me keep a clipping file. I hired a clipping service for her."

"Did she ever come out to look at it?"

"Once a year. She'd stay here, and we'd go over her affairs. She usually came out in February or March so we could take care of tax business at the same time." He went over to the chair, and took a seat. Then he placed the file on the coffee table and opened it up.

Charlotte stepped over a pile of papers on the floor, sat down in the other chair, and put on her reading glasses, half glasses with tortoise-shell frames that gave her a professorial air.

"These are the clippings." He started leafing through the articles. "As you can see, it's just the usual stuff. Until about two years ago, when we started getting these." He lifted an article out of the file. "This one's from *Variety*." But there were dozens of them.

It was a classified advertisement, with the bold-face heading CASH REWARD. The rest of the ad read "Information wanted on the whereabouts of Iris O'Connor, Hollywood screenwriter from 1939 to 1952." This was followed by a phone number with a Hollywood exchange.

"This was the first. As you can see, it's dated February, 1988. They ran in the entertainment press for about four months, and then stopped."

"Did you ever call the number?" she asked.

"Yes. The party wouldn't give me his name. The reward was substantial: five thousand dollars."

"Someone wanted to find her badly."

He nodded. "I offered to hire a private detective to track down the person who had placed the ads, but Iris would have nothing to do with it. I think she knew, or suspected, who was trying to find her."

"Do *you* know who it was?" she asked, knowing that even if he did, he wouldn't have told her.

He shook his head. "But I know who might know."

"Who?" asked Charlotte.

"Charlie Perkins," he replied.

"Charlie Perkins!" she exclaimed, repeating the name out of the past. At one time, it had been one of the most hated—and feared—names in Hollywood. A former FBI agent, Perkins had been HUAC's chief investigator in Hollywood; some would have said its chief inquisitor.

He nodded.

Why would Charlie Perkins know who was after Iris? she asked herself. She stared at Ron's long, bassett hound face, and he stared back as if to say, "Figure it out for yourself."

"Iris testified in executive session," she said.

Ron nodded. "Didn't it ever occur to you to wonder why she and the others with whom she testified were permitted to testify in closed session while everybody else had to go to Washington and take the witness stand?"

"As I recall, there was some explanation; that it was a rehearsal for a public session, or something. But what you seem to be suggesting is that she made a deal: closed session in exchange for naming names."

"I'm not suggesting anything," he said.

Iris had left Hollywood shortly after testifying, and it was widely assumed that she had been blacklisted, but if what Ron was hinting at was true, maybe she had left because she couldn't live with herself anymore.

"Are you telling me that Iris was a friendly witness?" Charlotte asked, talking as much to herself as to him. "You are! And you're also telling me that someone had been trying to find her. Probably someone whose life was ruined as a result of her HUAC testimony."

Ron sat quietly smoking his cigarette.

God knows, enough lives were ruined, Charlotte thought. She also thought of what Tracey had said about Pamola being a ghost out of Iris' past who had come back to haunt her. Maybe his comment had been more prescient than either of them had realized at the time.

"You're getting warm," said Ron as he took a handful of peanuts. "You haven't come by your reputation as a detective undeservedly."

"Some detective. The thought never even occurred to me that Iris might have left town for another reason. But how do you know that the person who's looking for her is looking for her because of her HUAC testimony? Why not a long lost cousin or someone she owes money to? And why all these years later?"

"I don't know," he replied. "I'm just guessing. The first ad appeared in February of 1988, just after an article appeared in the L.A. *Times* containing previously unreleased testimony from the executive session in which Iris testified. The reporter had gotten the transcripts through the Freedom of Information Act."

"In other words, the person who placed the ads might have just found out that Iris was a stoolie."

He nodded. "A lot of people were out turning over rocks after that article appeared: scholars, victims, relatives of victims. Iris wasn't the only one who was exposed as a friendly witness."

"You're the one who should be the detective, not me," she said. "I didn't know about any of this. I must have been in New York when the article was published. Did you represent her at the executive session?"

Ron nodded.

"Then you know who this person might be."

He nodded again. "But you're not going to get any more out of me. I'll get you Perkins' address," he said.

"I'm surprised he's still alive," Charlotte said. Somehow she always expected villains like Perkins to have succumbed to their own venom.

"Alive and well, like a lot of other scoundrels," said Ron.

Going over to his desk, he placed a call to his secretary, and returned a moment later with a slip of paper bearing an Orange County address. "Let me know how it goes," he said.

Charlotte rose to leave. "Ron, about the cancer . . ." she said. "I hope . . ."

He waved a dismissive hand. "It's just as well. I don't have any fight left in me anymore."

"I find that hard to believe."

"I don't care," he explained. "Like this case I'm working on now. A rock musician who smeared shit all over the walls of a hotel room. In the old days, when people got into trouble, they at least did it with style."

"Polito in a pinch," she said, repeating a slogan from the old days. Then she reached out—it wasn't up anymore, she noted sadly—to give him a hug.

"Don't ever say Ron Polito never did anything for you," he said as he held out her jacket for her.

"You know I would never say that."

As he closed the door behind her, she thought of how many secrets he would be taking to the grave with him.

· 13 ·

AFTER LEAVING RON'S office, Charlotte bought a map and located the street where Perkins lived. She felt like a Nazi-hunter who's finally discovered that the villain he's been searching for is living in a suburb of Buenos Aires. She drove out there after getting a bite to eat at the hotel. Perkins lived with his wife in a tract house in a development; like a thousand others in his town, like a million others in California. Three bedrooms, two and a half baths, a small backyard with a high fence. Talk about the banality of evil, she thought as she rang the doorbell. She hadn't called in advance for fear that he wouldn't want to see her, but she needn't have worried. He welcomed her as warmly as he might have an old high-school acquaintance. As far as he was concerned, they were both products of the same era; the fact that they had played on rival teams didn't seem to matter. After proudly introducing her to his wife, he ushered her into a wood-paneled family room, where the television was tuned to a popular quiz show, and asked his wife to bring them some cake and coffee.

Though she had seen Perkins' photograph in the newspapers many times during the blacklist era, Charlotte had never actually met him before. He still looked much the same as he had then, with the addition of a couple of extra chins. He belonged to the type that could be labeled genial all-American: tall, beefy, and blond (now gray). He looked like everybody's favorite high-school football coach.

Actually, there were many people, even those who had played on the opposing team, who had not disliked Perkins, recognizing that although he had chosen a contemptible career, he had carried out his job with competence, and, to the degree that it was possible, fairness.

"I've come about Iris O'Connor," she said, once she was settled in on the couch with her cup of coffee.

"What about her?" he asked.

"I want to know how she testified. Everyone in Hollywood thought she left town because she was an unfriendly witness, but I have recently learned that she was in fact a friendly witness." She didn't let on that her reason was Ron Polito.

Perkins gave her an appraising stare from the depths of his plastic-covered recliner. "I don't suppose it makes any difference if I tell you," he said finally. "The records are all open to the public now anyway, if you wanted to take the time to seek them out."

"I'm in a hurry," she snapped.

Perkins leaned his head back against the recliner, and stared out at the spinning wheel on the game show. "As I recall, she testified in Los Angeles in the winter of 1952, in executive session."

Charlotte nodded.

"I actually remember it very clearly," he said. He looked over at Charlotte and smiled. "She testified third; she was wearing a green suit."

He was playing this for all he could, Charlotte thought.

"She named all the usual names—no surprises there."

Those who were subpoenaed had often tried to get off the hook by naming self-confessed Communists who had already been disgraced in the eyes of the Red-hating public, and had nothing more to lose.

"To our surprise, really, she didn't stop there," Perkins continued. "She went on to implicate others, people whose names had never come up before. I remember it so clearly because it was such a coup for us."

"Who were they?" asked Charlotte, who had never had much patience for this kind of game-playing.

He smiled again. "You know the answer already. That's why you're here. To confirm your suspicions." He nodded slightly at her, signaling an affirmative reply. "Well, your suspicions are correct."

What was he talking about? she wondered. She hadn't even told him about Iris' murder, much less about her theory that the murderer was someone who was out to avenge Iris' testimony.

He shifted his attention from the show back to Charlotte, baffled by her puzzled reaction. "Isn't that why you're here?"

"Isn't *what* why I'm here?"

"To confirm that she testified against you."

"She testified against me!" she repeated dumbly.

"Yes. You, among others. But your name was the real coup for us. Her associate, Charlotte Graham—who would have thought that you were a Communist?"

"But I wasn't a Communist!" she protested.

"Yes, but you associated with Communists, didn't you? Iris O'Connor foremost among them."

"Iris was my screenwriter for ten years. We did seventeen films together. Of *course* I associated with her." She paused for a moment to calm herself; she was practically yelling at him. "But even she wasn't a member of the Party. Not that I knew of, anyway."

"The Screen Writers' Guild was infested with Communists," he said.

The logic was mind-boggling. Iris was a Communist because the Screen Writers' Guild was infested with Communists. Charlotte was a Communist because she had known Iris. "Talk about guilt by association!" she said. It was almost as bad as the actor who had been at the same bullfight with Picasso.

Perkins merely shrugged.

And what about the effects of Iris' testimony on her own career? she wondered. In one overpowering wave, it all became clear to her. The reason she hadn't been able to get work wasn't because she had been too old to play young women and too young to play old women, but because she had been blacklisted.

"I was blacklisted?" she asked.

But even as she spoke, she knew it didn't make sense. People who were blacklisted knew it, and had the opportunity to salvage their careers by renouncing their Communist pasts. Ron Polito, for one, had made a career out of guiding blacklisted actors and screenwriters through the tricky waters of rehabilitation. But no one had ever told her that her name was on a list.

"A better term would be graylisted."

"Ah! Graylisted," she repeated. Graylisted explained it, she thought. Tarnished enough that no one would hire her, but not black enough to be rehabilitated. A gorge of bitterness rose in her throat. Iris must have known what she was doing. You didn't name names to HUAC—even just as an associate—without recognizing what the consequences would be.

For a moment, she felt faint. How could she not have realized what was going on? All that time, she had thought the reason she wasn't getting work lay with *her*. All those years she had felt guilty for not doing enough to help, when she had unwittingly been cheated out of ten years of her career.

"Who *else* did Iris list as her associate?" She spat out the last word.

"Let me think," said Perkins, leaning his head back against the recliner again, his hands folded calmly over his bulging belly.

"Or, better put," she said, "what other lives did she ruin?"

Perkins didn't seem to take offense at the venom in her voice. She supposed that forty years of such questions had inured him to their sting.

"She named a lot of names. Well over fifty . . ."

Charlotte gasped. Where was Iris' sense of morality, her self-respect? She hadn't just sung the same old song, she had sung a whole repertoire.

"Almost all of them were people whose lives had already been ruined, to couch my reply in your terms," he said amiably, "except for—" He raised a finger. "There *was* someone else."

"Who?" she prompted.

"Linc Crawford."

Charlotte leaned back as if the wind had been knocked out of her. She remembered that afternoon well—it had been at the Marmont, in fact, when Linc had been called away from the poolside for a phone call.

He had returned a few minutes later, his tanned, handsome face ashen. "Jesus!" he had said. "That was J. Edgar Hoover calling to tell me that my passport's been revoked. He said it wasn't in the best interests of the United States for me to travel abroad. I have to testify before HUAC."

Unlike Charlotte, Linc had actually attended a few Communist Party meetings in his youth. Partly idealism, partly curiosity, he said. Partly stupidity, he said in retrospect. But he had also served with distinction in the Army during the war, and was about as loyal an American as they came.

After Hoover's call, he had gone to Washington to testify. He had admitted attending a couple of Party meetings, but he denied that he was a Communist, and he refused to name anyone he had encountered at those meetings.

"War Hero Admits He's a Commie!" the headlines had screamed. "Crawford Bares Commie Past"; "Crawford Confesses All"; "Screen Idol is Ex-Red."

He had taken the honorable path. He wouldn't even hire someone like Ron to stand by his side, much less stoop to signing on with one of the "smear and clear" organizations—if you named names, they'd get you cleared. Or even worse, buy a clearance, in the same way that medieval sinners bought indulgences from corrupt clerics to save themselves from perdition.

He had paid dearly for his scruples. He didn't go to jail, but he didn't get any work either. He slipped into a

depression, started to drink. His wife sued for sole custody
of their two sons, and won. Even his life insurance was
canceled because his chances of living out a normal life
were too slim. "On a par with a gangster or a steeplejack,"
the insurance agent had told him.

Then, four years later, came *Red Rocks*. A talented, icono-
clastic young director named William Ireland had been willing to thumb his nose at the studios, and take a chance on
Linc. From the start, everyone involved knew that *Red Rocks*
was going to be a classic. It was also going to be Linc's
comeback vehicle.

But by the time *Red Rocks* was released, he was dead. The
insurance agent had been right about his chances of living
out a normal life.

Charlotte had never quite gotten over Linc's death. If she
couldn't punch Perkins in his fat, smug nose, she at least
wanted to leave him with some stinging retort, but she was
too stunned to say anything, and ended up stumbling blindly
out of the antiseptic tract house and into the opaque sunshine
of the late California afternoon.

She remembered nothing about the drive back to Hollywood, except a stupefying numbness. And the glare of the
freeway: the harsh, disconnected light that reduced everything it touched to the flat, emotionless status of an object,
that penetrated into every corner and ground down every
projection. She had the feeling that the soft underside of her
own life, and that of Linc's as well, had just been exposed
to such a light, a light that revealed secrets that had long
been concealed, and that accentuated the deep wounds and
the ugly scars. She wanted to just switch it off, and go back
to that soft darkness, but now that she had seen what was
there, there was no getting it out of her mind. With time,
she hoped, the harsh glare would fade. The wounds and
scars would still be there, of course; but they would be less
disturbing if their ragged edges were allowed to recede back
into the shadows.

Without even realizing it, she had driven back to the Marmont. She had been planning to stay at her co-op in West Hollywood, but now that she was here, she realized that she needed to go back to the place where she and Linc had spent so much time together. She also needed the comfort of being near a friend who had also lived through those crazy times.

A few minutes later, she was standing at the door of the bungalow.

"Oh, Ron!" she cried as he answered the door. Then she fell into his arms.

It was the next morning before she was even able to think. She had ended up spending the night in one of the two bedrooms at the bungalow, unable to forsake its cozy comfort. Awakening to the smell of roses and the chattering of the birds, she remembered why she was there. She sat up in bed, and went over again what she knew: someone was looking for Iris, probably because of her testimony before the HUAC inquisitors. Everyone Iris had named was a known Communist, and had nothing more to lose by being named yet again. Except for two: herself and Linc. She was out: her life hadn't been ruined by Iris' testimony. Or at least, not that she had been aware of until now. Which left Linc. Or rather, Linc's sons. They were the only ones she could think of who might have wanted to avenge Linc's ruined career. They had been small when she had known them; the elder, Brent, had been only eleven when Linc died, and the younger, Johnny, seven or eight. But they had loved their father. Linc's being branded a Communist had given his ex-wife the ammunition she needed to prevent him from seeing them. According to Linc, she was a selfish, lazy, bitter woman, who only wanted the children to get back at him. Subject to outbursts of bizarre behavior, she had later been hospitalized for schizophrenia. Though Charlotte had seen the boys often on their frequent visits with Linc before the custody battle, she had lost touch with them after his death. What had become of them? she wondered. Then she remembered Linc's sister. Maybe she would know. Charlotte and Linc had visited her several times in the New Jersey suburb where Linc had grown up. Could it be that she still lived there? Charlotte tried to remember her married name: Kelly, no; Kenney, no; Kinney, yes. Elaine Kinney. Her husband had been a Bill.

Picking up the phone on the bedside table, she called long distance information and asked for the Kinneys' number. To her astonishment, the operator gave it to her right away. They still lived on the same street. Then she called Tracey and told him what Perkins had said about Iris' testimony, and that she was planning to talk with Linc's sister about the boys.

She left Los Angeles a day later, after a meeting at the Beverly Wilshire with her agent and a producer about a movie project that sounded as if it were about to die in development hell, as ninety percent of them seemed to do. Which left her back where she had been before: facing the twice-postponed deadline on her autobiography, a matter that she would rather not have thought about at the moment (though at least she now had something to say about the middle period of her life). On the plane ride back, she turned her thoughts instead to the case, remembering the feeling she had had at the beginning that the pieces of Iris' life didn't add up. Now she had the missing piece: the piece that was the link between Hollywood and Maine. Or maybe it was just *a* missing piece; she was sure there would be others. With an important piece now in hand, she lined up what she had in her head, the way a jigsaw puzzle player lines up the pieces he thinks will be needed for a particular section. After betraying her friends (just thinking about it made Charlotte want to spit), Iris had left Hollywood—not on account of being blacklisted, not even on account of world weariness or the desire for solitude—but out of self-loathing, and perhaps, fear of being considered a pariah by her friends.

She retired to Hilltop Farm with her bottle, and developed the Thoreau connection. How, Charlotte still wasn't sure—not that it was important. If she'd been a friendly witness, it wasn't on account of *Civil Disobedience*. Maybe it was just on account of being in Old Town.

Reminded of that essay, Charlotte remembered a line that Thoreau had quoted to her character, Margaret Fuller, in *On Walden Pond*: "Is there not a sort of blood shed when the conscience is wounded? Through this wound a man's real manhood and immortality flow out, and he bleeds to an everlasting death." Iris had chosen to bleed to an everlasting death in Maine, by living a life of austerity and solitude. Perhaps she had adopted Thoreau's philosophy not out of conviction, but as a form of self-recrimination, his words and his way of life being a penance for her sins. Why else would she have set up that secret altar to her past in the green-wallpapered room? Charlotte asked herself. If she had truly taken Thoreau's philosophy to heart, she would simply have buried her past in the same way that that young vision quester had buried his past in the grave in the dingle next to Little Beaver Pond, and started over. But by keeping a light burning at the altar of her misdeeds, it seemed to Charlotte that she had in some sense been opening the door to the retribution of the fates. Instead of ignoring her dark side—or getting rid of it in any of the many ways one could—by burying it, laughing at it, rising above it—she had appeased it with offerings, and it had responded by coming back for more. Pamola had been her nemesis.

The idea that Iris may have been murdered by a specter out of her past was an intriguing one: it appealed to Charlotte's dramatic sensibilities. But when she looked at it more rationally, it sounded quite fantastic. First there was the basic question: Would the forty-year-old ruin of a career be motive enough for murder? Then there were the more ordinary ones: How would one of Linc's sons have ended up on a mountain in Maine with a pistol crossbow? How would he have known that Iris would be climbing the mountain

that day? How would he have known of Coley's camp? Her
head spinning, she dismissed the premise of one of Linc's
sons being the murderer as being too farfetched. Keith was
the far more likely suspect, especially when one considered
that the probable weapon was a crossbow with an Indian
charm on it. He had called Coley one of Black Elk's Blue
Men—a man driven by jealousy and greed—but maybe it
was *he* who was the Blue Man. Keith had criticized Coley
for being a self-appointed shaman, but it seemed to Charlotte
that he was playing the same game, albeit more subtly and
with more success. "Keith is a pipe-carrier," Didias had
informed her with the utmost solemnity. Which meant that
he was the king of his own little spiritual realm. It seemed
to Charlotte, as she came across reproductions of medicine
shields and kachina dolls everywhere she went, that Native
American spirituality was going to be to the nineties what
Eastern spirituality had been to the sixties and seventies.
How much better to be king of a bigger spiritual realm,
by riding the crest of a wave of New Age fascination with
Native-American ways?

Especially when you would be getting in on the ground
floor with a million-dollar foundation.

She arrived at JFK Airport at five, exhausted from her
quick trip back and forth across the continent. When she
got back to her town house in Turtle Bay a short while
later, she went promptly to bed, and didn't wake up until
seven the next morning. After a breakfast of bacon, eggs,
home fries, and coffee at her local luncheonette, she went
back home to call Elaine Kinney. She wanted to put the
possibility of one of Linc's sons being the murderer to rest.
She figured that if she eliminated the least likely possibility,
that would free her mind to concentrate on the most likely
one. Occam's Razor again. She had to admit, however, that
some of her zeal to find Iris' murderer had abated. She no
longer felt any obligation to an old friend, that was for sure.
In fact, the vindictive side of her wanted Iris' murderer to

get away with it, wanted even to give him a medal. But whatever vindictive feelings she may have harbored were overshadowed by the need to figure it all out, to subject Iris' death to the same unyielding light that had just been shone on the corners of her own life. Charlotte's friend, Kitty Saunders, who was fond of doing character readings—from the Tarot cards, tea leaves, the palms of the hands, you name it—had always described Charlotte as a wanderer, a person who thrives on the fuel of new experiences. Which was true. But she was a wanderer who relied heavily on her compass. In the wilderness, she needed to know where north was, and where south, east, and west were; where up was, and where down was.

She had yet to find her way in the wilderness that was Iris' murder.

An hour later, she had retrieved her car from the garage, and was on her way out to Ho-Ho-Kus, the northern New Jersey suburb with the Indian name that never failed to elicit some comment from whoever heard it, to say nothing of being the bane of copy editors: one unbroken word (Hohokus) or hyphenated? And if hyphenated, upper or lower case for the second "Ho" and the "Kus"? Though Linc had left town for good when he was eighteen and had been dead for over thirty years, he remained Ho-Ho-Kus' most famous former resident. And if there was ever a chance that the townspeople might forget that one of Hollywood's greatest stars had grown up there, there was always Elaine to remind them. In fact, their middle-class upbringing was one of the things that had drawn Charlotte and Linc together. In a town in which many had clawed their way up from the bottom, such a background had been a rarity. And perhaps the reason they both had ended up in Hollywood instead of going on to lead comfortable lives in Ho-Ho-Kus, or, in Charlotte's case, Hartford, was that their middle-class backgrounds had rested on such shaky foundations. Charlotte's father, a successful attorney, had

walked out on his family when Charlotte was a girl, and
although he had paid for Charlotte's tuition at a posh finishing school, he had paid for little else, which meant that
her mother had always had to struggle to support Charlotte
and her sister. Linc's mother had married twice after his
father died, in both cases to unreliable men with drinking
problems whose priorities did not include providing for their
families.

As Charlotte headed over the George Washington Bridge
into the New Jersey suburbs on the other side of the Hudson,
she considered what excuse she was going to use for her visit, and how she was going to raise the subject of Linc's sons.
She also wondered what it was exactly that she wanted to
find out about them. On the first point, she decided to lie, her
talent for dissimulation being a skill that she had parlayed
into a lifetime career. She would tell Elaine that she had
been in Ho-Ho-Kus for whatever reason, and, remembering
that Elaine lived there, decided to drop by. On the second
point, she decided to play it by ear: one advantage of being
a wanderer was that you recognized that new discoveries
were often made despite the fact that you might not have a
destination in mind.

She pulled up in front of the Kinneys' house forty-five
minutes later. It still looked exactly the same: a small,
charming faux-Tudor cottage on a quiet tree-shaded street
lined with other small, charming faux-Tudor cottages. Elaine
greeted her warmly, and escorted her into a neat living
room.

The first thing Charlotte noticed was a picture in a silver frame on an end table. Identical to one in Iris' green-
wallpapered room, it showed Iris standing between Charlotte
and Linc, with her arms around their waists. Just seeing it
almost made her choke.

Charlotte needn't have worried about how to bring up the
subject of Linc's sons. The subject was a natural one for two
people who had absolutely nothing in common but the boys'
father.

"And what about Brent and Johnny?" Charlotte asked, having heard in tiresome detail about Elaine and Bill's recently purchased retirement home on the inland waterway in south Florida.

Elaine sighed. "It's a sad story. As you may know, Gloria was hospitalized for schizophrenia in 1961," she said, referring to Linc's wife.

Charlotte nodded. She had heard about it through the grapevine.

"She never came out again," Elaine said. "She died there last year. After she was committed, the boys continued to live with their stepfather, but from what I understand, he pretty much left them to take care of themselves—that is, when he wasn't being abusive."

"How sad," said Charlotte.

Elaine nodded. "We wanted to take them in, but Bill was out of work. Nor was there anything from Linc; as you know, he was broke when he died. In fact, he still owed money to the lawyers who represented him in the custody battle. I felt terrible about it, but I don't think we would have gotten them anyway."

"Why not?" Charlotte asked.

"Gloria had named the stepfather as their legal guardian."

Charlotte had assumed that the boys had gone to live with Elaine after Gloria's hospitalization. Elaine's news left her feeling conscience-stricken as well. "I feel terrible," she said. "You should have contacted me. Maybe there was something I could have done."

"What?" said Elaine. "If we couldn't get custody, there wasn't any chance that you would have been able to."

Elaine was right. "Maybe I could have looked after their interests in some way," she said. "Protected them."

"How? We had no way of knowing that their stepfather was abusing them. It only came out later on. Anyway, it wasn't so bad for Brent. He was sixteen by then, and he just took off on his own after a year or so. He's done very well. He even worked his way through college."

Named after the actor Brent Fogarty, who had been Linc's closest friend, Brent had been the spitting image of his father. Charlotte could still remember his pale white face at the funeral, a miniature of Linc's own. "And Johnny?"

"John's a bum. He hitchhikes around the country, working at odd jobs here and there. By the time he was in his early twenties, we were back on our feet financially, and we offered to send him to college. But he just turned his nose up at our offer. It made me pretty mad."

"I can imagine," said Charlotte sympathetically.

"He had this anti-materialist ethic. He also had a very big chip on his shoulder. He said that he was the way he was because of his upbringing. Well, if you ask me, that's a cop-out. There are lots of people who have difficult upbringings who don't turn into bums."

Charlotte nodded in agreement.

"We had a big scene here one night, during which he set fire to the last of his money at the kitchen table." She nodded toward the kitchen at the back of the house. "To show his contempt for money, and for our middle-class values."

"Where is he now?"

Elaine shrugged. "I have no idea. I haven't heard from him in a couple of years. But he'll show up eventually. He always does."

"And Brent?" she asked.

"We're still in touch with Brent. He lives out in Colorado, near Linc's old ranch in Ouray. He's happily married, with two children. We don't see him much. He won't come East; he says he can't stand the congestion. But we get out there to visit him every couple of years."

"What does he do out there?"

"He has a sort of dude ranch. Hunting, fishing, whitewater rafting."

Charlotte could easily picture Brent in such a setting. As she remembered, he had his father's adventurous streak.

Linc's ranch in Ouray had been his favorite place, and the boys had spent a lot of time there. It would make sense that Brent would be drawn to that life.

Elaine had now moved on to the careers of her own children.

Charlotte, who had been lulled almost to stupefaction by Elaine's nonstop recap of thirty years of family history, suddenly snapped to attention. Colorado! The Ford Bronco that Jeanne had noticed at Hilltop Farm had had a Colorado license plate. Could it be? she wondered.

She endured a few more minutes of conversation and then, after thanking Elaine for the visit, beat a hasty retreat to the nearest pay phone. Thank goodness Tracey was at the barracks. "Howard!" she said, almost breathlessly.

"Ayuh!" he said, in his usual laconic tone. "This Charlotte?"

"Yes. Listen. I need some information right away. I'd like you to find out what make of car is registered to a Brent Crawford of Ouray, Colorado."

"Gonna tell me what this is all about?" he asked.

"Not quite yet," she replied.

"It's gonna cost ya."

"Cost me to get the information or cost me that I'm not going to tell you what it's all about?" she teased.

"The latter. You're going to owe me one. The former's free. Though it'll take a few minutes to check with the DMV out there. Where are you, anyway?"

"In New Jersey. But I'm on my way home."

"I'll call you there in an hour."

Charlotte was unpacking her bag on her bed when the phone rang an hour later, on the dot. It was Tracey. "It's a black Ford Bronco," he said, and proceeded to give her the license plate number.

Charlotte had found the trail, and she didn't like where it was leading. It was Brent whose black Ford Bronco Jeanne had seen parked on Stillwater Avenue, and once, on the grounds of the farm itself, when she had noticed the driver studying the house through binoculars.

"It seems to me that I remember a vehicle fitting that description having something to do with the case we're working on now. Remember that case?" Tracey asked. "It's a murder case."

"I remember," she said.

"I also seem to remember your telling me just yesterday that Linc Crawford's son might have a motive. May I remind you that the withholding of information in a murder investigation is a crime?"

"Now, don't go getting all huffy on me. I'm not withholding anything. In fact, I'm going to need your help following up on this. Has Pyle been calling the hikers who were signed out to Katahdin?"

"Yep," Tracey replied. "Found one who saw Jeanne Ouellette on Hamlin Peak, which confirms her alibi."

"Has he got the entrance permits there at the barracks?"

"Copies of 'em," said Tracey. "We left the originals back at park headquarters. They're right here on my desk."

"Great. Can you look through them for one with the name of Brent Crawford, and the Colorado license plate number? He probably would have entered the park on June eighth, the day before the murder."

Charlotte watched the traffic passing by outside on East Forty-ninth as she waited impatiently for his answer. She could hear the soft rhythm of his breath, and the rustle of papers being shuffled.

Then he replied: "I've got it!" he said. "Brenton Crawford. He entered on June eighth, stayed overnight at Abol Campground, and left the next day. He signed out for Katahdin at the Abol hikers' register."

How had she ever missed his name? she wondered. But then, why would she have noticed it? She hadn't thought about him in years. Moreover, she had never known that his name was Brenton, and Crawford was a common-enough surname that it wouldn't have attracted her notice.

Sitting down on the edge of her bed, she took a deep breath. She couldn't believe it! Linc's son. He might have followed Iris up to the mountain from Old Town, but that still didn't explain how he had known about Coley's camp. No, she thought, something didn't add up.

Then she remembered what Haakon Hilmers had said about seeing a man who looked like Linc on the Abol Trail. Hilmers had said that he appeared to be arguing with Mack, or a man fitting Mack's description.

"I guess we'll have to track this guy down and bring him in for questioning," said Tracey, thinking aloud.

Charlotte, too, was still thinking. Even the entrance permit didn't add up: What murderer would give his real name? He might as well have put down "to commit murder" as the purpose of his visit. "Were there any prints on the crossbow?" she asked.

"Nope," said Tracey. "Wiped clean."

Scratch that idea.

Tracey continued. "Though Henry Clough said the heads of the bolts we found at the camp matched the entrance wound. Which means that the murderer used those bolts or ones identical to them."

No, Charlotte was thinking, it wasn't enough for her that she had tracked Brent to Katahdin. She needed to know the route he had taken to get there.

"I'll let you know what happens," said Tracey. "Are you planning to come back up here anytime soon?"

"I don't know," she said. The thought of seeing Linc's look-alike son struck panic into her heart. "I'll check back with you tomorrow."

"Thanks," Tracey said as he hung up. "I think we've got a real lead here."

But Charlotte wasn't so sure.

·14·

AFTER TRACEY HAD hung up, Charlotte sat on the edge of her bed for a moment, thinking. If Brent had wanted to find Iris, he might have put the ads in *Variety* and the other trade papers, but he also might have taken steps on his own to find her, the logical first step being to ask her friends and associates if they knew where she was. Of Iris' friends, Charlotte knew little; but associates were a different matter. There had been precisely two: herself, and the director Harold Ames. They had been a threesome—Iris, Charlotte, and Harold—and together they had made some of the best movies ever turned out by Hollywood—movies with class, not the garbage that they turned out today. Not that Hollywood hadn't turned out garbage back then as well, but at least it hadn't been all garbage, the way it was now.

Closing her empty suitcase, she carried it up to the storage room on the fourth floor, which was also where her office was located. After putting the suitcase away, she looked up Harold's number, and dialed.

A maid answered the phone, and she gave her name.

In a minute, the director was on the line. "How are you, Charlotte?" he asked. His voice was thin and quavery. He was getting very old. A generation of Hollywood history was marching toward the grave.

For a moment, they exchanged greetings. Charlotte saw him fairly often, so they didn't have a lot of catching up to do. "I have a favor to ask," she said finally, getting right to the point.

"You know I'm always ready to help, Charlotte," he said.

She could picture him sitting in his elegant home, wearing white Viyella trousers and a white V-neck tennis sweater. Always impeccably dressed; always impeccably mannered. A gentleman of the old school in a town full of sharks.

"I'm calling about Iris O'Connor. I'm still working on my autobiography, and I'd like to talk with her about the good old days, but I lost touch with her ages ago. Did you ever hear what had happened to her?"

"I ran into Iris a few years ago," Ames replied. "On the street in front of Polito's office. She'd been in to see him. I hardly recognized her: her hair had turned snow white. I thought I told you about it at the time."

"I don't think so."

"I meant to. Must have forgotten. Anyway, I asked her what she was doing. She said she'd become a follower of that nature philosopher from Massachusetts. The transcendentalist."

"Thoreau?" prompted Charlotte.

"That's right, Thoreau. I have no memory for names anymore. I asked her to lunch, but she was on her way to Massachusetts to deliver a paper about Thoreau and the Maine Indians at the Thoreau Lyceum. That's all I know."

"Harold," she said, "has anybody else asked you about Iris recently? Say, within the last couple of years?"

There was silence on the line while he thought for a moment.

"Any phone calls, for instance?" she prompted.

"There *was* a phone call, now that you mention it. Two years ago, maybe more. It was from one of Linc Crawford's sons. He also wanted to know what had become of her. I told him roughly the same thing I just told you. He said he was still trying to work out that business at the Chateau Marmont."

"You mean Linc's death?"

"Yes," he said. "The boys were there, remember?"

Charlotte thought back to that horrible day. There was a lot that was a blank—it had been such a tremendous shock—but she did have a vague memory of Linc having been with his sons.

"One of them found the body, as I recall."

"But what would that have to do with Iris?" she asked.

"Iris had been there too. Just before Linc died."

"I didn't know that."

"I didn't either. The son told me. He didn't know who she was until that L.A. *Times* article came out about the blacklist, in which it was revealed that she had testified against Linc. He later saw an old photograph of her, and realized that it was she whom he had seen in the room just before Linc died."

"What was she doing there?"

"Probably dropping off the rewrite of the script for the film I wanted to do with Linc. That was why he was there, to talk about it with me. I wanted to make sure he was committed before I started moving mountains to get studio approval to use a blacklisted actor."

Charlotte didn't think she'd ever known why Linc had been at the Marmont that day, but there was a lot about that day that she'd never known, or, if she had known, had buried somewhere in her memory.

Harold continued. "The boys had come along with him. He was seeing them so infrequently at that point—that was after the custody battle—that he was reluctant to get a babysitter. So I told him to bring them along."

"*Would* the studio have approved?" she asked, curious about the turn Linc's life might have taken, had he lived.

"I think so. There was already a sense that *Red Rocks* was going to be a blockbuster. If they hadn't approved then, they certainly would have by the time *Red Rocks* was released. They had nothing to lose; Ireland had already tested the waters for them."

"But why was Iris doing the script? I thought she'd left

town five years before, that she was well out of the business by then."

"She *was* out of the business. I contacted her through Polito. I wanted the best, and she was the best. I had told her to drop the script by my suite at the Marmont when she got into town. But I never made the connection between the woman who came to the suite and Iris."

"Where were you during all of this?"

"I only remember that I'd gone out, and was delayed in getting back. I had called the hotel, and asked the desk clerk to see to it that Linc and the boys were let in. Of course, you know what I found when I finally got there."

Charlotte didn't want to be reminded.

Harold continued: "Iris delivered the script to me a few days later. She never said anything about having gone to the suite earlier." He paused for a moment and then continued. "It was a peculiar thing about that script . . ."

"What was peculiar?"

"It was so crass and heavy-handed. She'd lost that wonderful butterfly touch that she used to have. She was like a concert violinist who wakes up one day and finds she can no longer play cadenzas. I always wondered if her muse had been dependent on her being in Hollywood."

No, Charlotte thought, it wasn't that. It was that her creative blood had flowed out through the wound in her conscience. It was time for Charlotte to confess. "I'm afraid I misled you, Harold," she said. "It's true that I'm interested in finding out about Iris for my autobiography, but I'm also interested for another reason."

"What?" he asked.

"She's dead," she replied. "Murdered."

There was a stunned silence on the other end of the line.

"The police didn't know it was her, at first. She was living in Maine under her married name." She took a breath, and then said, "One of the suspects is Linc's son, Brent." She proceeded to tell him how Iris had died, and about Brent having been seen on the mountain at about the time of her death.

"I see," Harold said. "I don't remember the name of the son who called."

"Did you tell him where Iris was living?"

"I didn't know where she was living. But I suppose he could have tracked her down through the Thoreau Lyceum. Do you think he thought Iris was responsible in some way for Linc's death?"

Charlotte thought: a ruined career as a motive for murder—no; but the conviction that Iris had indirectly caused his father's death? Yes, indeed. Her pulse quickened; she was on the trail again. "I don't know. Maybe something happened that day to give him that idea."

"Like what?"

The wheels in Charlotte's brain were turning. "Maybe Linc had found out somehow that it was Iris who had testified against him, and confronted her about it when she showed up at your suite."

"An altercation of some sort," offered Harold.

"Which was witnessed by Brent," Charlotte added.

"My memory's hazy," Harold said. "But I think I remember something about an argument. Wait a minute. I would have the newspaper clippings about Linc's death in one of Miriam's scrapbooks."

"Ah, yes, Miriam's scrapbooks." Harold's wife had kept scrapbooks of references to her husband and his movies for over fifty years. Charlotte had used them several times in researching her autobiography, but she had skipped the volumes that covered her black years.

"What year was that?"

"Nineteen fifty-seven," she said. "April. April twenty-sixth, to be precise. He was pronounced dead at five fifty-four P.M."

"I'm sure it's a date you'll never forget, Charlotte," he said softly.

Though she knew the date and the time, she knew few of the other details surrounding Linc's death. People had kept that information from her, and she hadn't asked. All she could remember was several weeks of stupor induced by the sedatives that had been prescribed by her doctor.

Harold was back in a minute with the scrapbook for that year. "I was right," he said. He read:

" 'A room service waiter reported hearing an argument between Crawford and an unidentified woman shortly before the body was found by Crawford's son Brent. The woman had entered the director's hotel suite about twenty minutes earlier.' "

That's why Charlotte hadn't known anything about this. *An unidentified woman*: people would have thought Linc was cheating on her.

"Where was Brent during the argument?" she asked.

She waited while Harold scanned the article. "Here it is: 'Crawford's son was unable to identify the woman. He said his father had sent him and his brother into an adjoining bedroom to watch television when the disagreement with the woman broke out.' "

Charlotte wondered whether Linc's heart attack had come before or after Iris left. If she'd walked out on a dying man, his death would have been that much more on her conscience.

"What do you think?" asked Harold.

"I think the scenario might have gone something like this. Woman enters room, argument breaks out, father sends son out, son returns to find father dead. Son thinks the shock of the argument brought on heart attack. Son tracks the woman down and kills her in revenge."

"Sounds pretty plausible to me."

"I'm not sure I'm ready to deal with plausible," Charlotte said. "The prospect of unveiling Linc's son as a murderer is not one that's pleasant to me, even if he thought he was avenging Linc's death." She paused, then asked, "Do you think you could make copies for me of those articles?"

"Do you have a fax machine?" he asked.

"As a matter of fact, I do," she said. It was a recent acquisition with which she had yet to get acquainted. But she did have the number, and she gave it to him. Then she thanked him, and said goodbye.

A moment later, her phone rang to alert her that the fax was coming through. While the machine was spewing out papers, Charlotte went back to the storage room and retrieved her suitcase.

When she got back to her office a few minutes later, the machine had finished printing the copies. Taking them out, she folded them and stuffed them into her pocket. She would read them on the plane.

She had decided to take the next shuttle to Boston.

The evidence against Brent seemed overwhelming, Charlotte thought as she repacked her bag. He was on the mountain at the time of Iris' death, and he had a strong motive: he may have believed Iris to be indirectly responsible for his father's death. He had been tracking her for some time; putting ads in the papers, calling her former associates, even parking in front of her house. But she still had major problems with Brent as a suspect. First, if he had been intending to kill her, why put an ad seeking her whereabouts, with a phone number that could be traced to him, in the entertainment press? Why tell Harold about her being in the hotel room just before Linc's death? These acts would most certainly have linked him with her murder, to say nothing of his name on the park entrance permit. One explanation was that he hadn't been planning to kill her. His intent may only have been to track her down for the purpose of clarifying the events of that day in his mind, just as he had told Harold. The other explanation was that he had been counting on her death being ruled an accident. Or, if it *was* determined to have been a murder, on the victim being identified as Iris Richards, a wildflower nurserywoman from Old Town, Maine, rather than Iris O'Connor, the Hollywood screenwriter.

In any case, there was still a big gap in the trail of evidence between Brent's conversation with Harold and the summit of Katahdin. To find out how he had ended up on the Knife Edge, Charlotte had to follow in his footsteps. And the next place his footsteps had taken him was probably the Thoreau Lyceum. Checking in her Thoreau Association file, she turned up a membership card that gave the Lyceum's hours as nine to five daily. It was now only a little after noon. She would have plenty of time; Concord was only an hour at the most from Logan Airport. Depending on what she found out, she would then either go back to Maine or return to New York. It was a lot of running around, but she was used to that. She even liked it; it reminded her of her old days on the road. As her friend Kitty had said, she was a wanderer. Her suitcase packed, she called the Lyceum to make sure it would be open. The woman who answered said she would be there until seven. Then she wrote a note for her secretary, Vivian, telling her where she was going. That done, she headed out to the street to hail a cab for the airport.

Riding through the Queens-Midtown Tunnel, the thought struck her that she probably should have called Tracey. It would be only polite to let him know what she was up to. But she decided instead to call him after her visit to the Lyceum. Maybe then she would have something to report.

The Thoreau Lyceum was located in a small Colonial house on a side street in downtown Concord. She later learned that it was next door to the house in which Thoreau had grown up. She entered a large room filled with display cases containing artifacts from Thoreau's life. The walls were hung with photographs of Thoreau and the other members of the Concord Authors' Circle—Ralph Waldo Emerson, Bronson Alcott, and Nathaniel Hawthorne among them—as well as with large wood-block prints illustrating some of America's most quotable writer's most quotable quotes, including "If a man does not keep pace with his companions, perhaps it is because he hears a different drummer"; "I have travelled a good deal in Concord"; "The mass of men lead lives of quiet desperation"; and Charlotte's favorite, "It is a great art to saunter." A bulletin board on one wall displayed some of the junk mail that Henry David had received in recent months: a notification that he was eligible for a VISA gold card, a promotional brochure for a condominium development in Phoenix named Walden Acres, a notification from the Publisher's Clearing House that he was eligible to win the grand prize of two million dollars, and a get-to-know-us invitation from the Bank of Boston.

As Charlotte stood looking at a chunk of brick and mortar from the site of Thoreau's house at Walden Pond, which was displayed in a lighted Plexiglas box as if it were a crown jewel of the British Empire, a stout old woman with gray hair fixed in a neat bun at the back of her neck emerged from the adjoining gift shop and introduced herself as the docent.

Upon learning that Charlotte was a member of the Association—moreover, a member who had never had the opportunity of visiting the Lyceum before—she waived the two-dollar admission fee, and welcomed her with open arms.

"We're not a museum," the woman explained, reiterating the point she had made on the phone. "We're here to answer questions about Mr. Thoreau's life and philosophy, to shatter the romantic illusions, so to speak. We like to say we deal with Mr. Thoreau the person, not Mr. Thoreau the phenomenon."

"That's good, because I have some questions," said Charlotte. "But not about Mr. Thoreau himself. About his modern-day followers."

"Oh, he has plenty of those," she said. "As you can see from the guest register." She waved an arm at the book that lay open on a lectern near the door. "We had nearly six thousand visitors last year, from twenty-eight different countries. Would you like to sign?"

"Certainly." Charlotte went over to the register. "I'm interested in a particular visitor you may have had," she said as she added her name to the list. "He would have been a man in his forties, from Ouray, Colorado. He would have visited here about two years ago."

"We get so many people fitting that description," the docent said. "But you can look through the guest register for that year if you like." She pointed to a stack of volumes on the lower shelf of the lectern. "We keep the old registers right down there."

"He would have been looking for a woman named Iris Richards, who had delivered a paper here some time before on Thoreau and the Maine Indians."

"Oh, I remember that man now. Iris Richards was one of our founders. We know her here very well. He came here looking for her almost exactly two years ago, just after our Thoreau Association meeting. It was held on July twelfth; it's always on Mr. Thoreau's birthday."

"Please, go on," Charlotte prompted.

"He puzzled me at first because he asked for Iris O'something."

"O'Connor?" asked Charlotte.

"That was it, yes. When he told me that she'd delivered a paper on Mr. Thoreau and the Maine Indians to the Association, I figured that he must be talking about Iris Richards. I don't recall that he was from Colorado, though."

She pulled out one of the old registers and set it down on a nearby table. Then she opened it up and leafed through the pages until she reached the entries for July.

"I also remember him very clearly because he arrived only a few minutes after a man from India who'd been an associate of Gandhi's. It was Mr. Thoreau's essay, *Civil Disobedience*, that inspired Gandhi to follow a path of nonviolent resistance in his quest for independence from British rule."

"I didn't know that," said Charlotte.

"Yes. Mr. Thoreau's ideas have inspired a lot of political protests—not all of them worthwhile, I hasten to add. His brand of radical individualism can be misinterpreted to justify all manner of immoral behavior," she said cheerfully. She ran her finger down the list of entries. "Here it is."

Charlotte looked over her shoulder at the page of entries.

"His name was Gupta. J. D. Gupta. He arrived in a cab from the airport, just as you did. He said he had wanted to visit Concord all his life. When he left here, he was going out to Walden Pond." She moved her finger down to the next line. "And this must be the person you're looking for."

Charlotte looked at the entry: the signature wasn't that of Brent Crawford, but of a man named J. MacKenzie Scott. The space for the address wasn't filled in. The name Scott was a common enough one, but Charlotte had a distinct memory of having seen it recently. Then she remembered the wooden sign on the side of the horse trailer on South Water Street. J. MacKenzie Scott was Iris' friend, Mack! But what would he have been doing here? Then she realized the answer to that question as well. Her memory relinquished the long-forgotten fact that Gloria's second husband had been named Scott. J. MacKenzie Scott, otherwise known as Mack, must be Linc's younger son, the one whom she had known as Johnny, and who had burned the last of his money at Elaine Kinney's kitchen table.

Stunned by this revelation, she took a seat on one of the wooden folding chairs that lined the walls of the room.

"Are you all right?" said the docent, taking notice of Charlotte's distress. "Would you like me to get you a drink of water?"

"I'm fine," Charlotte replied. "Just a little dizzy, is all."

It made sense, she thought, as she regained her composure. If Scott had been Johnny's guardian, it would have been natural for Johnny to take his name, while Brent, who had been older and had taken off on his own, retained the Crawford name. Just to make sure, she asked the docent what Scott had looked like.

"Not too tall," she replied. "About five foot ten, I'd say, with a stocky build. Light-colored eyes, if I remember right.

A big head of curly hair, dark blond. A reddish beard, rosy cheeks."

It was Mack, all right. "Did you give him Mrs. Richards' address?"

"I don't remember. There would have been no reason not to. But if I didn't, he could have looked it up. We have our members' names and addresses on cards in this box." Opening a file box on the table, she showed Charlotte the collection of cards. "Here she is," she said, pulling out Iris' card.

A group of visitors had just entered.

"Excuse me," the docent said as she moved off to greet the new arrivals. Then she turned back to Charlotte. "I'll be giving a lecture on Mr. Thoreau's life in a few moments, if you'd like to stay."

"Yes, I would," she replied.

Sitting down again, Charlotte pulled out the copies of the newspaper clippings about Linc's death. She would read them while she was waiting. She had meant to read them on the plane, but had fallen fast asleep.

The first one was from the *New York Herald News*. The information she was looking for was in the first paragraph:

The dead body of actor Lincoln Crawford was discovered yesterday in a suite at Hollywood's posh Chateau Marmont Hotel by his two sons from his marriage to the actress Gloria Smithson.

The boys, Brent, 11, and John, 7, had been with their father when he paid a visit to a suite occupied by the director Harold Ames. The boys found their father's body when they returned to the living room of the suite from an adjoining bedroom.

The boys reported that they had been sent into the bedroom to watch television after an argument broke out between Crawford and a woman caller. The boys were unable to identify the woman, who had left the room by the time they emerged from the bedroom.

*   *   *

The article went on, but there was no need for Charlotte to read any further. It wasn't just one son who had discovered the body, but both. John MacKenzie Crawford, now known as Mack Scott, had also been present at his father's death.

Putting the clipping away again, Charlotte asked the docent if she could look through the guest register for the current year.

"Certainly," the woman said.

When Charlotte and Tracey had spoken with Jeanne, she said she'd noticed the Ford Bronco about a month before, which would have been about two weeks prior to the murder. Charlotte went back through the pages until she got to the middle of May, and then started looking through the entries.

There it was, on May twenty-second: Brenton Crawford, Ouray, Colorado. God only knew how Brent had tracked his brother to the Thoreau Lyceum, but he had. And from there, he'd tracked him to Old Town, Maine.

Standing there, Charlotte at last started fitting the pieces of the puzzle together. After their custody battle, the boys' idyllic days with their father are over. (If anyone was ever suited to being a father of boys, it was Linc: fishing, hunting, horseback riding, ball games; their boyhood as Linc's sons must have been a boys' heaven.) They now spend almost all their time with their crazy mother, who has married Scott. Then Linc dies, thereby eliminating any hopes they may have had of living with him. Their mother's mental health deteriorates, and she is committed. Scott becomes the boys' guardian. Brent takes off not long afterward, but Johnny is left with a cruel and uncaring stepfather. For him, it must have seemed as if the moment when his childhood came to an end could be pinpointed to that afternoon at the Marmont when he found his father lying dead on the floor. And who better to blame than the woman who had quarreled with him immediately before his death? She could imagine him in his room at Scott's house, wondering who the woman was, dwelling on his memory of this one fateful event. Then he finds out that it was Iris who fingered his father, who launched him on the downhill spiral that ended in his death. He sets out on a quest to find her. Maybe he just wanted to confront her at first: to face the woman who had brought him so much misery. Or perhaps he had always planned to find her some day, and take his revenge.

Then he drops out of sight.

It was Charlotte's guess that Brent, suspecting that his brother was on a mission to kill Iris, had tracked him to Old Town. Hence the Bronco parked on the street in front of Hilltop Farm, hence his presence on the mountain. The next question was: Had he been trying to stop his brother, or to help him? What had they been arguing about when Haakon Hilmers spotted them on the Abol Trail?

Thanking the docent, who was about to start her lecture, Charlotte excused herself and went back out to her waiting cab. She had decided not to go back to New York after all.

An hour and a half later, she was airborne again, this time en route to Bangor International Airport. She had followed the brothers' trail three-quarters of the way: from California to Concord, and from Concord to Old Town. As in Thoreau's dream, she had emerged from the deep woods onto the open ridge, but she still had to find her way to the summit. Metaphorically, and literally. It was the last leg of the boys' journey that was stumping her; the leg that went from Old Town to the summit of Katahdin. The leg that featured the most elusive aspect of the case: the weapon. But the fact that it was Mack instead of Brent whom she now suspected of being the murderer would probably make it easier to track the weapon down. She could work from the assumption that the weapon had come from Old Town, rather than from, for instance, some second-hand sporting goods store in Colorado. It also helped that it was such a distinctive weapon: not a modern crossbow that might have come from any mail-order sporting goods catalogue, but a weapon that had been carefully made by hand many years ago, and that was decorated with a unique Indian amulet.

A thought struck her as the plane circled Bangor—a few high rises surrounded by a wilderness of green. Jeanne Ouellette had been an archery champion at the age of fourteen or so. At that age, one didn't suddenly develop an overwhelming interest in archery. One had to have been encouraged by an older person—a coach, a teacher, most likely a parent. And Jeanne's father was still alive, living in a senior citizens apartment in Old Town, according to Doug Pyle. If indeed it had been Jeanne's father who promoted her interest in archery, he might know what had been going on in Old Town in terms of archery at that time, and specifically, who might have made a pistol crossbow.

She called Jeanne from the airport. Why, yes, she said, it was her father who had encouraged her interest in archery. He had been an avid bow hunter. *Would he like to talk with Charlotte about archery?* (In other words, was he *compos mentis?*) Yes, he would be delighted. He was eighty-four and crippled by arthritis, but he still had all his marbles. (Jeanne had recognized Charlotte's question for what it was.) He lived at the Bickmore Manor, a senior citizens apartment building on South Main Street. *Would he know who in the area might have made a pistol crossbow?* Why, yes, he probably would, Jeanne had replied, adding, "Now why didn't I think of that?" She obviously recognized the weapon Charlotte was talking about as the one that had killed Iris. In response to Charlotte's inquiry, Jeanne provided her with directions to the Bickmore Manor, and told her that if her father, whose name was Earl, wasn't at home, he could probably be found playing gin rummy with his buddy Reggie Pyle at the senior citizens center at St. Joseph's Church, across the street.

But Charlotte did find him at the Bickmore Manor, which was an old three-story red brick building located next to the headquarters of the United Paperworkers International Union, Local #80. He was sitting on a bench out in front, watching the traffic on South Main Street go by. His walker stood on the sidewalk next to the bench.

A big man with a thick head of snow-white hair, Earl Ouellette bore a strong resemblance to his daughter. His brown eyes carried the same glint of suspicion, and he had the same bump on the bridge of his nose.

Charlotte broke the ice by asking about the bas-relief frieze of a pair of draft horses that crowned the arched doorway of the building. Above the relief was a panel which read "1812 DOCTOR 1906."

"They used to manufacture the gall cure here," Ouellette replied. "I worked here then. There's a relief of a horse inside over the mantelpiece, too. It's part of the apartment on the first floor now. Can't see it, unless you know Bessie Cyr." He nodded at the first-floor windows. "She lives there."

Charlotte just listened.

Ouellette continued. "Then the newspaper was here. The *Penobscot Times*. I worked there too. Linotype operator. Twenty-seven years for the gall cure; fifteen years for the newspaper. Then the building was converted into senior citizens apartments, and I signed right up."

"The tenants changed, but you stayed on."

"Yup." He chuckled. "I've been living with this building for more than fifty years. Longer than I lived with my wife." He looked over at Charlotte. "What can I do for you, young lady?"

Charlotte smiled. She liked the "young lady" part. "Your daughter Jeanne sent me over," she said. "I'm here to talk with you about archery. Jeanne said you were the one who encouraged her as a girl."

"Yup. Started a trend here in Old Town, too."

"I heard. How did you get interested in archery?" she asked, just to get the conversation rolling.

"During the war in Europe I was a commando, see. We

used crossbows because they were silent, and easy to lug around. You could shoot a German sentry and nobody would know the difference."

"I'm interested in crossbows myself," she said.

For the first time, he took a good look at her, as if to say, "What would a woman like you be interested in crossbows for?"

"Not for myself," she added by way of explanation.

That was enough to satisfy him. "I guess I know a bit about crossbows. I was president of the Maine Crossbow Association. What do you want to know?"

Charlotte improvised; she was good at that. "I bought an old crossbow at a yard sale here in town for my nephew. He's interested in archery. It looks as if it was made by hand. The body is made out of wood, and it's painted in a green and brown camouflage design."

He looked over at her, his interest piqued.

"I'd like to be able to tell him a little bit about it," she went on. "Do you have any idea how old it might be, or where it might have come from?"

"Guess I do," he said laconically.

She wanted to grab his arm, and shout "WHAT?" but she had enough experience with Mainers to know that she just had to wait.

"I used to make crossbows like that myself," he said. "As far as I know, I'm the only one who ever made 'em. I used to make a lot of stuff. I had a shop in my garage: birdhouses, gliders, wooden toys. Can't do it anymore, on account of my arthritis." He pronounced it arthuritis.

Charlotte held her breath. She was getting very close now.

"I stopped making crossbows when they made 'em illegal for huntin' and fishin'. You could still use 'em for target practice, but that wasn't enough of a market." He looked over at her again. "Was it a pistol crossbow?"

She nodded. "It had a little beaded bag with a claw in it hanging from the trigger guard," she said.

"That was mine, all right. An old Penobscot gave me that charm for good luck. You hung it from the trigger guard to help you shoot straight. Guess you got it at my daughter Doris' yard sale. She lives in the house now. She told me she was going to sell all that stuff in the garage."

"Where does she live?"

"Three twenty-two South Water Street," he said. "Down by the railroad tracks. Is that where you got it?"

She nodded.

"Where does your nephew live?"

"Ontario," she replied. It was the first place to pop in to her head.

"Good," he said. "That's one of the few places where crossbow huntin' is legal. Those pistol crossbows are good for fishin', too. I used to rig some of 'em up with a line so you could reel the fish right in."

"Sounds like a good idea," Charlotte said.

"Damn right it was. I used to pull some mighty nice salmon out of the river. That was before the pollution from the paper mills killed 'em all off. Course, they've been comin' back in recent years. I read in the paper that last year's run was four thousand."

He paused for a moment to look up at the frond-like branches of the mountain ash trees that lined the walk, which waved in the breeze against a sky of cerulean blue. They were a lovely sight.

"The crossbow I bought from your daughter had a coil of line for fishing," Charlotte said. "I also bought the bolts, which had cartridge tips."

He nodded. "I used to use those bolts for rough fish. The summer isn't a game animal season, but you can keep in practice by goin' after rough fish, see. If I was goin' after salmon or bass, I'd use a harpoon-type arrow with a barb, so I could haul 'em in."

Another mystery explained, she thought.

"I used to keep a rowboat on the river bank. There was a nice salmon pool over on the Milford side. It was by the mouth of a stream; they liked to lay off in the cool water, see. When they was runnin', I'd row over and shoot me a salmon for dinner. It was like shootin' fish in a barrel."

It sounded like the same salmon pool that Mack had talked about.

"I bet you could shoot some mighty nice fish in that pool today," Ouellette said. "Now that they've come back."

"I bet you could," she agreed.

After leaving Bickmore Manor, Charlotte hopped back into her rental car and headed down to South Water Street, which was only a stone's throw away. She followed the same route she and Tracey had taken to Mack's trailer, down Sawyer Street to the river. At the foot of Sawyer Street, she turned right. A dozen or so houses lined the road between the railroad yard at one end and the municipal sewage treatment plant at the other. Across the road, a locomotive stood on one of the tracks, its engine throbbing. As Mack had pointed out, it was hardly the city's most prestigious address, and she could readily see why Jeanne had been willing to suffer Iris' tyranny for the privilege of living at Hilltop Farm. She pulled over next to the tracks and parked. As she got out, her sense of smell was assailed by the noxious odor of rotten eggs. It was so bad that it made her nose twitch, though not as bad as it used to be, Tracey had assured her on their earlier visit. There had been a time when the air pollution from the mill would peel the paint off the houses.

Charlotte didn't know if it was air pollution or lack of money that was responsible, but most of the houses on the street looked as if they could use a coat of paint. Number 322 was one of the better-maintained of the lot: a tiny matchbox of a house with a tiny front porch and a tiny front yard planted with flower seedlings. The one-car garage in which Ouellette had had his wood shop was visible at the back of the house.

The door was answered by a short, plump, red-cheeked woman with gray hair.

"I'm looking for Doris Ouellette," Charlotte said.

"Haven't been a Ouellette for forty-three years, but I guess you've got the right person," she said, opening the door.

"I'm sorry," Charlotte said. "It was your father who referred me to you, and he didn't mention your married name."

"That's okay," she said. "I'm a widow now, anyway."

"You must look like your mother," Charlotte said.

"Spittin' image. I look just like my mother, my sister looks just like my father, and the other five are a combination."

Charlotte found it hard to imagine nine people living in this tiny house.

"People couldn't believe me and my sister were related. They still can't: one's short and fat, and the other's tall and skinny." She laughed. "C'mon in," she said, opening the door wider. "What can I do for you?"

"Thank you," said Charlotte. She entered a small, spotless living room with a painting of Jesus hanging over the sofa, and a row of African violets on the sill of the window overlooking the tracks.

"Would you like a cup of coffee?" the woman asked.

"No, thank you," said Charlotte. She decided she might as well be up front about the reason for her visit. "I'm helping the police with the investigation into Iris Richards' death," she said. She didn't bother introducing herself. She didn't want to get into that.

"Please," Doris said. "Sit down." She took a seat herself and waited, a worried expression on her face. Did she think her sister was about to be arrested?

"As you may know, the weapon was a pistol crossbow," Charlotte began, taking a seat in a cushioned rocking chair by the window.

"I saw the picture of it in the newspaper," Doris said.

"With the medical examiner?" Charlotte asked.

She nodded.

"That picture was printed before the actual weapon was found," Charlotte explained. "The weapon that was used in the murder was quite different. It was old, and the body had been handmade of wood. It was painted in a green and gray camouflage design."

Doris' face showed no signs of recognition.

"Your father said that he used to make pistol crossbows like that in his wood shop. He told me he thought there might have been one or two among the things you sold in the garage sale."

Doris' eyes widened as she realized what Charlotte was talking about. "I remember that old thing now! I didn't know what it was. It was in an old cardboard drum with a bunch of other stuff. Do you think the murderer used it to kill Iris Richards?"

"We don't know for sure," said Charlotte, "but it appears likely. Do you remember who bought it?"

Doris' thick gray brows knitted in concentration. "That was one of those things I didn't put a price on because I didn't know what it was. I didn't know what half that stuff was. I just let people rummage around, and if they wanted something, make me an offer. I don't remember anybody buying it."

"What happened to it, then?"

"I think it was in the stuff that I put out at the curb for the garbage collection after the sale. I threw away most of the stuff I didn't sell. I wanted to get rid of it all because I needed the garage for my car. Most of it was junk anyway; Dad is a pack rat."

"So somebody could have picked it up off the street?"

"Could, and did. Most of that stuff was gone by the time the garbage truck came around a couple of days later. I like to put stuff like that out early in hopes that someone can find some use for it. I don't like to see things goin' to waste. Know what I mean?"

Charlotte did. "Did you see who picked it up?"

"Naw. I work down to the pie plate. I'm not usually home

during the day. I took the day off today because of a doctor's appointment."

"What's the pie plate?"

Doris stared at her in astonishment. "You must be from away."

"I am," Charlotte said.

"It's a mill up on North Main," she explained. "We make pie plates." Seeing Charlotte's puzzled expression, she went on to explain. "They're those cardboard discs that they put under the cakes you buy at the bakery."

Charlotte nodded in recognition. Of course! Doris worked down to the pie plate. Just like her father had worked down to the gall cure.

Charlotte thanked her for her help, and left.

·15·

SHE WAS SURE of it, she thought as she got back into the car. It was Mack who had picked the pistol crossbow out of the cardboard drum full of junk on the curb. Not only was picking garbage his career, he lived just a hundred yards down the street. Maybe he had intended to use it at first for fishing. Maybe he even *had* used it for fishing. He too had bragged about the salmon that he'd pulled out of the river. The fact that crossbow fishing was illegal wouldn't have deterred him; as a follower of Thoreau, he would have believed that laws oppressed the individual. Besides, he would have thought that poaching was okay because he was fishing for sustenance, not for sport. It was probably only later, as he was considering how to murder Iris, that the virtues of the pistol crossbow as a murder weapon became apparent, particularly when used with a bolt with a cartridge tip: it was quiet, it was accurate, and the bolt could be withdrawn, making it appear as if Iris had died from the fall. He had no doubt assumed that the entry wound would be overlooked, which might have been a valid assumption in other rural states, but not in Maine. Henry Clough might have been the chief medical examiner in a state in which there were fewer homicides in a year than in New York City in a week, but that didn't mean it was easy to pull the wool over his eyes.

There was only the final section of the trail left now, she thought as she sat there, staring out at the giant mill: the section that ran between Katahdin's summit and Lorne

Coley's camp at Klondike Pond. How would Mack have known about the camp? The obvious answer was that he had heard about it from Coley himself, or from some other Penobscot. No sooner had she posed the question in her mind than the image of the twin pyramids of bottles stacked against the end wall of the camp came to mind. Bottles! That was it. If Coley had done his share of emptying them, he had probably done his share of returning them as well. In the currency of recycling, whiskey bottles represented the highest denomination. In all probability, Mack and Coley had met at "work," which is how Mack had referred to the railroad station that now served as the municipal redemption center.

Eager to confirm her theory, she got out of the car and headed back down South Water Street to the redemption center.

The ramshackle old railroad station was well-matched to the derelicts who not only earned some extra money by collecting bottles for recycling, but provided their own raw materials as well. The sagging ridgepole looked as if it was about to snap, and the windows at one end were boarded up, but the overall air of dereliction was brightened somewhat by a red, white, and blue flag, which proclaimed that the center was "Open." Another sign said "True Count." Below that was written "Recycling Can Work When We All Pitch In—Reduce, Reuse, Recycle. Please separate glass, plastic bottles, and metal cans."

Opening the door, Charlotte found herself on the threshold of a large room with a low, tin-paneled ceiling and stained fiberboard walls. It was filled with long tables on which stood dozens of boxes, each labeled according to their contents: Coke, Pepsi, Miller, Bud, and so on. The room smelled like a fraternity house rec room after a party weekend. A clean-cut young man who looked like a college student stood behind the counter next to a sign publicizing a bottle drive on behalf of the Old Town High School band's proposed trip to Washington. A radio on a shelf blared out rock music.

As Charlotte stepped up to the counter, the clerk went over to the radio and turned down the volume.

"Thanks," Charlotte said. "Is your name Richie?" she asked, remembering that Mack had mentioned his "boss's" name in their previous conversation.

"That's me," he said. "What can I do for you?"

"I'm here to inquire about someone who may have been one of your customers. His name is Lorne Coley. He's a Penobscot Indian: about forty-five, medium height and build; long black hair, worn loose; usually wears a beaded medicine bag around his neck."

"I know the guy," he said.

"Is he a customer?" she asked.

"He comes in sometimes. He used to come in three or four times a week. Now he only comes in once a month or so. He's been off the sauce for a couple of years now, so he doesn't come in as often."

"I was wondering if he knew one of your other customers."

"Who might that be?"

"Someone named Mack Scott."

"Sure, he knows Mack. They used to pick together sometimes. Before he stopped drinking, Coley used to hang out on the river bank with the canned heaters. That's what they call themselves. It's a joke. They don't really eat Sterno. They drink more classy stuff. Like Thunderbird." He laughed.

"And Mack hung out with them too?" she asked.

"Mack doesn't drink," he said. "Do you know Mack?"

Charlotte nodded.

"Then you know that he's an eccentric. He lives in an old horse trailer right down the street, across the tracks from where the canned heaters hang out. They've got a hobo camp down there."

"Then he was socializing with the neighbors."

"Yeah," he said. "I guess you could call it that." He looked at her more closely. "Why do you want to know, anyway?"

Charlotte was uncharacteristically slow in coming up with a reply.

"Well, I guess it's none of my business," he said cheerfully.

"Is there a pay phone around here?" she asked.

"At the Mobil station just up the street."

She thanked him and left.

She was headed back to her car when she noticed a footpath on the other side of the tracks that appeared to lead down to a peninsula that jutted out into the river; she could see the tops of the trees sticking up above the tracks. Concluding that this was the site of the hobo camp, she crossed the six rows of tracks and followed the path down into the grove of trees. She wanted a close-up look at the magnificent river that was second in importance only to Katahdin in the eyes of the Penobscots. The path emerged at a circle of cast-off chairs surrounding an old oil drum, which was probably used for a fire when the weather got cold. There was also an old picnic table, which looked as if it had been carted away from a highway rest stop. One would have expected to find such a spot littered with whiskey bottles and beer cans, but there were only a few; the rest had probably been turned in at the redemption center.

It was a lovely spot that the canned heaters had picked for their camp, shaded as it was by the overhanging willows, which were now tinged with gold by the low-lying sun. Subject to flooding, though, Charlotte thought as she felt the squish of the muddy black earth beneath her feet, and not exactly quiet. She was just turning back when she noticed a turnoff leading through the trees to a clearing. And there, in the clearing, was an old straw archery target mounted on a metal stand. So this was where Mack had honed his archery skills! It also appeared to be the point of disembarkation for his fishing trips: tied to a tree on the river bank was an old wooden rowboat.

She was headed back up the path when she ran into Mack himself. He was carrying a garbage bag full of bottles over his shoulder, and looked, with his bushy beard, like Old Saint Nick with a pack full of Christmas toys. A pang of fear shot through her at the sight of him, but it subsided the moment she had a chance to think. Mack had been a conceptual killer: his murder of Iris had been like a work of art, carefully planned for years in advance. He wasn't a murderer who would act on impulse.

Or so she hoped. She remembered with some degree of apprehension his statement that the only reason Iris hadn't dropped him too was that his behavior was so far beyond the pale that there was no point in even trying to hold him to civilized standards.

"Hello," he said, pleasantly enough. "I was just going to rinse these bottles out in the river. Richie told me that you were inquiring about me."

His eyes told her that he knew that she knew. Why else would she have been asking Richie about Mack's connection with Coley?

"Yes. How did you know I was here?" Now that she knew who he was, she could see some resemblance to his mother. But he also had his father's long, straight nose, and pale skin, which, like his father's, was weather-beaten and sprinkled with freckles.

"Richie said he saw you come down here."

Standing aside to let him pass, Charlotte said, "I didn't tell you my name when I met you last week. I'm Charlotte Graham, the actress. I knew you when you were a little boy."

He stared at her. "Lottie," he said, using the name that he had used for her as a child. "You used to bring us gummy worms. 'For your little chicks,' you used to say." He paused. "You haven't changed much."

"You have," she said.

He looked at her appraisingly. "So you know," he said.

She nodded.

"Lieutenant Tracey called me in when he found the photographs of me in the locked room at Iris'. I've been on your trail for over a week now. I just figured out the last piece: how you knew about Coley's camp."

"I've got to put this bag down," Mack said. Continuing on down the path, he set the bag down in the middle of the clearing, next to the oil drum. Then he took a seat in a rusted folding chair.

Charlotte followed him, reassured by the fact that Tracey was on his way. If Richie had told Mack where she had gone, he would tell Tracey too. She sat down in another chair. Two chairs for friendship, she thought with irony.

For a moment, Mack stared out at the river, the pale eyes under the brim of his engineer's cap unreadable. "Have you reported me?" he asked.

"No," she lied.

"I could kill you now too," he said, echoing her thoughts. "Toss your body in the river. No one would ever know."

She quoted from *Walden*: " 'Life is sweetest closest to the bone,' " she said flippantly, as if they were having a normal conversation. In reality, she was poised to up and run.

He smiled. "Touché. I know you reported me," he said. "Richie told me you made a phone call from the Mobil station."

"Why don't you tell me about Iris?" she said.

"Okay," he replied, and proceeded to tell his tale. "Brent and I had the best father in the world," he said. "He was the one who raised us." He looked over at her. "As you well know. Then she got sole custody. That was in 1952, after his HUAC testimony." He spoke bitterly. "Never mind that the committee never proved he was a subversive, never mind that it wouldn't have mattered to us if he'd been Stalin himself. It was the ammunition my mother needed to keep him from seeing us. Not that she really cared about us. She just wanted to get back at him. That's how screwed up she was. She'd take off to God-knows-where and leave us to fend for ourselves. We subsisted on TV dinners, if we were lucky. Sometimes she didn't even leave us anything to eat. Then she married Scott in 1955. He'd get drunk and rough us up. We would run away, but they would always catch us. Once we tried to hitchhike to the ranch. It was our dream to be reunited with Dad, a dream that was kept alive by our infrequent visits with him. But as time went on, we realized that that wasn't ever going to happen. Nor was it the same when we were with him; he was a broken man." He paused for a moment, and then said, "Then came that day."

"April twenty-sixth, 1957," said Charlotte.

He nodded. "We were at the Chateau Marmont. He had a meeting with Harold Ames to talk about a project. We were waiting in Ames's suite for him to arrive. Dad had just finished filming *Red Rocks*, which was his first film in—I don't know—three or four years."

"Four years," said Charlotte.

"He hadn't been feeling well—he said he thought he was coming down with the flu—but he was in a great mood nevertheless. Ames' interest had confirmed his feeling that *Red Rocks* was going to be his comeback picture. We were having a wonderful time. He ordered up banana splits from room service."

"I remember those banana splits they used to make for you at the Marmont," said Charlotte. "They were enormous."

"Then *she* arrived. I didn't know who she was, then. All I knew was that they had an argument. Dad sent us into the bedroom to watch television. I even remember the show: it was Kate Smith; she was singing 'When the Moon Comes Over the Mountain.' I guess he didn't want us to hear what they were saying."

"Were you listening?" she asked.

He nodded. "We turned Kate down so we could hear. I never could stand that woman, anyway." He smiled. "Dad was very angry. There was shouting; it was ferocious. Then there was silence. We were afraid to come out: he'd told us not to."

"Or else," said Charlotte, remembering Linc's disciplinary tactics.

He nodded. "Or else. When we finally did open the door, he was lying there on the carpet. I'll never forget the color of his skin, how gray it was. A heart attack, the hotel doctor said. But she was the one who killed him."

Leaning over, he picked up a whiskey bottle and put it into his bag. "Some of my best picking's right here on my doorstep," he said.

Charlotte leaned over and picked up another one for him.

"Thanks," he said. Then he continued. "It was in that moment that all hope disappeared from our lives. *Poof.*" He snapped his fingers. "Like that. Dad was dead. There was no chance that we'd ever be reunited. It was only a few years after that that my mother was committed. We stayed on with our stepfather. Or rather, I stayed on with him. Brent was lucky enough to get away."

"Your Aunt Elaine told me," Charlotte said. "I went to see her."

"Then you know the rest. Bleak, bleak, bleak. Except for one spot of brightness: the hope that some day I would find out who the woman was who had ruined our lives, and avenge Dad's death. It was that thought, and that thought only, that's kept me going for thirty-three years."

"How *did* you find out who she was?" Charlotte asked. "Through the article about HUAC in the L.A. *Times*?"

He waited for the sound of couplings clashing from the railroad yard to subside before he answered.

He nodded. "Brent saw it. He wanted to track her down too. He didn't want to kill her. I don't even think he wanted to see her. He just wanted to know what had become of her. If she'd been rich and successful he might have wanted to expose her for the stool pigeon she was."

"But knowing what had become of her wasn't enough for you," said Charlotte. "You wanted vengeance."

"Yes, but in a special way. I didn't want to just polish her off; I could have done that a million times. I wanted the satisfaction of planning and executing a murder that was suited to her crime."

"That's why you insinuated yourself into her life."

"Yeah," he said. "It wasn't hard. One of the things I'd inherited from Dad was his old copy of *Walden*, with his favorite passages underlined. I had read it a lot over the years, and its philosophy had always made a lot of sense to me, too. To pass myself off as a Thoreauvian was a natural."

"Then the dogeared, marked-up copy of *Walden* that you talked about last week was Linc's," she said.

"Yes," he said. He cocked his curly head in the direction of the road. "It's on my bookshelf at Heritage Farms."

"I always wondered what had happened to it."

Mack continued. "Once I'd found out about her, I became even madder. If ever there was a woman whose life was a contradiction of everything that Thoreau stood for, it was Iris. And here she was passing herself off as a Thoreau authority. It infuriated me."

And what about his own life? Charlotte wanted to say. She was reminded of what the docent had said about Thoreau's radical individualism being used to justify all kinds of immoral behavior. Mack was a perfect example.

"Is that why you chose to kill her on Katahdin—because Thoreau had written about it?" she asked.

"Yes. Her annual climb was symbolic for me of her arrogance, not only before Thoreau and the natural world, but before the people she had ratted on as well. Thoreau said Pamola was always angry with men who had the daring and insolence to climb to Katahdin's summit."

"Weren't you worried that she'd recognize you?" Charlotte asked. "You said she had good eyesight—for aluminum, anyway."

"She did have good eyesight, but I was behind her. Just to make sure she wouldn't spot me, though, I took off this hat, and put on a balaclava hat that covered my beard; it was cold enough up there for one. I also put on a windbreaker on over my green and black plaid jacket."

"And why did you ditch the crossbow at Coley's camp?"

"I didn't want to get caught with it, of course. I also didn't want it to be found. I figured no one would find it there."

"And if they did, the murder would be blamed on Coley?" she asked, thinking of what Coley had said about Indians always being the scapegoats.

"Something like that," he replied.

Charlotte also remembered the subtle way in which Mack had directed their suspicion toward Jeanne; and, for that matter, Keith.

But Mack's attention was no longer on their conversation; it was as if his mind had been carried off by the swift current of the river.

Finally, he spoke. "Iris' mistake was that she only paid lip service to Pamola. You can't just climb up to his lair once a year, offer him a bottle of rum, and then slam the door on him. He'll pester you to death. What you have to do is invite him down to meet your friends, and to dine at your table."

"Yes," Charlotte agreed. "But after you've made your peace with your demon, you have to kick him out. Otherwise, he'll move right in and take over."

Mack looked over at her. "Maybe there are people who *like* having a demon around. Sometimes a demon is the only friend you have."

For a moment they sat in silence, looking out at the wide, gray river, swollen with the snowmelt from Katahdin's stony flanks.

Then the silence was interrupted by the crunch of tires on gravel. A state police cruiser had just pulled over next to the tracks. A door slammed and Tracey and Pyle came hurrying down the path.

"I guess that's my ride," Mack said.

When Tracey called him about Mack's arrest, Brent Crawford booked a seat on the next plane out of Colorado,

braving the East's congestion for the second time on his
brother's behalf. He sat now in Tracey's office, having just
returned from a trip to Bangor to visit Mack at the Penobscot
County Jail. He was a tall, lanky man with his father's clear
blue eyes, narrow nose, and pale, freckly skin, which, like his
father's, had been cured to the color of rawhide by the strong
sun and harsh winds of the Rockies. It made Charlotte's
heart melt just to look at him, so strongly did he resemble
Linc. He even dressed the way Linc used to: cowboy shirt,
dungarees, work boots. Charlotte remembered the first time
she had looked in Linc's closet. There had been a dozen
cowboy shirts, neatly lined up on hangers, and that was it!
If ever there was a man who had taken to heart Thoreau's
admonition to beware of enterprises that require new clothes,
it was Linc. "If I need anything more," he had always said,
"I can get it from the wardrobe department."

Brent also had his father's natural dignity. The cowboys
Linc had played might have been rough around the edges,
but he had always had the grace of the natural aristocrat.
He had been a kind man too—a man who never could have
found it in his heart to hate anyone, and Charlotte sensed
that about his son as well. She was sure that had Linc lived,
he would have forgiven Iris, however angry he might have
been with her in the scene at the Marmont. That was the way
he was. Mack was more like his mother, in temperament as
well as appearance. They had clung to their obsessions like
dogs to a bone, never willing to bury them and move on.

It turned out that Brent had tracked Mack down on the
suspicion that he was out to harm Iris. At the least, he had
wanted to see what Mack was up to. He had followed him
up the mountain, but he'd been too late.

He had told the story in Linc's deep, mellow voice, less
crusty for lack of the cigarettes that Linc had chain-smoked.
How the boys would lie awake in their room at their mother's house, inventing ways of murdering the woman who
had taken their father away from them: stabbing, hanging,
drowning, shooting.

"It was a game for us; or rather, it was a game for me," he said. "I guess it wasn't a game for Mack." He took a deep breath. "At one point we actually *did* make a game out of it. We got the idea from Clue, the board game."

"Colonel Mustard did it in the library with the wrench," said Tracey.

He nodded. "We had our own set of rules, in which the victim was always Miss Plum. In later years," he continued, "I didn't think much about her. Then came the article in the L.A. *Times*. Shortly after that, I saw a picture of her somewhere, and figured out that she was the woman at the Marmont. I wanted to track her down, just to talk with her. It was an unfinished part of my life that I wanted to put behind me. I put the ads in *Variety*, and the other trade papers. Then I found out that Harold Ames was still around, and I called him. What he told me was enough to lay her to rest for me. I had no desire to find out more."

"But Mack did," said Charlotte.

"Yes," he said. "After my conversation with Ames, Mack told me that he was going to go to the Lyceum to find Iris. When he dropped out of sight right after that, I didn't think anything of it. He was always dropping out of sight. Then I got a postcard from him. It was of the Indian Island bridge. There was only one sentence: 'It's going to be a bow and arrow.'"

Brent shifted the position of his long legs. "I didn't know if it was a joke, or what. But I didn't want to just let it ride. There had always been this streak in Mack that was—I don't know—extreme."

"Your Aunt Elaine told me how he had burned all his money at her kitchen table as a symbol of his contempt for material values," Charlotte said.

Brent held out an enormous hand, which was just like his father's. "There you go," he said. "A perfect example. You never knew what he was going to do. Anyway, I decided to drive out. I would be needing a car; besides, Mack never did anything fast. I got to the Lyceum in two days. When

I asked about a Thoreau authority who lived in Old Town, the woman there gave me Iris' name. Then I drove up to Old Town and staked out her house for a couple of weeks. Mack came by a few times, and I got the sense that they were friends, which really set me wondering. Why would he have befriended her?"

"Unless he was planning to kill her," said Tracey.

Brent nodded. "When I saw her and her companion packing up for the camping trip, I suspected that Mack's plan was about to go down. I couldn't decide whether to follow Mack or Iris. By then, I knew that Mack was living in the trailer. I decided on Mack, which was where I went wrong. Had I stuck with Iris, maybe it wouldn't have happened. Anyway, I followed him to Katahdin, and even stayed in the same campground. In the morning, I followed him up, and then watched while he and Iris ate lunch at Thoreau Spring."

"From where?" asked Charlotte, thinking of her conversation with Hilmers.

"From the spot where the Abol Trail comes out on the Tableland."

She nodded.

Brent went on. "Then she headed up to Baxter Peak, and he headed back down. I was waiting for him just below the Tableland. I asked him what he was doing. I was confused by then. Why was he coming down, if she was going up? He told me that he was following in Thoreau's footsteps, and that Thoreau had only come as far as the Tableland. He was mad that I had followed him. When I asked him about the postcard, he said it was part of our game."

"Part of the game," Tracey repeated.

"Yeah. That Indian Island had been the inspiration for a new murder weapon to add to our make-believe arsenal. I didn't know what to think. I asked him about his friendship with Iris. He went on in a convincing way about their shared admiration for Thoreau. I knew he'd always been a Thoreau fan, so that made sense to me. Since I didn't see any bow sticking out of his backpack, I assumed I'd been wrong."

"Then what?" asked Tracey.

"Then we quarreled. He told me to stay out of his business. Then he continued on down the trail. I went up; I figured that as long as I had come that far, I might as well go to the top. I passed Iris on Baxter Peak—she was just sitting there—and continued on across the Knife Edge. I was resting on Pamola Peak when I saw it happen."

"You saw it?" said Charlotte.

He nodded. "She was standing on the tip of one of those knobs, looking out. All of a sudden, I saw her totter; she reminded me of my daughter's Gumby, one of those blow-up figures that are weighted at the bottom. She rocked back and forth a couple of times, and then she went over. I had a front row seat for the fall. It was gruesome."

"Where was Mack?"

"I couldn't see him. At first, I thought she'd had a stroke or a heart attack. Then I saw Mack scrambling up South Peak in the direction of Baxter. He was wearing a balaclava hat to cover his beard, and a navy windbreaker over his jacket. But I knew it was him. I recognized the orange backpack, too."

Charlotte remembered that backpack from the trailer. She leaned back against her chair. "Phew!" she said.

"How come you didn't come to us?" said Tracey.

Charlotte knew that Tracey had to give the impression of being hard-nosed, but she doubted he would take any action against Brent.

"He was my brother," Brent replied. "Also, I didn't actually *see* him do anything. It looked like she just fell to me."

After Tracey had given him the requisite lecture about being an accessory to a murder, Charlotte spoke:

"I didn't tell Mack the real story of how your father died, but I'll tell you. You can tell Mack if you want to." She paused, and then continued. "Your father didn't die of a heart attack. At least, he didn't die of a heart attack brought on by the argument with Iris."

Though Charlotte had been spared many of the details of Linc's death, there was one detail she hadn't been spared: the autopsy report. Gloria had sent her a copy, for what reason Charlotte had never figured out. She had read it and reread it and reread it, trying to make some sense of Linc's death.

That's why she could remember it so well now.

"What did he die of, then?" Brent asked.

"The official diagnosis was first-degree heart block, subsequent to mild cardiogenic shock induced by a kick in the chest from a horse."

Brent stared at her. "But he hadn't been at the ranch," he said.

"It didn't happen at the ranch. It happened during the shooting of *Red Rocks*. The kick damaged the part of the heart that carries the electrical impulses that keep it beating. His heart hadn't been working right for two weeks, and finally it just stopped."

"We see that in auto accidents sometimes," said Tracey. "When people get hit in the chest by the steering wheel."

"But . . ." Brent began, his handsome face torn with confusion.

Charlotte held up a hand in demurral. "I know," she said. "I'll backtrack a little and fill in the holes. As you know, Linc hadn't worked for four years when he got the lead in *Red Rocks*."

Brent nodded.

"He got it because William Ireland was as much of a renegade as he was. He didn't care that your father had been blacklisted; he'd been blacklisted himself. He was using his own money to finance the picture. If he wanted Crawford, he was going to have Crawford. But it quickly became apparent, to me anyway, that there was an unhealthy chemistry at work between the two men."

"In what way?" asked Brent.

"Ireland was a man's man, like Linc was . . ."

"Or had been, before he met you," interjected Brent.

She nodded in agreement. "I don't know if it was me, or that he was getting older, but it's true that he'd given up a lot of that. Ireland, however, was still going strong. He reminded me of Linc's father," she said. "In the way he flaunted his masculinity in that Hemingway-esque way: boozing, carousing, showing off; refusing to be impressed by the exploits of other men."

"He could still afford to; he was younger than Dad," said Brent.

"By fifteen years or so," she agreed. "Anyway, being with Ireland revived all of that for Linc. His virility complex, I called it. To impress Ireland, he decided to dispense with the stunt man."

"He did all the stunts himself?" Brent said.

She nodded. "He'd come home night after night covered with scrapes and bruises. One day he did fifteen takes of a scene in which he roped a wild stallion. Another day he was dragged by a rope for four hundred feet."

"I remember that scene," said Tracey.

"Every night, I'd rub him down with Ben-Gay, give him an aspirin, and put him to bed. I think his wanting to do everything himself also came from not having worked for so long. He wanted to prove he could still do everything he used to. In that sense, perhaps Iris *was* indirectly responsible for his death."

"Didn't anyone ever tell him he was too old for that?"

"Myself, among others," she said. "But you knew your father."

He nodded. "Stubborn as a mule."

"He wouldn't even wear gloves in the roping scenes," Charlotte said. "He'd come home with his hands looking like raw hamburger meat. Anyway, it was in one of those roping scenes that a stallion kicked him in the chest."

"We didn't know," he said.

"Why would you have known? Everyone was trying to shield you from what was going on. There was no reason to explain the details to you; as far as you were concerned, a heart attack was all the explanation that was necessary."

"Did you know about the kick in the chest?"

"Not until your mother sent me the autopsy report. I did know that he hadn't been feeling well for a couple of weeks. He complained about feeling tired; he thought he was coming down with the flu. He had even thought about canceling the meeting with Harold Ames."

"I see now why you said I might not want to tell Mack," Brent said. "I'd be telling him that he killed Iris for nothing."

"I don't think it matters. It was his own hate that killed Iris, a hate that he'd nursed for thirty-three years, until it became so big and strong and dark that there was no escaping it."

"How's he doing?" asked Tracey.

"Okay," Brent said. "It sounds odd to say, but I think he's quite content in his cell. He doesn't seem to mind it a bit. I suppose it's not that much different from his horse trailer."

Charlotte was reminded of a young follower of Thoreau's whom she had read about in the bulletin of the Thoreau Association, who had shed family, friends, and possessions for a life of simplicity in the Alaskan wilderness. Neglecting to prepare properly, he'd been caught by the Alaskan winter without enough food, and had starved to death. In describing the youth, the author had used the phrase the "euphoria of dispossession" to describe his mania for doing without.

The author of the article had commented that it was as if, by subconscious design, the youth had sought death as the ultimate act of renunciation. Similarly, it was as if Mack had sought out the loss of his freedom, and his status as an outcast from society.

"Well," said Brent, standing up to his full height of six foot four. "I guess I'll be getting back to the airport."

"Did you get everything out of the trailer?" asked Tracey.

He nodded. "I'm having the stuff he wanted to save sent back to Colorado. There wasn't much; it was mostly books. He didn't even want his clothes. Oh, I almost forgot." He pulled a book out of his carry-on bag, and handed it to Charlotte. "He said he wanted Lottie to have this."

"Lottie?" said Tracey.

"It was our nickname for Charlotte," Brent explained.

It was Linc's copy of *Walden*. She slipped it out of its case, which was covered in brown and burgundy marbleized paper, and ran her fingers down the leather spine. Then she opened it up. It fell open to the section on Economy. One sentence was underlined:

"There is no odor so bad as that which arises from goodness tainted."

·16·

FOR OVER AN hour, Charlotte and Tracey had been climbing Katahdin. They had decided to give it a try just after Mack's arraignment. They both felt as if they had an appointment to keep with the mountain, as if the case wouldn't really be closed until they, too, had made their pilgrimages to the summit. For Tracey, it was an appointment with an old acquaintance; for Charlotte, it was a first-time meeting, an effort to square the mountain of her imagination with the real thing. After camping overnight at Chimney Pond, they had set out first thing in the morning in order to reach the summit at a reasonable hour. The campground ranger, Chris Sargent, had assured Charlotte that as long as she was fit (which she was), there was no reason why she couldn't go to the top. Many people her age and older had done it; it just took them longer. He advised them to plan on four hours instead of the usual two. As their ascent route, they chose the Dudley Trail, the easternmost of the four trails leading to the rim of the basin from Chimney Pond, and the only one whose terminus was Pamola Peak. They would descend the same way, the only alternative being to cross the Knife Edge to Baxter Peak, which neither of them was eager to do.

It seemed to Charlotte as if they'd been climbing over outcrops and boulders forever, but they were barely past the turn-off for Pamola's Caves, a group of slab caves that were only about a quarter of the way up. The hike up to Chimney Pond from Roaring Brook, which had seemed so overwhelming three weeks ago, now seemed like child's play next to this. The palms of her hands were raw, and her shoulders ached from lifting herself up onto boulders and then lowering herself back down again. She now knew what the park authorities meant when they advised hikers not to underestimate the mountain. Its unique personal quality—the fact that it wasn't part of a chain, but an individual mountain standing alone—made it seem approachable, but to think that it was easy to make Katahdin's acquaintance was a serious miscalculation. The trail was steep, and the rocks were sharp and slippery. Katahdin, like the man who had written most eloquently about it, was a mountain that spurned society.

As she climbed, Charlotte was reminded of her friend Larry Olivier, who had died a year ago to the day. In his obituary, he was quoted on his secret for good acting. It was "Remember your feet." The writer had treated this as a flip remark, but Olivier had been very serious. Keeping your feet on the ground was the secret to good acting, and it applied to mountain climbing as well. As in acting, the trick was not to think about how far you had to go, or, for that matter, how far you had come. To consider either was to divert your attention from the present, which required every ounce of your physical and mental energy. The trick was to stay with the moment, to concentrate on the simple matter of where to put your hands and feet next. The second trick Charlotte had discovered was to maintain the pace: not to shrink back at the tough spots, but to keep going—around, if possible; or over, if necessary. Likewise, not to tarry in the easy spots. It struck her what valuable lessons these were for life, as well. As Thoreau had said—it was a great art to saunter.

As she climbed, Charlotte found herself thinking about Mack again. She had spent a great deal of time thinking about him over the last two weeks. Mack's problem had been that he'd gotten hung up on an obstacle way back at the beginning of the trail. It had been a sizable enough boulder, but instead of finding a way around it, he'd let it block his way. All his hatred had become fixated on that boulder. There had been ways of getting around it, but his obsession had blinded him to them. He was another of Black Elk's Blue Men, blinded, if not by greed, then by hatred and rage. If only he could get rid of that boulder, everything would be fine. Finally, he had blasted it away, and was left only with a swath of rubble so wide and so deep that it would be years, if ever, before he would be able to work his way through it and get back on the trail again.

Once they emerged from the scrub onto the ridge, the going was a bit easier, and they made faster progress. It was like walking up an inclined plane: a straight, steep, open path leading directly to the summit. At Index Rock, just two tenths of a mile short of the summit, they decided to take another break. By now, they had been on the trail for three hours, and had stopped a number of times. Index Rock was a giant boulder—as big as a full-sized car—that had been deposited on the ridge by the retreating glacier, what the trail guide called a glacial erratic. They sat with their backs against it, drinking tea that Charlotte had packed in a Thermos, and looking down on Chimney Pond fifteen hundred feet below.

So far, the weather had been with them, but it was beginning to look dicey, Charlotte thought as she gazed out at the horizon. For the past hour, a fog had been creeping across the landscape, leaving only the distant mountain peaks protruding above it, like volcanic islands in a South Pacific sea. The ranking at the ranger's station was for a Class II Hiking Day, which meant that the trails above the tree line would be open but were not recommended because of the possibility of thunderstorms. They had decided to chance it. Perhaps it had been a mistake.

After finishing his tea, Tracey stood up and went around to the other side of the rock to assess the weather conditions. He was back in an instant. "Looks like we're in for some weather," he said, nodding up at the rim.

Charlotte stood up and went around the rock to take a look: above loomed the jagged gray peak of Pamola. Beyond that, a huge black thundercloud was advancing rapidly toward the Knife Edge from the back side of the mountain.

"Uh-oh," she said as she came back around.

"Time to get out the rain gear," said Tracey. Squatting, he removed his rain gear from his backpack.

Charlotte could already feel the first drops of rain. Not little sprinkles, but big, heavy drops. They were in for a real storm.

"There's a place on the other side of the rock where we can take shelter," she said. "It's a good thing we got here before the storm broke."

"You can sit under that rock if you want to," said Tracey. "But I'm not going to get fried by a lightning bolt."

Charlotte gave him an inquiring look as she donned her rain gear.

"It's the biggest thing around," he explained. "It will be the first place that lightning strikes."

"So what do we do?"

"Sit right out in the open," he said. "Below the ridge. We don't want to be up on the ridge, either." His rain gear on, he led the way to a spot about ten feet down the slope.

At Tracey's direction, Charlotte sat on top of her backpack with her legs crossed to avoid being electrocuted by ground currents. "It's a good thing I'm with you," she said. "I would have done all the wrong things."

No sooner had she spoken than the storm broke with a crack of thunder. For fifteen minutes, they sat in the pouring rain and watched as the storm raged around them. Each thunderclap was followed by rumbles and rolls so loud that the ground seemed to shake beneath them. As the thunderclaps came closer and closer, the rumbles and rolls and crackles and booms bounced back and forth across the basin, as if the basin itself were a gigantic kettle drum. The wind roared, bending the tops of the fir trees lining the basin, and the air seemed to almost hum with electricity. Rivulets of water cascaded down the mountain. From their vantage point, they had a fine view of the lightning striking the rim, which was spread out before them. At one point, Charlotte counted five bolts striking the Knife Edge at once, like the fingers of a fiery hand reaching down from the heavens. Below, the clouds whirled around in the basin, as if they were being whipped up by a giant egg beater.

"Pamola's artillery," said Tracey, after a particularly loud boomer.

"I'm glad we're not up there," said Charlotte, nodding at the Knife Edge. Had they been faster, they would have been on the summit when the storm struck, she thought, concluding that there were some benefits to old age.

"A number of people have been struck by lightning on the Knife Edge," Tracey said. "Some of them fatally."

Charlotte shuddered. It was a frightening display of the power of Pamola, the storm bird. But that's why they had climbed the mountain: to experience nature in the raw. She would have felt cheated if they'd seen only sunshine.

And then, just as suddenly as it had come on, the storm was over.

Forty-five minutes later, they were sitting on a knob of grim, frost-riven granite nearly a mile high under a cloudless blue sky, eating their lunches. It had taken them three hours and forty-five minutes to reach the summit, almost two hours longer than usual. But they had made it, and had added their rocks, symbolic of having made it to the top, to the monument at the summit. It was an amazing feeling, being at this spot where the earth and the heavens came together; to be in contact with the earth, yet in the midst of unimpeded space. Spread out below was a vast vista of green, dotted with countless lakes. Charlotte remembered Thoreau writing that it was as if a mirror had been broken into a thousand pieces and scattered over the landscape, each piece reflecting the blaze of the sun. Ahead of them, the Knife Edge Trail followed the narrow rim of the basin over to Baxter Peak. Charlotte was very glad that they hadn't decided to attempt it: it started out with a near vertical descent of one hundred yards into a notch between Pamola and Chimney Peaks, the latter being named for the Chimney leading down the headwall to the basin floor, which was strictly for technical climbers. Just past the Chimney was the gully where Iris' body had been found. The notch, or col, between Pamola and Chimney Peaks was the most difficult section of the Knife Edge, Tracey said. Once you were past that, the rest was easy. Charlotte had no desire to try it, however easy it might have been past the first scary section. "The most difficult nontechnical route east of the Rockies," which was how the Knife Edge was referred to in her trail guide, might be a little on the ambitious side for an over-the-hill movie star with a weakness for Manhattans and marzipan.

On the other side of Chimney Peak, she could see a pair of hikers, a young man and a young woman, traversing the Knife Edge at about the spot where Iris had been killed. Below, the headwall fell away: a sheer drop of two thousand feet. Charlotte and Tracey watched the couple's careful progress over the most narrow and dangerous section. They were at the head of a group of half a dozen other young adults, who were strung out behind them like birds on a wire.

"Looks like we're about to have some company," said Tracey.

For a moment, the leader disappeared behind Chimney Peak. When he reappeared a few minutes later on its summit, Charlotte recognized him with a start as Keith Samusit, and was reminded of the translation of his name, which meant line walker. He was certainly walking a line now.

Keith and his companion, who turned out to be Didias, reached them a short while later, after their descent down to the floor of the col, and their climb back up the other side.

"Fancy meetin' you here," said Tracey. "I thought the Penobscots had a superstition about going above the tree line."

"Some Penobscots do," said Keith.

"The ones who are smarter than we are," said Didias.

"Did you get caught on the rim in the storm?" Charlotte asked.

Keith nodded. "We had just come up the Saddle Slide. When we saw the storm coming, we turned around and went back down. But we were caught on the rim during the storm for a few minutes. It was pretty hairy," he said.

"Who are the others?" asked Tracey.

Keith turned around to look at the other hikers, the first of whom was just starting the descent into the col.

"Vision questers," he said. He removed his pack, and set it down. Then he sat down next to them. "We've added the ascent of the mountain to our curriculum. It's the first thing we do now. It's a way of getting them to leave their everyday routines behind."

"I'll say," said Tracey.

Opening his pack, Keith pulled out a package of chocolate bars and offered it around.

"Speaking of vision questers," said Charlotte as they sat on the mountaintop, eating their chocolate, "have you decided yet what you're going to do with the money Iris left the Katahdin Foundation?"

"Yes," he said. "I've been talking about it with the board. We'd like to expand the center into a national center for the study of Native American rituals. Slowly," he added. "We don't want to move too fast."

"We want to help carry out Black Elk's vision," said Didias. "To bring Native American ways into the mainstream of American life."

"The first thing we'd like to do is build a dormitory," Keith went on. "As it stands now, we're only available to people who are willing to rough it, which is fine, except that it excludes a lot of people."

"Like families," Didias added.

"Yes," said Keith. "We'd like to have day care available too so parents could come and be confident that their children were well taken care of. But we're not going to be as rich as we thought we were going to be."

"What do you mean?"

"I talked with your friend Ron Polito the other day. He says the novels that Iris wrote since she came to Maine aren't any good. He'll still be able to sell them based on the popularity of her other books, but he doesn't think they're going to be best sellers."

It was like the script she had done for Harold Ames, Charlotte thought.

"There will still be the income from her other books, though. By the way," he added. "He's very sick."

"I know," said Charlotte.

"I mean, I think he's dying," he said. "When I called him back yesterday to clarify some questions I had, his secretary told me that he was in intensive care. Apparently, his cancer has spread."

Charlotte felt a wave of heaviness wash over her. Another one of her old friends, checking out. Was this the way it was going to be for her in years to come? Each taking with them a part of her life, a part of her history.

For a moment, they watched the progress of the first of the vision questers as he began his steep descent into the col.

Then Keith asked, "What brings you up here?"

"Don't ask me," Tracey replied. "Miss Graham here got me into this." He nodded at Charlotte. "Wouldn't take no for an answer."

The pair's attention shifted to Charlotte. She addressed Keith. "Do you remember Louis Neptune?"

"Do you mean the Penobscot who was supposed to be Thoreau's guide on his trip to Katahdin, but who didn't show up?"

Charlotte nodded. "Do you remember him telling Thoreau in *The Maine Woods* about planting a bottle of rum on the summit to pacify Pamola?"

"Sure," he said. "That's why Iris always took a bottle of rum along on her annual climb. That and her own personal reasons," he added, alluding to her history of alcoholism.

Charlotte reached over to her backpack. Unzipping it, she rummaged around for a minute and then produced a bottle of Mount Gay. "I figured that I had some unfinished business to take care of on Iris' behalf."

"You lugged that all the way up the mountain!" said Tracey.

"You'd better be glad I did," Charlotte said. "We want to keep Pamola happy. Do you want him to put us through another thunderstorm like that one?"

Keith smiled. "I like that," he said. "Finishing Iris' business. You asked what we're going to do with Iris' money. One of the things we want to teach is the importance of creating ritual in everyday life."

"Would you like to officiate at this ceremony?" she asked.

"Keith, you have your drum!" Didias said.

"That I do," he said. "We did some drumming before we set out," he explained. Reaching into his backpack, he produced a hand drum, and a drumstick wrapped with leather strips. "I'll do a chant," he said.

For a few minutes, Keith pounded on the drum, a fast, steady beat. Then he began to chant. It started out low, and then rose in volume and pitch, like the wind that had roared through the basin a short while before.

It was an eerie, primitive sound; a sound that had reverberated in the Maine wilderness for ten thousand years.

Keith chanted for ten minutes to the accompaniment of the drum. When he had finished, Charlotte unscrewed the cap of the bottle, took a swig, and passed it around. They each took a drink.

"Iris would have thought of this as drinking the blood of the enemy," Keith said as he took his swallow.

*

Then Charlotte stepped over to the edge, and emptied the contents of the bottle into the void. "For Pamola," she said.

And also for Iris, for Linc, for herself, for Ron Polito, and for the dark side of Hollywood history.

EARLENE FOWLER

Introduces Benni Harper, curator of San Celina's folk art museum and amateur sleuth

> Each novel is named after a quilting pattern that is featured in the story.

"Benni's loose, friendly, and bright. Here's hoping we get to see more of her..."–<u>The Kirkus Reviews</u>

__FOOL'S PUZZLE   0-425-14545-X/$4.99

Ex-cowgirl Benni Harper moved from the family ranch to San Celina, California, to begin a new career as curator of the town's folk art museum. But one of the museum's first quilt exhibit artists is found dead. And Benni must piece together an intricate sequence of family secrets and small-town lies to catch the killer.

"Compelling...Keep a lookout for her next one."
    –<u>Booklist</u>

The latest Earlene Fowler mystery
A Berkley Prime Crime hardcover

__IRISH CHAIN   0-425-14619-7/$18.95

When Brady O'Hara and his former girlfriend are murdered at the San Celina Senior Citizen's Prom, Benni believes it's more than mere jealousy. She decides to risk everything–her exhibit, her romance with police chief Gabriel Ortiz, and ultimately her life –uncovering the conspiracy O'Hara had been hiding for fifty years.